OTTO PENZLER PRESENTS
AMERICAN MYSTERY CLASSICS

THE CASE OF THE BAKER STREET IRREGULARS

ANTHONY BOUCHER (1911-1968) was an American author, editor, and critic, perhaps best known today as the namesake of the annual Bouchercon convention, an international meeting of mystery writers, fans, critics, and publishers.

Born William Anthony Parker White, he wrote under various pseudonyms and worked in a number of genres outside of mystery, including fantasy and science fiction. He served as the mystery fiction reviewer for the *New York Times* for over twenty years, writing a total of 862 columns on the subject.

OTTO PENZLER, the creator of American Mystery Classics, is also the founder of the Mysterious Press, a literary crime imprint; MysteriousPress.com, an electronic-book publishing company; and New York City's Mysterious Bookshop. He has won a Raven, the Ellery Queen Award, two Edgars, and lifetime achievement awards from NoirCon and *The Strand Magazine*. He has edited more than 70 anthologies and written extensively about mystery fiction.

THE CASE OF THE BAKER STREET IRREGULARS

ANTHONY BOUCHER

Introduction by
OTTO PENZLER

AMERICAN MYSTERY CLASSICS

Penzler Publishers
New York

Published in 2020 by Penzler Publishers
58 Warren Street, New York, NY 10007
penzlerpublishers.com

Distributed by W. W. Norton

Cover image: Andy Ross
Cover design: Mauricio Diaz

Paperback ISBN 978-1-61316-182-1
Hardcover ISBN 978-1-61316-181-4
eBook ISBN 978-1-50405-734-9

Library of Congress Control Number: 2020912987

Printed in the United States of America

9 8 7 6 5 4 3 2 1

THE CASE OF THE BAKER STREET IRREGULARS

INTRODUCTION

NOT LONG ago, I was stunned to learn that a friend who is otherwise quite rational, and even intelligent, believes Sherlock Holmes is a famous fictional detective created by Sir Arthur Conan Doyle. What's more, hers is not an isolated case. Extraordinary as it seems, many others share this delusion. They don't question it or think twice about it. They just accept it as fact, the way seven-year-olds used to *know* (before they got so sophisticated) that the moon was made of green cheese.

It looks as if the astronauts have settled the green cheese theory of moon matter once and for all—even to the satisfaction of all but the most obstinate seven-year-olds. Now someone has to rectify the Holmes misconceptions.

As any member of the Baker Street Irregulars knows, Sherlock Holmes is not a famous fictional detective. He is a famous real-life detective, born in Yorkshire, England, on January 6, 1854. His most dramatic adventures were recorded by his friend and associate, Dr. John H. Watson. Conan Doyle, although his heirs brazenly dispute it, served the secondary, if valuable, role of Watson's literary agent.

Furthermore, it is inaccurate and premature to discuss Holmes in the past tense. He still lives, of course (has anyone read his obituary?), on the Sussex Downs, quietly keeping bees.

He is old now, having learned the secrets of long life from the Dalai Lama on a trip to Tibet, and he does not receive visitors or accept cases. He does, however, continue to work on a monumental book, *The Whole Art of Detection*, which should be published in the near future.

To what secret, esoteric knowledge are the Baker Street Irregulars privvy that they know all this? None. It is all there, in black and white, in the four novels and fifty-six short stories that comprise the Canon, as it is respectfully called. If the tales are read carefully, in the proper spirit (and perhaps with the proper spirits), ideally on a cold, foggy March night, where the rattle of a horse-drawn hansom cab just might be heard to echo in the distance, the reader could easily become a Baker Street Irregular.

The requirements for becoming an Irregular are not great. They were outlined some years ago by the late Edgar W. Smith, a Vice-President of General Motors and the long-time head of the society. An Irregular, he said, is any kindred soul "who feels his pulse quicken and his steps seem lighter whenever, in a darkling world, he turns the corner of reality into the most magic of all streets."

In several cases, Holmes employed a gang of street urchins to help gather information. To make the tongue-in-cheek distinction between them and the regular officials of Scotland Yard, he called them his Baker Street Irregulars. Sherlock Holmes admirers have taken the name for themselves, ever since the first annual dinner nearly ninety years ago.

It was a fitting evening. The air was heavy with damp, the ground covered with a thick, grey-colored soup that moments before had been powdery white flakes. A small handful of men tramped through endless slush until they reached the unmarked door. On the other side were warmth, smoke thick enough to be worthy of the vilest fog on England's moors, and smooth amber liquid to help erase the icy memory of the bitter December night air.

On just such a night in 1895 London, Sherlock Holmes might have called to his roommate, "Come Watson, quickly. The game's afoot!" On this night, in 1934 New York, a few enthusiasts met to celebrate the birthday of the man they most respected, admired and loved. The Baker Street Irregulars were officially born.

Alexander Woollcott, the noted actor and critic (the titular character of *The Man Who Came to Dinner* was based on him) rolled up to the door in a somewhat shabby hansom cab, wearing a cape and preposterous red deerstalker cap which he insisted on sporting for the entire evening.

William Gillette, who made a career of portraying Holmes on the stage, was there. So was Gene Tunney, the former heavyweight boxing champion, Frederick Dorr Steele, the finest illustrator of the Holmes stories, and Christopher Morley, perhaps the most beloved man of letters in American literary history.

The ranks of the Irregulars, past and present, include Frederic Dannay, half of the Ellery Queen collaboration; Franklin D. Roosevelt, even during the presidential years; Robert L. Fish, who wrote the book on which *Bullitt* was based and then wrote stories about Schlock Homes of Bagel Street; Rex Stout, creator of the eccentric fat detective Nero Wolfe; and Isaac Asimov, the prolific science and fiction writer.

The annual dinner now attracts more than 200 Irregulars from every part of the country and around the world.

Members reminisce about Dr. Roland Hammond, who once created quite a stir at the august Racquet and Tennis Club. Ordering three carcasses of beef to be hung in the club's dining room, he set upon them like a madman with a cataract knife to prove a theory about a point in one of the stories. The bloody demonstration, although effective, was not enthusiastically received by the club and new quarters for the annual dinner were mandated.

Older members remember Laurence Paine, who returned from the annual dinner meeting of the Baker Street Irregulars to find his apartment burglarized. He could not work up the courage to report it to the police. He was too embarrassed about having to tell them where he'd been.

And all the members of the Baker Street Irregulars remember Tony Boucher (rhymes with "voucher"), one of the first, one of the most learned, one of the most beloved, and one of the most talented of all the stars who illuminate the annual celebration.

The by-line on this volume is the pseudonym of William Anthony Parker White (1911-1968). Born into a family with backgrounds in medicine, law, and the Navy, Boucher originally wanted to become an admiral, but while he was attending Pasadena High School, he decided to be a physicist. Later, at Pasadena Junior College, he again changed his mind and studied linguistics, his goal being to teach languages. He received a bachelor's degree from the University of Southern California in 1932 and a master's degree in German from the University of California in 1934, at which time he was elected to Phi Beta Kappa.

He later became sufficiently proficient in French, Spanish, and Portuguese to translate mystery stories from those languages into English, but after spending much time in acting, writing, and directing in the little theater movement while at school, he decided to become a playwright. He was unsuccessful but did manage to gain employment as theater editor of the *United Progressive News* in Los Angeles (1935-1937). He wrote a mystery novel in 1936 and sold it the following year. During the next several years he wrote a mystery novel every year, including two under the pseudonym H. H. Holmes (a famous murderer); later he signed that name to his science fiction reviews for the *Chicago Sun Times* and *The New York Herald Tribune* (1951-1963).

In the late 1930s Boucher became interested in science fiction and fantasy and, in the early 1940s, wrote stories in this genre as well as mysteries for pulp magazines, which were more remunerative that books were. After spending the years from 1942 to 1947 as a book reviewer specializing in science fiction and mysteries for the *San Francisco Chronicle*, he reviewed mysteries for *Ellery Queen's Mystery Magazine* for sixteen months. While employed by the *Chronicle*, he edited the anthology *Great American Detective Stories* (1945). In 1949 he cofounded and became coeditor of *The Magazine of Fantasy and Science Fiction*. He later returned to review books for *Ellery Queen's Mystery Magazine* for eleven years (1957-1968).

In 1951, Boucher began writing the "Criminals at Large" column for *The New York Times Book Review*. He continued in this position until his death and contributed 852 columns. His mystery criticism brought him Edgar awards for 1945, 1949, and 1952 from the Mystery Writers of America.

Boucher was married, had two sons and lived in Berkeley, California. His interests, in addition to Sherlock Holmes, included theological speculation, party politics, cooking, poker, cats, opera (he once conducted a radio series, *Golden Voices*, in which he played recordings and discussed opera), football, basketball, true crime (he edited *The Pocket Book of True Crime Stories* [1943], and *True Crime Detective* magazine), and collecting old records. He was a member of the Mystery Writers of America, for which he served as national president in 1951.

Boucher died of lung cancer in 1968. On learning of his death, Frederic Dannay said, "In his chosen field Tony was a Renaissance man, a complete man—writer, critic and historian. He was conscientious and a fine craftsman."

Although Boucher's status as a critic overshadowed his reputation as a writer, his talent for inventing entertaining and well-plotted puzzles established him as one of the leading mystery writers of the late 1930s and early 1940s.

His first novel, *The Case of the Seven of Calvary* (1937), features Dr. John Ashwin, professor of Sanskrit, who acts as an armchair detective when a series of bizarre murders are committed in an academic setting, with the only clue the baffling and obscure symbol referred to in the title.

He also published two novels as H. H. Holmes. *Nine Times Nine* (1940) is a locked room problem set against the background of a weird Los Angeles cult called The Temple of Light. It was dedicated to John Dickson Carr and solved by Lt. Marshall of the Los Angeles Police Department and Sister Ursula of the Sisters of Martha of Bethany. The next Holmes effort, with the same investigative team, was *Rocket to the Morgue* (1942), the main interest of which is its setting among science fiction writers and fans; Boucher himself appeared in a minor role.

Much of Boucher's subsequent short fiction was of the science fiction-fantasy variety, but he occasionally published notable detective stories in *Ellery Queen's Mystery Magazine*. His Nick Noble series—written mainly in the 1940s—concerns a disgraced former policeman turned wino who sits in a cheap bar drinking sherry and trying to shoo an imaginary fly away from the tip of his nose while solving baffling crime problems brought to him by a policeman friend. Boucher once wrote: "Good detective stories are, as I have often quoted Hamlet's phrase about the players, 'the abstracts and brief chronicles of the time,' ever valuable in retrospect as indirect but vivid pictures of the society from which they spring."

Probably his most memorable fictional creation is Fergus O'Breen, a Los Angeles private detective who runs a one-man agency. He is Irish. He is, in fact, *very* Irish—his hair is bright red, and he has the reputation of being a wild man.

Born about 1910, O'Breen never knew his mother and his father was an alcoholic whose interests did not extend to his children. His older sister, Maureen, had the responsibility of bringing up Fergus and did a more than satisfactory job.

O'Breen has been described as "cocksure," "curious," "brash," and "colorful" (he has the habit of referring to himself as "The O'Breen"). All these qualities seem to be the instinctive camouflage of a man who, in another age, might have been a bard, a crusader, or possibly a prophet. He is moderately successful in a financial sense, and his clients, usually pleased with his efforts, speak highly of him and call him a thoroughly nice young man.

His hobbies are reading, cooking, football, and classical music. His allergy to cats makes him sneeze exactly seven times. Many of his cases are set in Hollywood and are often brought to his attention by his sister, the head of publicity at Metropolis Pictures and one of the smartest women in the industry.

O'Breen appears in three major cases: *The Case of the Crumpled Knave* (1939), which deals with the death of an elderly inventor whose anti-gas weapon could be of incalculable value during wartime; *The Case of the Solid Key* (1941) concerns a little theatre group whose managing director is found dead in a locked room; and his last book-length adventure, *The Case of the*

Seven Sneezes (1942), set on an island off the California coast on which murder repeats a 25-year-old pattern at a silver wedding anniversary. A short story in *Far and Away* (1955) also features "The O'Breen."

One of the great triumphs of the O'Breen family involved Maureen. *The Case of the Baker Street Irregulars* occurs when a movie studio sets out to make the greatest Sherlock Holmes film of all time. To ensure authenticity, the producer and his publicity girl, Maureen, conceive the plan of inviting members of the Baker Street Irregulars to the studio lot to give their views. The screenwriter, as villainous a devil as Professor Moriarty himself, appears briefly but violently, and the discovery of his body quickly sets off a series of Sherlockian adventures so bizarre that no one can give them credence.

James Sandoe, the two-time Edgar-winning critic, regarded this volume as Boucher's best, calling it "a cheerful Sherlockian frolic."

It is that, to be sure. It is one of the few Sherlockian mysteries in which Holmes himself does not appear, either under his real name or using some inane bastardization of it, such as Sheerluck Jones or Herlock Soames or Picklock Holes or any of the dozens that have found their way into print.

At the time of the book's publication, 1940, the last Sherlock Holmes story by Dr. Watson was only 13 years old. Since it was published, there have been scores—no, hundreds—of imitations, but few rank as highly as this for ingenuity. A Sherlock Holmes novel was a rarity in 1940; today, more than ninety years after the death of Watson's literary agent, it is commonplace. But Holmes is no fad, no cult figure. He will endure when we have all been forgotten. He epitomizes another age, a more peaceful and stable one. He is dependable, when all else seems uncertain. His justice invariably triumphs, in an era when justice is beleaguered. He is the symbol of Good, in a time when Evil too often has the upper hand. He is a fixed point in a changing world.

As Vincent Starrett, the dean of Sherlockian scholars once wrote of Holmes and Watson: "...they still live for all that love them well/ in a romantic chamber of the heart/ in a nostalgic country of the mind/ where it is always 1895."

OTTO PENZLER
New York City

BIBLIOGRATITUDE

A full bibliography would, I am happy to say, be out of place in this volume; but I wish here to express my special indebtedness to Vincent Starrett's classic, *The Private Life of Sherlock Holmes;* to Edgar W. Smith's less-known but almost equally invaluable *Appointment in Baker Street;* to the many bits of Baker Street illumination scattered through the files of *The Saturday Review of Literature;* and above all to the reminiscences of John H. Watson, M.D., quotations from which appear in this book through the courtesy of Doubleday, Doran and Company, Inc., Harper & Brothers, A. P. Watt & Son.

All characters portrayed or referred to in this novel are fictitious,
with the exception of Sherlock Holmes,
to whom this book is dedicated

METROPOLIS ★ PICTURES

F. X. WEINBERG

Memo to RESEARCH

Get me information at once on Baker Street Irregulars and why should they send me threatening letters.

F. X. Weinberg

METROPOLIS ★ PICTURES

RESEARCH DEPARTMENT

Memo to F. X. WEINBERG

Little material available on Baker Street Irregulars. Apparently an informal organization of Sherlock Holmes enthusiasts founded through Christopher Morley's column in *The Saturday Review of Literature*. No formal list of members on record, but includes big names—Woollcott, Bottomley, Starrett, O'Dab, etc. Activities recorded principally in *SRL*, with one write-up by Woollcott in *The New Yorker*, 12/29/34. Attached find constitution as published in *SRL*, 2/17/34. (Exhibit A.)

Also attached is manifesto recently sent to Irregulars and others. (Copy obtained from Author's Club of Los Angeles.) This should explain threatening letters. (Exhibit B.)

—GG

3

EXHIBIT A

ARTICLE I

The name of this society shall be the Baker Street Irregulars.

ARTICLE II

Its purpose shall be the study of the Sacred Writings.*

ARTICLE III

All persons shall be eligible for membership who pass an examination in the Sacred Writings set by officers of the society, and who are considered otherwise suitable.

ARTICLE IV

The officers shall be: a Gasogene, a Tantalus, and a Commissionaire.

The duties of the Gasogene shall be these commonly performed by a President.

The duties of the Tantalus shall be these commonly performed by a Secretary.

The duties of the Commissionaire shall be to telephone down for ice, White Rock, and whatever else may be required and available; to conduct all negotiations with waiters; and to assess the members pro rata for the cost of same.

BUY LAWS**

1) An annual meeting shall be held on January 6th, at which these toasts shall be drunk which were published in

---

*   This means A. C. Doyle's Sherlock Holmes—GG.
**   This is not a misprint—GG.

The Saturday Review of January 27th, 1934;* after which the members shall drink at will.

2) The current round shall be bought by any member who fails to identify, by title of story and context, any quotation from the Sacred Writings submitted by any other member.

> *Qualification A.*—If two or more members fail so to identify, a round shall be bought by each of these so failing.
>
> *Qualification B.*—If the submitter of the quotation, upon challenge, fails to identify it correctly, he shall buy the round.

3) Special meetings may be called at any time or any place by any one of three members, two of whom shall constitute a quorum.

> *Qualification A.*—If said two are of opposite sexes, they shall use care in selecting the place of meeting, to misinterpretation (or interpretation either, for that matter).
>
> *Qualification B.*—If such two persons of opposite sexes be clients of the Personal Column of *The Saturday Review,* the foregoing does not apply; such persons being presumed to let their consciences be their guides.

4) All other business shall be left for the monthly meeting.

5) There shall be no monthly meeting.

---

* "It was agreed that the first health must always be drunk to '*The* Woman.' Suggestions for succeeding sentiments, which will have their own overtones for all genuine Holmesians, were: 'Mrs. Hudson,' 'Mycroft,' 'The Second Mrs. Watson,' 'The game is afoot!' and 'The second most dangerous man in London.'"

EXHIBIT B

MANIFESTO

TO ALL TRUE LOVERS OF BAKER STREET AND MORE ESPECIALLY TO THOSE STYLING THEM-SELVES ITS IRREGULARS GREETINGS

BE IT KNOWN THAT Metropolis Pictures has announced its intention of filming that episode of the Sacred Writings known as *The Adventure of the Speckled Band.*

THAT this is a worthy and laudable intention, particularly as the chronicler of the Master himself considered this episode especially adapted to dramatic form.

THAT the cast announced is no more unworthy of the Writings than mortals must inevitably be, with the exception of the late William Gillette.

BUT THAT the delicate and responsible task of transferring this adventure to the screen has been entrusted to the typewriter of Stephen Worth.

BE IT FURTHER KNOWN THAT this man Worth, hereinafter to be known as *that rat,* is the author of many stupid and illogical mystery novels of the type known as hard-boiled and is therefore to be considered as an apostate from the teachings of the Master.

THAT that rat was once himself a private detective, of the lowest divorce-evidence, strike-breaking type, and therefore feels himself to be an authority upon the art of detection.

THAT that rat's personal life has been such as to bring disgrace upon the profession of crime and even upon the more tolerant profession of letters.

AND THAT that rat has many times expressed in public print his contempt for the exploits of Holmes and his desire "to show up that cocky bastard for what he is."

BE IT THEREFORE RESOLVED THAT it is the duty of all true Holmesians to write, wire, or otherwise express their sentiments to the producer F. X. Weinberg, Metropolis Pictures, Los Angeles, California, demanding in the name of all honor and decency that Stephen Worth be purged from the task of adapting the Sacred Writings.

By the Sign of Four, the Five Orange Pips, the Dancing Men, and the Dog in the Night-time, we conjure you to do so.

THE BAKER STREET IRREGULARS
in session extraordinary by Rufus
Bottomley, M.D., Tantalus

METROPOLIS ★ PICTURES

F. X. WEINBERG

Memo to PUBLICITY, ATTN. M. O'BREEN

Maureen, have you, for God's sake, any ideas about Worth? I have Irregulars on my tail.

F. X.

Chapter 1

THE MAIN trouble, thought Maureen, is the ideas Worth has about me. It had not been a pleasant scene that morning. At the thought, she smoothed her dress as though to wipe off the touch of Stephen Worth's hands. But personal revulsion and defense of one's virtue shouldn't interfere with handling publicity contacts, and F. X.'s memo sounded really worried. Dutifully she ran a comb through her short black hair, gave a moment's perfunctory attention to her face, and went off down the corridor to Mr. Weinberg's office.

That executive was crouched over a paper-strewn desk, shouting into a speaking apparatus. "So I don't want to see any professor! I don't care who he has letters from. One hundred and eleven insulting letters I have yet on my desk and I should talk to professors? He should live so long!"

Maureen couldn't resist it. "He says he wants to give you English lessons, Mr. Weinberg," she said in Miss Blankenship's squeaky voice.

"English lessons!" Mr. Weinberg bellowed into the apparatus. "I'm Hermann Bing maybe, or Mike Curtiz? English lessons he wants to give me! I—" Some instinct warned him to turn. He saw Maureen. Slowly the little executive's gargoyle features went through a double take.

9

The Weinberg double takes are a Hollywood legend, as famous in their way as the corrosive wit of Dorothy Parker, the discomforting ribs of Vernon Crews, or the magnificent verbal creations of Samuel Goldwyn. Paul Jackson had once said that these retroactive reactions could be equaled only if Lubitsch were to direct Horton in slow motion. Such a triumph of the mobility of the human countenance is not easily to be described. The effect, however, for those unwise in theatrical argot, may be roughly compared to the appearance of a man with pixies in his brainpan slowly recalling what he said to the hostess last night.

"It's you," he pronounced, somewhat in the tones Selznick must have used when he saw Vivian Leigh's test for Scarlett O'Hara. "You're a smart girl, Maureen. You tell me what I should do."

Maureen read the constitution, the manifesto, and the incredible series of missives which the latter had evoked. At last she shook her head sadly. "There's nothing to do," she said. "You've got to fire Worth."

The thing on the desk buzzed. "Eleven thirty, Mr. Weinberg."

Automatically the executive reached out for the water carafe and the packet of sodium bicarbonate. "Give me a reason," he said.

She waved at the papers. "There's a hundred and eleven reasons, if you counted right. Look at the names signed to those— Christopher Morley, Rufus Bottomley, Alexander Woollcott, Vincent Starrett, Harrison Ridgly, Elmer Davis, John O'Dab. Why you simply can't afford to have these men against you, F. X. Take Woolcott alone. If he came out for a boycott on *The Speckled Band*, you'd never even get your investment back on it, let alone a cent of profit. I'm trying not to let my personal feelings about

Worth influence me. Just from a business standpoint, you've got to get rid of him."

The little man smiled. "You *are* a good girl, Maureen. You don't yes me; no, you do better than that. You tell me what I wanted to be told. I was afraid maybe because I've been sore at Worth . . . But now I know I'm right. So tomorrow I get rid of Stephen Worth."

"And just how do you propose to do that?"

Mr. Weinberg sprang from his bent-chromium chair and stiffened to his full five feet four inches of height. "Where did you come from, Worth?"

Even beside an ordinary man, Stephen Worth was a giant. Next to Mr. Weinberg he seemed nothing less than a titan. But he did not take advantage of his full height. He merely leaned heavily against the wall and answered in one syllable—a syllable which his publisher's reader had been forced to strike out with dogged monotony from page after page of his hard-boiled detective stories.

The buzzer sounded. "He just pushed his way in, Mr. Weinberg," Miss Blankenship's voice squawked. "I tried to tell him you were busy, but he just went right on in. I'm terribly sorry, Mr. Weinberg, but—"

"That's all right." Mr. Weinberg switched off the apparatus and turned to glare at the writer.

But Stephen Worth's eyes had lit on Maureen. "Hiya!" he said. "If it isn't the darling of the publicity office—the little colleen that plays hard-to-get when a man makes a pass at her and then comes sneaking into the boss' office."

Maureen dexterously avoided his outstretched arm. "I was meaning to ask you, F. X. Can I bill the studio for a new bra? Damage incurred in the line of duty?"

Mr. Weinberg looked up at the ex-detective with such concentrated scorn that he seemed to be looking down into a measureless and fetid abyss. "Mr. Worth," he announced, "you and Metropolis are through."

Stephen Worth laughed softly to himself—a rumbling laugh of self-conscious virility. "I thought you'd say that, F. X. When do you want me to leave?"

"You can't bluff me out of this," Mr. Weinberg continued. "I'll have you out of this studio if—" He cut himself short, and one of the Weinberg double takes began its slow progress across his face. "So when do I want you to leave?" he muttered. "When do I—? Today. This minute. Right away. As soon as possible." He was almost choking with relief. "Now," he added, to leave no doubt as to his meaning.

Stephen Worth dropped his heavy body solidly into the chromium chair meant only for little Mr. Weinberg. "Swell. You want me to leave, as you so succinctly put it, now. All right. What happens then? First of all you've got to tell A. K. Now I owe that bastard four thousand dollars on the races and twenty-three hundred at roulette; he wants me around here, earning the studio's good money, or he knows he'll never see that sixty-three hundred again."

"So I'll answer for A. K.," Mr. Weinberg spluttered. "If he wants his six thousand so bad, he should sue you."

"Gambling debts aren't recoverable—that's one of those little points, F. X., that have made me the success I am. But what happens next? My agent comes to see you and calls your attention to several little clauses in my contract. You send him away with a bug in his ear, but he comes back. He comes back with a representative from the Screen Writers' Guild. And now you're beginning to get into real trouble. No, F. X., it isn't any use grabbing for the bicarb. That won't make you feel any better. You'll have to just get used to seeing me around here—at any rate till I've finished *The Speckled Band.*"

Mr. Weinberg looked at the pile of Irregular messages on his desk. "All right. So I can't throw you out. Such a *Schlemiel* I must keep on the payroll. All right. But I tell you this: you don't adapt *The Speckled Band.* That property I turn over to somebody else. And you," he concluded in tones of excommunication, "you will write *Speed Harris and His Space Ship,* in twelve breath-taking episodes."

Worth snorted. "To put it briefly, F. X., like hell I will. Don't bluster. I've got you over a barrel, my fine Semitic friend, and your pants are slipping inch by inch. Read my contract, and learn what dimwits you've got in your legal department. They let a honey slip by them that time. You can switch me off to *Speed Harris* if you want; but if you do, you'll never produce *The Speckled Band.* I've got it in black and white—either I write that picture or nobody does."

"To me all this should happen!" Mr. Weinberg moaned plaintively. "But why, Mr. Worth? What has Metropolis done to you?"

Stephen Worth grinned unpleasantly. "Polly hasn't done a damned thing to me. It's just that this is my chance to show them up."

"Show who up?"

"These cockeyed pantywaist deductionists. These silly-frilly nancy-pantsy dabblers who think they can write about detectives. Solving murders oh! so cutely with a book on Indo-Arabian ceramics when they'd faint at the sight of a nosebleed. Holding hands in a ducky little daisy chain while they all murmur the sacred name of Sherlock Holmes. Sweet Christ, but they're going to learn something in this picture, and they're not going to like it."

"So because you were once a detective, we should ruin Metropolis? Mr. Worth, couldn't we—?"

Buzzer. "It's that professor, Mr. Weinberg," Miss Blankenship explained. "He says was that Stephen Worth he saw going into your office, because if it was he wants to come in, too. He says to tell you it's about the Baker Street Irregulars, whatever that is."

Worth guffawed. "A professor on my tail! That's a sweet one."

"Tell him I'm gone," Mr. Weinberg snapped. "Tell him I strangled Worth in cold blood. Tell him I'm a fugitive from justice. Tell him—" Slowly a new comprehension began to replace his annoyance. "Did you say the Baker Street Irregulars?"

"I think that's what he said, Mr. Weinberg."

"So tell him to come in. Tell him to come right in."

While he had sardonically debated matters of contract, Stephen Worth had seemed almost sober. Now, as he jerked himself up from Mr. Weinberg's beautiful chair, a heavy flush crossed his face, brutalizing the handsome irregularity of his features. Maureen shrank back into a corner; she had seen him like this before.

"Baker Street Irregulars," Worth muttered with utmost loathing. "Baker Street Irregulars! . . ." His growl rose almost to a roar.

Then Professor Furness came in. He was not the elderly academician that Maureen had subconsciously expected, but a lean man of thirty, dressed in what was obviously his Good Blue Suit. Lean, in fact, was a flattering adjective—scrawny might be better. His collar fitted badly, and his nose seemed too thin to support the pince-nez which were poised as though ready for instant flight.

All these details Maureen took in at first glance. Then the picture was shattered by the terrific swing of Stephen Worth's left.

Before Professor Furness could say a word, he lay stretched out cold on the polished, rugless floor of the office. Stephen Worth loomed above his carcass, swaying a little and rubbing his knuckles.

"See you in story conference, F. X.," he said, and swung out of the room.

At once Maureen was beside the poor professor, applying first aid from F. X.'s water carafe, and thinking rapidly. "Hush," she said at last, cutting across her employer's dire groans and predictions. "There's no danger of a suit. I'll have a talk with the professor and turn on the old charm. Things have come to a pretty pass if a smart Irish girl can't handle him."

Mr. Weinberg brightened a little. "My mother was Irish," he said wistfully, "but nobody ever believes me."

"And it's a good thing he came here," she went on rapidly. "It gives me a bright idea. Look. If these Irregulars are so interested in Holmes that they'll actually come here to Polly to protest . . ." Deftly she sketched out the plan.

Chapter 2

I
METROPOLIS ★ PICTURES

June 26, 1939

Mr. Harrison Ridgly
Editor, *Sirrah*
New York, N. Y.

Dear Mr. Ridgly:

Your protest against the assignment of Stephen Worth to the script of *The Speckled Band* has been received and personally considered by me. Unfortunately, contractual arrangements, which I am sure you as an editor will understand, prevent me from altering this assignment; but I have hit upon an arrangement which will, I hope, satisfy you.

I am inviting you and a group of your associates among the Baker Street Irregulars to be my guests in Hollywood during the making of this picture. You will have complete advisory authority over all details of adaptation and be in a position to guarantee authenticity and fidelity.

I will not affront your devotion to the literature of Sherlock Holmes by offering you a salary as technical advisor. As I say, you shall be my personal guest, with all travel and living expenses cared for and a liberal drawing account for personal expenses.

I hope you can see your way clear from your editorial duties during this slack summer season to accept my offer and render this service to the memory of Sherlock Holmes by guaranteeing him a worthy immortality on the screen.

I take this opportunity of expressing the longfelt gratitude of Metropolis Pictures for the treatment which its products have received in the review columns of *Sirrah*. Even your adverse criticisms have stimulated us as a needed, if sometimes harsh, corrective.

Sincerely yours,
F. X. Weinberg
FXW/RS

SIRRAH
The magazine of male modernity

June 30, 1939

Mr. F. X. Weinberg
Metropolis Pictures
Los Angeles, California

Dear Mr. Weinberg:

Will a small black arm band, neat but not gaudy, be out of place in your select advisorial house party?

You could, of course, hardly know that your invitation reaches me so shortly after the death of my sister that it finds me hardly in the mood for critical sportiveness. Nevertheless, I am inclined to accept, if only because I hope that a change of scene may prove consoling.

It is perhaps as well that I am dictating this letter to one of my more efficiently prim stenographers. You are thus spared the rather ghastly stream-of-consciousness on Life, Death, Futility, and other such sophomoric capitalizations which are at present all too apt to pour forth from me at the thought of what my eminent father calls "our shocking bereavement."

In short, I have made up my mind in the course of this babbling dictation. I gladly accept your summons, if you are willing to number among the party the bright corpse which I must henceforth always carry with me. I owe a certain duty, I suppose, to the shade of Sherlock Holmes. Moreover, I am more than a little anxious, Mr. Weinberg, to see you execute a double take.

I have extended your longfelt gratitude for our treatment of Metropolis pictures to Harold Swathmore, our third-string reviewer. I am sure that it will keep him in a warm glow all through the next Kane Family opus.

Sincerely yours,
Harrison Ridgly III
HR/NP

Miss Purvis (known to the staff of *Sirrah* as "Impurvis" because she could take Harrison Ridgly's dictation without blinking an eye) finished reading back the Weinberg letter and looked up from her notebook. "Do you want it sent just like that, Mr. Ridgly?" she asked.

Beside his neat and tasteful desk Harrison Ridgly stood tall and straight and dark. His lips barely stirred with speech, and not another muscle moved visibly in his body. "Yes," he said, "just like that. It's a stupid letter, committing me to a stupid action. You will send it as it is."

Miss Purvis' pencil lingered longingly over the sentence

about the bright corpse, which could be so easily stricken out. "You're sure, Mr. Ridgly?"

A muscle in his brown forehead flicked tautly. "Yes."

"If you'd let me make it a little more formal—"

"Please!" The word burst out as though it were a curse. Its noise hung for a moment in the still room like smoke after an explosion.

Miss Purvis snapped the notebook shut. "Very well, Mr. Ridgly. Anything else?"

"Yes. Make arrangements with Fisher to take over my work while I am gone. He will disapprove strongly of my desertion, as he will doubtless term it, and resolve to do my job so well that the owners will consider giving it to him permanently. You may wish him luck from me."

"Is that all?"

"Yes. I shall sign the letter after lunch. Now go."

Harrison Ridgly had not moved all the time that Miss Purvis was in the room. He had not dared to move. Now he turned and looked across the room to the chastely framed photograph of the young girl in her coming-out gown. He could hardly focus his eyes to read the familiar inscription, in that foolish round hand. *To the world's best brother from his Phillida.*

He moved toward the picture. He had been wise to remain still while Miss Purvis was present. Movement requires coordination, and small rugs on smooth floors are a danger.

The cartoonists of rival publications (and even of his own) would have rejoiced in the sight of Harrison Ridgly III sprawled stupidly on the floor of his office. They would have thought it funny.

The perfectly *Sirrah*-styled suit was acquiring wrinkles which would have wrung its designer's sensitive heart. But its wearer had no thought for the things of *Sirrah* as he lay there, his eyes twisted upward to the photograph, his body shaken with horrible noises which he would have deemed ludicrous in another.

His mouth twisted. Perhaps he knew these sobs to be ludicrous even in himself. Even the grotesque sincerity of his woe could not keep the Ridgly mouth from twisting.

II
METROPOLIS ★ PICTURES

June 26, 1939

Mr. John O'Dab
c/o Mason and Morrison, Publishers
386 Fourth Avenue
New York, N. Y.

Dear Mr. O'Dab:

Your protest against the assignment of Stephen Worth to the script of *The Speckled Band* has been received and personally considered by me. Unfortunately, contractual arrangements, which I am sure you as an author will understand, prevent me from altering this assignment; but I have hit upon an arrangement which will, I hope, satisfy you.

I am inviting you and a group of your associates among the Baker Street Irregulars to be my guests in Hollywood during the making of this picture. You will have complete advisory authority over all details of adaptation and be in a position to guarantee authenticity and fidelity.

I will not affront your devotion to the literature of Sherlock Holmes by offering you a salary as a technical advisor. As I say, you shall be my personal guest, with all travel and living expenses cared for and a liberal drawing account for personal expenses.

I hope that this invitation is fortunate enough to reach you at a period between novels when you will be free to accept it. May I add that I strongly anticipate meeting the creator of that dashing criminal of the printed page and the silver screen, the Honorable Derring Drew. You will be pleased to hear that our motion picture, *Meet Derring Drew,* adapted from your *The Deeds of Derring Drew,* is a great success throughout the country from exhibitors' reports; *Variety,* in fact, describes it as "the socko B of the season." Your sequel, *The Grand Duke's Cigar Case,* will shortly go into production under the working title, *Derring Drew at the World's Fair.* You will doubtless be happy to learn that Paul Jackson, whose fan mail has mounted daily since he assumed the role of Derring Drew, will play a leading part in *The Speckled Band.*

Hoping that I shall soon receive a favorable reply from you, I remain

Yours sincerely,
F. X. Weinberg
FXW/RS

Columbia, Mo.
July 3, 1939

M. F. X. Weinberg
Metropolis Pictures
Los Angeles, California

Dear Mr. Weinberg:

You may well marvel at the postmark on this letter. A small Midwestern town—and an academic one at that—seems an odd place to encounter Derring Drew. But we were weary of the brilliant world, Derring and I, and in this out-of-the-way place we have found a restful charm.

Even a restful charm, however, palls on one in time. I myself, who am merely the humble narrator of dashing events, have found the seconds hanging heavy on my hands; and Derring has been veritably champing for action.

We have heard great things of your Hollywood. Perhaps it will live up to its promises, though I must confess that I am doubtful. Moreover, the honor of protecting the memory of Holmes appeals to me strongly.

Derring suggests scornfully that you might better make a picture about Raffles; but I tell him that such an act would in all likelihood merely cut the market out from under his own picture. Any psychoanalyst could tell him that all the bravura of his exploits results quite simply from a Raffles fixation.

But why should I tell the secrets of my hero? It is enough that he and I cordially accept your invitation.

Sincerely yours,
John O'Dab

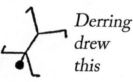

Derring
drew
this

For all its careful dashing air, this letter was written in a schoolroom—to be precise, in a classroom of Miss Aminta Frowley's Select Coaching School for Young Ladies. There were French verbs on the blackboard, and the air was heavy with chalk and the peculiar scent of janitor's sawdust.

The dry little man at the desk screwed the cap meticulously

back on his fountain pen. "That is a peculiarly silly letter, Fred, is it not?"

Fred, the janitor, leaned heavily on his pushbroom and peered through Woolworth reading glasses at the letter on the desk. "Don't seem to make much sense to me, Mr. Evans, and that's a fact; but there ain't no telling what them Hollywood people like. That's what I always say when I go to a movie: 'They don't know what we like,' I say, 'that's plain enough. So how's a body ever to know what they like?' I say."

"They seem to like Derring Drew, at all events," said Jonadab Evans, known to what Mason and Morrison term "his unending circle of readers" as John O'Dab. (Mr. Evans had once pointed out to them that all circles are unending by definition; but the thought had not discomposed the copywriters.)

"So do I," said Fred, pulling out a heavily caked corncob of the most primitive design. "Leastways I guess I do. It ain't what you'd call real convincing, but it sort of makes you forget things, and I guess sometimes that's a pretty good idea."

"Thank you, Fred. The literature of escape receives the endorsement of the proletariat."

"Is that what I am?" Fred slowly filled from a rubber pouch what little space remained in the pipe's bowl. "Can't say as I like the sound of it."

"I know. That's one of the consolations of democracy. No American workingman likes to be told that he's a proletarian."

Fred looked back at the letter as he struck a match. "So you're really going to Hollywood?" (He said it in the tone of "So you're leaving for Mars after all?") "What are you going to say to Miss Frowley?"

"There, Fred, is a problem. What would you say to Miss

Frowley if she came in now and caught you smoking in the classroom?"

Fred grinned. "I'd say I was helping out her old man. He made his money out of corncobs, and I always say there ain't a sweeter smoke in the world than a good Missouri meerschaum."

"That," said Mr. Evans judiciously, "is as it may be. But for all my fine words to Metropolis Pictures, I don't quite know how to face Miss Frowley. I may not be able as a writer to understand Mr. Weinberg's contractual difficulties, but I certainly do as a teacher."

"Why don't you just tell the old lady to go to blazes? I would, Mr. Evans; I certainly would, if the movies was buying my books."

"I know, Fred; but the trouble goes back to old Mr. Frowley. He was such a good businessman that he passed on his tricks to his daughter. And I, like an innocent lamb, signed the contract she gave me. For seven years. Four years I've been here—ever since dear old Sampson Military Academy died. Four years of coaching the young ladies of Missouri, winter and summer, and three more years to go. Ever since the Derring Drew stories were accepted, I have been hinting to Miss Frowley that I might like to leave; but she as good as brandishes the contract in my face, and here I am still."

"Pick a fight with her," Fred suggested. "Get her mad and she'll break the contract her own self."

Mr. Evans shuddered delicately. "Please, Fred. You know Miss Frowley. Do you imagine that I have the courage to pick a fight with her?"

Fred looked him over at some length. "No-o-o-o. Guess not. Can't say as I blame you. Ain't got that much guts myself."

He set down the corncob and picked up his bucket of cleansing sawdust. "Well, I got to be getting along to the other rooms. Wish you luck, Mr. Evans."

"Thanks." The door closed behind Fred. Mr. Evans picked up his optimistic letter to F. X. Weinberg and reread it. "A trifle coy," he commented distastefully. "But then people seem to expect that of such a *dashing* writer." He turned again to Mr. Weinberg's own epistle, and clicked his tongue over the disgraceful misuse of "anticipate." "And I do wonder," he murmured, "just what a 'socko B' might be."

The door swung open again. Mr. Evans looked around, to see the whole of the good-sized doorway obscured by the formidable bulk of Miss Aminta Frowley.

"Working late, Mr. Evans," she observed in a thin voice— quite out of proportion to her vast size and therefore all the more terrifying.

"Why . . . ah . . . yes," he fumbled. "Exercises, you know. Correcting them. That Loring child will never understand the imperfect subjunctive." Miss Frowley was ominously stiff and silent. He babbled a bit. "That might be a good sign, you know. She may end by speaking like a true native—so few of them understand it, either. Ha ha," he added. It was not a laugh—just the two syllables *ha ha*. It sounded pitifully helpless before Miss Frowley's glaring silence.

Slowly she cleared her throat and then spoke with measured sharpness. "Mr. Evans, there is tobacco smoke in this room."

He looked. There in front of him lay Fred's well-seasoned corncob, still smoldering. And in a second he knew what to do. He stuck the stem in his mouth, cocked the pipe at a grotesque angle, and looked up. "So there is," he said.

Miss Frowley's eyebrows all but met the gray roots of her black hair. "You know the rules of this institution, Mr. Evans," she said.

"And if I do?" he ventured bravely.

"You know how strongly I am opposed to the weed in any form, in spite of my father's ill-gotten wealth."

"I know." He tried to send a sizable puff straight into her face, and almost made it.

Miss Frowley glared. "There is only one answer then, Mr. Evans, much though I have admired your work. There is no room in the Frowley School for a—a *corncob!* I shall see my lawyer tomorrow to draw up a release from your contract. You may well shudder, Mr. Evans! Good day!"

But Jonadab Evans was not shuddering in awe of Miss Frowley's wrath. Neither was he shuddering in blissful expectation of the delights of Hollywood, nor yet in uncanny prescience of the events which were to befall him there. Mr. Evans, in the triumph of his first acquaintance with Missouri meerschaum, was only wondering if he could reach the men's room in time.

III
METROPOLIS ★ PICTURES

June 26, 1939

Rufus Bottomley, M.D.
c/o Venture House
20 East 57th Street
New York, N. Y.

Dear Dr. Bottomley:

Your protest against the assignment of Stephen Worth to the script of *The Speckled Band* has been received and personally considered by me. Unfortunately, contractual arrangements, which I am sure you as a professional man will understand, prevent me from altering this assignment; but I have hit upon an arrangement which will, I hope, satisfy you.

I am inviting you and a group of your associates among the Baker Street Irregulars to be my guests in Hollywood during the making of this picture. You will have complete advisory authority over all details of adaptation and be in a position to guarantee authenticity and fidelity.

I will not affront your devotion to the literature of Sherlock Holmes by offering you a salary as a technical advisor. As I say, you shall be my personal guest, with all travel and living expenses cared for and a liberal drawing account for personal expenses.

Since you have retired from active practice, I hope that you have no other commitments at this time which will interfere with your accepting this invitation.

I should also be glad of the opportunity to confer with you on the sale of screen rights to your deservedly best-selling book, *G. P.* Your agents report that you are adverse to selling, because of our notion of introducing a romantic interest; but I hope that I can persuade you personally of the wisdom of such a move. As a doctor, you must know the value of sugar-coating a bitter capsule.

I look forward warmly to our meeting.

Sincerely yours,
F. X. Weinberg
FXW/RS

New York
June 30, 1939

Mr. F. X. Weinberg
Metropolis Pictures
Los Angeles, California

Dear Mr. Weinberg:

Do you expect me to resist?

Lovingly,
Rufus Bottomley

P.S. Romantic interest indeed! We'll see about that.

R.B.

P.P.S. Do you know anything about Otto Federhut? Austrian scholar—eminent jurist—brilliant critical mind—do I have to add that he's a refugee? Wrote an amazing work called *Der Holmes-Mythos und seine Entwicklungen, mit einigen Bemerkungen über das Watson-Problem.* Just about as fine a piece of mock scholarship as I've ever encountered. We're initiating him into the Irregulars next week, if he passes our examination—as I've no doubt he will. He might add color to our party—to say nothing of aiding the refugee cause. You can reach him c/o the APRP—Association for the Placement of Refugees in the Professions. Give him my love.

RB

P.P.P.S. You don't sugar-coat capsules.

Dr. Rufus Bottomley was sealing his letter as the house phone rang.

"Hello." He listened a moment, then burst into an expansive

roar of welcome. "Fine. Good to hear your voice again. Come on up."

He set to sprucing himself a bit. Now that he was an Established Author, with a room at the Algonquin when he stayed in New York, it was necessary to keep up appearances more carefully than when he had been a general practitioner—a G. P.—in Waterloo, Iowa. He brushed the pipe ashes off his vest. Then he took a comb and did perfunctory justice to his mustache and imperial. These were new since his days of general practice. He was modern enough to realize the unhygienic possibilities of facial hair. He realized, too, that his short paunchy body looked absurd with such elaborate ornamentation sprouting above it; but that aspect did not concern him. All his life, for some reason, he had wanted an imperial—and there was no valid reason now why he shouldn't have one.

A knock on the door came as he was slipping on his coat. He left wrinkles unstraightened, and answered with a promptitude surviving from those days when a knock might mean anything from a fatal stroke for old Mrs. Wyatt to a new baby out at the Hobbses.

"Gordon!" he bellowed. "Great to see you! Come on in. Spot of whisky before we set out to paint New York?"

Gordon Withers, though by nature more restrained, was no less sincere in his greeting. "It is good, Rufus. And I will, if you don't mind."

"Fine." Dr. Bottomley occupied himself with pouring. "And how's the rest home?"

"Doing nicely. You've no idea what a boon the film industry is. Shooting schedules and nervous breakdowns form practically a definition of cause and effect."

Dr. Bottomley grinned. "No regrets for the quiet days when we ran a practice together?"

"None, Rufus. Oh, I know all your ideas about the true vocation of medicine. I've read your book, and God knows I've heard you talk. But if honest men didn't cater to this generation of neurotics, the quacks would. My conscience is clear—and that's more than you can say for the consciences of most of us who live off the colony."

"Strange place, Hollywood, from all I hear. Mrmfk! Wonder how I'll like it?"

"You, Rufus?"

"Me. Rufus. In person—and not, God grant, a moving picture. Here, take your drink."

"But what should bring you—"

"Out into your bailiwick? Matters of great moment, Gordon. Lo! And likewise behold!" He handed over F. X. Weinberg's invitation.

"So? . . . Well, I shall be glad to see you out there. I don't know quite what you'll make of it—"

"But I'll enjoy myself, Gordon. You may be sure of that. Cigar?"

Dr. Withers looked distastefully at the case of short black things. "Still at those? They look like torpedoes; but if I remember aright, they're infinitely more deadly. No thanks." He lit a cigarette. "But tell me—how's your book going?"

"Splendiferously. Right up in front with Heiser and all the rest. I expect the Writers' League of America to start issuing prescriptions any day—it'd be only a fair exchange. Mrmfk. Yes, everybody is unconscionably delighted with *G. P.*—all but a few misguided and probably misbegotten souls who thought it was a history of the Russian secret police."

Dr. Withers walked slowly over to the desk and laid his hand lightly on the vast calabash pipe that rested there in a specially constructed cradle. "Warm," he said softly.

Rufus Bottomley looked almost shamefaced. "Yes," he admitted.

"I've known you for twenty years, Rufus, and I know that the only cause that can drive you from your damned little torpedoes to a decent pipe is worry—and pretty serious worry at that. What is it now?"

Dr. Bottomley waved a plump hand helplessly. "What would it be?"

"Ann?"

"Of course. Two years, you know, doesn't make it hurt any the less."

"I know."

Dr. Bottomley's face was grave—so intensely grave that even the foolish imperial looked serious. "How is she?"

"My turn to give a helpless answer. How would she be?"

"I'll come to see her, of course. That's my main reason for accepting Mr. Weinberg's invitation so blithely. You probably guessed that?"

"Yes."

"Do you think—Is there any chance on earth that she might know me?"

Dr. Withers shook his head.

"If I ever know . . ." Rufus Bottomley muttered. "If I ever learn who . . ." His teeth were tight set under the flowing mustache. His hand clenched, and the black cigar within it slowly crumbled.

IV
METROPOLIS ★ PICTURES

June 26, 1939

Professor Drew Furness
Department of English
University of California at Los Angeles
Los Angeles, Cal.

Dear Professor Furness:

Miss O'Breen informs me that she has acquainted you with our plans for inviting the Baker Street Irregulars to act as unofficial advisors in the making of *The Speckled Band,* and that you, as a member of the Irregulars, are pleased with the idea.

However, let me take this opportunity of extending my own personal invitation to you to be my guest for this period.

I hope that in this way Metropolis Pictures may, to some small extent, make up to you for the inconvenience and humiliation which you suffered in my office the other day. I repeat the assurances, which Miss O'Breen has already given you, that I had no part in that shameful occurrence, and that I would gladly take punitive measures for what has transpired if only it was possible for me to do so. Our legal department, however, assures me that it is not. I hope and trust that you will accept, through me, the most sincere apologies of Metropolis Pictures.

Sincerely yours,
F. X. Weinberg
FXW/RS

11473 Shenandoah Road
West Los Angeles
June 27, 1939

Mr. F. X. Weinberg
Metropolis Pictures
Los Angeles, Cal.

Dear Mr. Weinberg:

Your plans, as Miss O'Breen outlined them to me, are indeed pleasing. I beg you to rely on my heartiest cooperation in your venture.

Your apologies, though gratefully accepted, are hardly necessary. I realized, of course, that the sole responsibility was that of Stephen Worth. Let us consider that the episode never took place.

Sincerely yours,
Drew Furness

The note finished, Drew Furness left the desk, settled his long frame in the Morris chair, and took up the latest copy of the *Journal of English and Germanic Philology.*

The little old lady on the sofa looked up from her crocheting. "Who were you writing to, Drew?"

"Whom, Aunt Belle," he said automatically.

"I don't know why you expect me to talk that way just because you're an English teacher. I know your grandfather wouldn't have stood for such highfalutin talk for a minute. Why, I remember . . ."

Drew Furness read calmly on until the familiar anecdote was ended and his aunt repeated her question. "Who's the letter to?"

"F. X. Weinberg. You remember, Aunt Belle—the cinema producer who's making *The Speckled Band.*"

"Oh." A crafty look came over Aunt Belle's round little face. "Tell me, Drew—is he one of them?"

"How should I know, Aunt Belle? He's Jewish, I think, if that's what you mean."

"You know very well that's not what I mean. I mean," she explained, "is he one of Them?"

"Now, Aunt Belle, let's not start that again."

"He beat you up, didn't he? You came home all black and blue after you went to see him. You can't fool me. What did he try to make you tell him, Drew?"

"Please. There's an interesting thing of Bretheridge's in here about the authorship of *Lust's Dominion*. He seems to upset quite a few of one's preconceived notions."

That seemed to hold Aunt Belle. She was silent. But Drew Furness did not return to the *JEGPh*. Instead he thought of that day in the studio and the absurdly humiliating scene in the commissary where that delightful Miss O'Breen had taken him for refreshment. He must, he feared, have cut a very sorry figure in that young lady's eyes—a figure hardly worthy of one of the foremost authorities on the problem of William Ireland and the sources of his forged plays. He wondered—

"Drew . . ."

"Please, Aunt Belle. Do let me alone. I have to study."

"Study indeed! A body'd think you were still a schoolboy instead of a professor. But you can't put me off like that. Drew, I saw a man in the street today."

"That's hardly surprising, is it?"

"He was lurking, Drew. Lurking right in front of this house. You can't tell me that doesn't mean anything. They're everywhere, They are. A person isn't safe in her own house any more, but They come spying around."

"Please. You go back to your knitting and let me read."

"That's just like a man," she sniffed. "Can't tell knitting from crocheting. And you're just as blind about what goes on all around you. But you'll find out someday. When They come into power, then you'll understand. Then you'll know what your poor old auntie used to try to tell you when you wouldn't even—"

"Hang it all, Aunt Belle!" Drew Furness cried in exasperation.

A resigned frown spread across the old face. "That's right. I knew it would come to this someday. Go on. Swear at me. Use your foul language—and you an English teacher. Someday you'll be sorry. Go right ahead—don't mind what I say. But you'll be sorry yet, Drew Furness, when They come . . ."

The dumpy little Cassandra gathered up her crocheting and majestically left the room, trailing doom behind her. Drew Furness sat still for a moment, trying faithfully to follow Bretheridge's intricate tables of run-on lines, but finally tossed the periodical from him.

These scenes brought on by Aunt Belle's unspecified phobia were frequent enough; but he could not get used to them. Quarreling, no matter how innocently, with an old woman always upset him. Besides, she had seemed worse of late. He began almost to wonder if there might be anything seriously wrong.

On an impulse he picked up the phone book and opened it to the O's. He ran his finger down the page: O'Boyle, Obradovich, O'Brand, Obrasky—O'Breen. And on Berendo Street—the address to which he had driven her home on that fantastic day.

He lifted the phone from its cradle, then slowly let it fall back again. Really that was a very foolish idea. What could Miss O'Breen and he have to talk about?

He went back to *Lust's Dominion*.

V
METROPOLIS ★ PICTURES

July 3, 1939

Mr. Otto Federhut
c/o The Association for the Placement
of Refugees in the Professions
New York, N. Y.

Dear Mr. Federhut:

You have no doubt heard from your new colleagues in the Baker Street Irregulars of my plans to invite the society to Hollywood to supervise the making of *The Speckled Band*.

If you are still unsettled in this country, I urge you to accept this invitation as applying especially to yourself. It is even possible that I can arrange some contacts for you here in Hollywood which will solve your problems for a time at least.

The motion picture, as the youngest and most progressive of the major art forms, owes it to society to do what it can in the defense of democracy; and I, as a representative of the industry, stand always ready to offer my aid to those who are victims of foreign tyranny.

I deeply hope that we can add your name to our roster of guests.

Sincerely yours,
F. X. Weinberg
FXW/RS

New York
7 July, 1939

F. X. Weinberg, Esq.
Metropolis Pictures
Los Angeles, California

My dear Sir:

This invitation that you offer to me is, I feel, a great honor, and I accept it with eagerness. Long have I admired the makers of American films—yes, and envied them when I have seen the propagandistic *Mischmasch* which our once great UFA has been forced to turn out. It will be a pleasant sight to behold an industry which is not dominated by Emil Jannings in an unending row of historical variations complete with costumes upon the role of Hermann Goring.

I hear—for in this land, thanks be to God, we may speak freely—that among the German colony in Hollywood the anti-Nazi movement is growing daily in strength and vigor. May it be that you could put me in touch with the leaders of such a movement that I may add my forces to theirs in our great work?

Believe me, even aside from these political considerations, I shall be more than happy to consider your invitation. In this world of strife and terror, it is happy to think again that free men may have sufficient cultural leisure that to them the treatment of Sherlock Holmes may seem a matter of weight and import. I shall enjoy joining in the sport.

Respectfully yours,
Otto Federhut

Otto Federhut wrote this note at a table in the Prater—a little restaurant founded by an Austrian *émigré* for his compatriots and fortunately still undiscovered by color-seeking New Yorkers.

Herr Doktor Federhut reread the note, passed it over to his companion, and sipped his coffee blissfully. It was highly sweetened coffee with a great island of whipped cream floating on it—the first such cup he had found in this benighted land.

His companion—a tall, heavy-set man with thick eyebrows and a striking saber cut across his left cheek—read the missive carefully and handed it back. "It is hard to adjust oneself," he said in German, "to the fact that in this land one may write what one pleases in a letter and have no fears as to who may read it."

Federhut nodded, with a shaggy toss of his leonine white hair. "It is a strange thing, this democracy. Sometimes it seems to me almost like a householder who says, 'No, I shall never lock my front door. That would infringe upon the rights of entry of my fellow man.'"

The heavy man smiled his agreement. "And now it is as though two of his fellow men should enter the house to find a safe dueling ground—two brothers who cannot fight their battle at home."

"Brothers!" Otto Federhut snorted.

"We are all Germans. That is not easy to forget."

"Does a German drink coffee and whipped cream?" the Austrian asked sardonically.

"Does an Austrian remain unmoved by Goethe, by Beethoven, by Wagner?"

"By Wagner, my friend, all too often. And if you have Beethoven, so do we have Mozart. But I will admit the brotherhood. More binds us now than a matter of names and nations. He has made us one in more ways than the world understands."

"Do you think that you will meet those of whom you have written there?"

Federhut laughed. "Do you think all the world a spy still, here in this free country? You recall the story of the three friends who met in a Berlin café"

"No."

"The first friend sat down in silence. The second friend sat down and sighed. The third friend sat down and groaned. Then the waiter came over and said, 'Gentlemen, I must ask you to refrain from this political discussion.'"

The thin edge of a smile met the saber cut. "Good," the man nodded.

"Good," Federhut agreed, "and true. But here we may speak out. So say it then—do I hope to meet in Hollywood these leaders of the refugee anti-Nazi movement?"

"Very well, I say it then. But do you?"

"Naturally. I hope to make contacts there invaluable to our cause. This F. X. Weinberg can hardly know with what eargerness I accept his invitation. It is sad," he went on hesitantly, "that brothers must suffer; but we have been patient long enough. Schiller was wrong in his *Ode to Joy*. Millions cannot be patient forever for the better world—not even courageously patient. We must act."

"We must act," his companion repeated.

Chapter 3

TIME: Monday, July 17, 1939
PLACE: 221B Romualdo Drive

Romualdo Drive is one of those curvaceous little streets that intertwine like a cluster of angleworms on the hill southeast of the Hollywood Bowl. F. X. Weinberg had pulled every conceivable wire with the City Planning Commission to have Romualdo Drive rechristened Baker Street, but the Commission had remained adamant. Romualdo was a fine old Spanish name of noble memory (a statement not likely to be disputed by the long-dead Indians who had suffered under the lash of Don Diego Arturo Romualdo y Vegas), and we Angelenos must preserve our traditions. Street numerals, however, can hardly be considered objects of traditional veneration; and 221B was allowed to stand in the middle of the 2700 block, to the rejoicing of all Baker Street devotees and the intense confusion of the mailman.

Thus the Baker Street Irregulars (such of them, that is, as had been able to accept Mr. Weinberg's invitation) were to be established in Hollywood proper, some ten minutes' drive from the Metropolis studios. Just what claim to existence Hollywood, as an entity, may have is a matter for argument. As part of the city of Los Angeles, it has no separate political being. The United States Post Office knows nothing of such a city. Most of the major studios have long since moved off to sprawl more contentedly in the open spaces. Actors and directors live where there is room for swimming pools and a chance of becoming an honorary mayor. The tourist hunting stars at play is advised to seek them in Beverly Hills or in the strip of resorts located along Sunset Boulevard in the county of Los Angeles.

All that Hollywood has left to distinguish it from any other comfortably bourgeois community within a city are the footprints in the forecourt of Grauman's Chinese, the corner of Hollywood and Vine, Morton Thompson, and the Brown Derby, where people lunch incessantly, hoping to be taken for actors by the others who are hoping to be taken for producers.

But Metropolis Pictures still remains in Hollywood, a desolate Casabianca. And in Hollywood, at 221B Romualdo Drive, Maureen was busy readying the household of the Baker Street Irregulars.

"This is your own bright idea, Maureen," Mr. Weinberg had told her. "So Feinstein can take over the office today. You run this."

And now it was four o'clock in the afternoon—a wonderful bright afternoon when you should be lying on the beach somewhere in the sun, or maybe better yet sitting under an umbrella beside a fountain of beer—and the press reception was at seven and nothing was ready. The house was of two stories— two big roomy stories—but at the moment it seemed to Maureen more like Groucho Marx's stateroom. There were the men from the caterers, the staff of servants for the reception, the decorator's men who had just remembered a few touches left unfinished, the cameramen from Maureen's department planning suitable angles, and enough unidentified extras to cast a de Mille production. But there was no Mrs. Hudson.

That had been Mr. Weinberg's own idea, after he had spent a hasty evening reading the Holmes works which he had purchased as story properties long ago. "At 221B Baker Street," he said, "they had a landlady named Mrs. Hudson. So all right— we won't give them a Japanese houseboy or a French valet. No— we'll give them a housekeeper named Mrs. Hudson. And you, Maureen, will make a release on that."

She had sent word to an employment agency: *Wanted: One housekeeper, must be named Mrs. Hudson, to report at 221B Romualdo Drive at twelve noon, July 17.* That morning the agency had phoned her. They had finally located a housekeeping Mrs. Hudson through their branch office in San Francisco. Should they have her fly down? They should, Maureen told them, and wondered at herself for taking such an utterly screwy commission in so calm a manner. She remembered when she had her first office job with the Atlas Paper Towel Supply Company and thought Mr. Murdock was eccentric because he smoked tiny cigars the size of cigarettes. Now an employer who smoked a hookah wouldn't surprise her, even if he sat on a specially constructed mushroom to do so.

The doorbell rang. Maureen, explaining to the caterer that he had sadly underestimated the liquor supply—this was a *press* reception—broke off and hurried to the door. Maybe this was Mrs. Hudson. She could turn over the household to this nice motherly soul and get back to finishing those damned releases to be handed out at seven.

But it was a messenger boy.

"For Stephen Worth," he said. "Sign here."

"Mr. Worth isn't here."

"O.K. Hold it for him."

"I don't know—"

"He'll be here, won't he?"

"I can't say. I—"

The phone rang.

"Listen, lady," the boy expostulated. "The guy that gave me this said this Stephen Worth was going to be here and I should leave this for him. Now will you sign for it"—the phone kept on ringing—"and let me get on with my job?"

"Oh—all right." Maureen scribbled her initials, snatched the plain white envelope, and hurried to the phone.

"Ha-lo," said a deep, vaguely foreign voice. "Two-two-one-B Bakair Street?"

"The City Planning Commission maintains it's still Romualdo Drive."

"Ah so? You are Miss O'Breen?"

"Yes"—impatiently.

"You will please to kindly inform Mr. Worth that I called and that I may see him later?"

"And what is your name?"

"Ah, that." The voice laughed—a hearty gurgle that seemed to Maureen, in her state of tension, almost ominous. "You are efficient, Miss O'Breen. You must know everything, no? Even if it is not good to know."

The doorbell rang.

"But how can I tell him you called if—"

"True. The admirable American logic. Na! You may tell him that I am concerned with Miss Gray, with Miss Amy Gray. Shall I spell it?"

"Amy Gray? All right. But if you would—"

"I hear that your doorbell rings. Goodby."

A click sounded in Maureen's ear. She made a hasty note on the back of the white envelope—that way Worth would be sure to get it, if indeed he came, which God forbid—and hurried to the door. Maybe this would be Mrs. Hudson.

It was a man who looked, oddly enough, as peculiar, with the same suggestions of the foreign and the sinister, as the voice on the phone had sounded. He was tall and bearded, with a felt hat pulled well over his face and, of all costumes on such a day, a heavy astrakhan-trimmed topcoat.

In silence he extended his card. Maureen looked up puzzled. "Whom did you want to see?" she asked, feeling as foolishly affected as she always did when trapped into a *whom* clause.

"Give this to Worth!" he commanded in a clear, unaccented voice. He gave a perfunctory tug at the felt brim, turned, and walked off, limping slightly.

She looked at the card. On one side was the name:

TALIPES RICOLETTI

On the other was drawn a string of little men, of the sort that have matchstick bodies and limbs and featureless dots for heads, dancing and cavorting in every imaginable manner. Some even stood on their heads, and others waved flags.

Maureen shook her head and went to place the card beside the white envelope. This she regarded curiously for a moment. It was of such thin paper that the note inside should have been dimly visible; but it was not. She held the envelope up to the light from the window. There was no paper inside it, but there was something else—something dry that rattled as she moved the envelope about.

She was saved the temptation of prying further by another ring of the doorbell. She hardly dared hope that this time it would be the missing Mrs. Hudson.

"If you want Stephen Worth," she was ready to say, "you can wait in hell. He'll be sure to show up."

But she fell back a little as she looked up at the gaunt frame of Professor Drew Furness.

He seemed not to notice her dismay. Instead he smiled with unexpected warmth and said, "Miss O'Breen! This is a delightful surprise."

"Isn't it!" she murmured.

He picked up a small suitcase and carried it into the hall. "I don't suppose you would know which is my room?"

"I don't suppose," she echoed, "that you'd know you weren't supposed to show up here until six at the earliest? There are, by actual count, seven hundred and sixty-three last-minute things left to do around here, and mostly just me to do them. And half the lunatic fringe of this town seems to think I'm hiding Stephen Worth under my skirts like Amy Robsart or whoever it is I mean—"

"Flora MacDonald," Mr. Furness interposed.

"Thank you. No, I don't thank you. This is a fine time to be accurate about things. The only thing I'd thank you for is if you were still wherever you ought to be, Professor, instead of—"

"Please," he protested gently. "Not 'Professor.' The academic man who uses his title in private life always seems something of a pretentious charlatan. Even the use of 'Doctor' is suspect. And besides, I am merely an assistant professor. So simply Mr. Furness, if you please, unless I dare—"

The phone rang.

"No!" Maureen snapped. "Leave it alone. Don't try to be helpful, for any sake." She took up the phone, leaving Mr. Furness looking very empty-handed and forlorn. "Yes, F. X. . . . No, she hasn't showed up yet. . . . All right, give them to me."

She stood silent, jotting down notes of instructions for the still-absent Mrs. Hudson. "All right. Fine. See you at seven, F. X., if I don't wind up in the Withers Rest Home before then. Now I've got the Professor on my hands. . . . What Professor? Don't you remember our pal? Canvasback Furness, the boys used to call him. . . . All right. Good-by, F. X." She turned back to Furness. "Now please," she began, "any minute Mrs. Hudson will be here and I'll have to start explaining—"

"Mrs. Hudson?" He smiled. "Surely 221B is not to be so realistic as all that?"

"Isn't it just?" For an instant she answered his smile. "Can't you see her? The old landlady in person—half admiring and half pitying the helpless males who need her—her—"

"Diurnal ministrations," Drew Furness suggested.

"There you go! I was just beginning to feel friendly again. Almost. But if you start pulling that stuff, out you go. Now—"

The doorbell rang.

"Now this, if the gods are good, will be Mrs. Hudson."

This was a tall, angular young woman, with rimless spectacles, black hair drawn back into a tight knot, and a dress which seemed to have been designed with far more of an eye to function than to form.

"Miss O'Breen?" she demanded.

"Look," said Maureen, "if *you* want Stephen Worth—which I admit seems damned unlikely—"

"My dear Miss O'Breen," the young woman announced, "I am Mrs. Hudson."

Maureen goggled. "Are you—God save the mark!—a housekeeper?"

Mrs. Hudson deigned to smile at the archaic word. "I am a

bachelor of science in domestic economics. Is this the household which I am to manage?"

"If Casting could get a load of this! . . ." Maureen muttered.

"Please!" the bachelor of science snapped. "Am I to stand here in the doorway all day? This *is* the right address, is it not?"

"Oh yes. Oh my, yes. Come on in, and God help you. Did they give you courses on the care and feeding of the press? But then that's up to the caterer. All you have to do is make five intellectual gentlemen comfortable and contented. And there's a sample for you."

Mrs. Hudson gave Drew Furness something the same glance he might have given a football star who wondered why he wasn't doing so good in Chaucer. "Hmm!" she remarked. "A special diet, I suppose?"

"Why, no. Not that I know of," he faltered absurdly, feeling as abashed under her gaze as he had always hoped (and vainly) that the football player might feel under his.

"Probably should have. Allergic type. Rash in the summertime?"

"Professor Furness," Maureen interposed, "is never rash."

"Miss O'Breen!"

"You asked for worse than that, barging in here. Now if you'll come with me, Mrs. Hudson . . ."

Drew Furness was left alone in the hallway—as alone, that is, as one can well be on a major thoroughfare. He spent the next ten minutes dodging the decorators' ladders, explaining to the caterer that he had no idea whether Mr. Weinberg wanted French or Italian in the Martinis, and letting the studio cameramen discover that there was no angle from which he could provide a presentable picture.

The phone put an end to his posing ordeal. There was still no sign of Miss O'Breen or Mrs. Hudson. After the fifth ring he picked up the handset himself.

"Is this the home of the Baker Street Irregulars?" a thick and somehow familiar voice wanted to know.

"It is."

"And who's this speaking?"

"Drew Furness."

"My pal!" The voice boomed so loudly in the receiver that Furness was forced to hold the instrument away from his ear. "Remember me, sister?"

Furness' voice grew dangerously cold. "Indeed I do, Mr. Worth."

"I'm glad I got you. Those other bastards don't know me so—let's say intimately, huh? They mightn't appreciate my friendly greetings."

"Is there anything in particular you wished to say?" Furness asked with frigid politeness.

"No. Nothing special. Just to tell you girls that I'll see you tonight. Your little reunion wouldn't be complete without me, would it now? You know you're just dying to see me, aren't you, ducky?"

"Mr. Worth, I warn you that if I see you again I shall—"

"I'll tell you what you'll do, Hyacinth," Worth cut in. And he proceeded to describe, in fantastic and unprintable terms, his notions of what Drew Furness could do to him—notions which entailed an incredible physical versatility.

Drew Furness thrust the receiver down on this farrago of obscenity with the gesture of one pushing the cork back on a jinni. His face was white when Maureen re-entered the hallway.

"Miss O'Breen," he began, "I—"

"Are *you* still here? Look. I thought I told you to scram till six. Just because you're a local boy in this galley is no reason you should have any special privileges. Bottomley and Ridgly and O'Dab are sitting pretty in their hotels and Federhut's still on the train, I suppose. They've got more sense than to come cluttering—"

"Miss O'Breen," he interrupted, "please be quiet for a minute." There was something close to authority in his tone, and not quite the authority of the classroom. "I did not come out here to clutter. My surprise at seeing you was, I confess, feigned. I learned from the studio that you were here, and because, ever since that mad day at Metropolis I have . . ."

He hesitated a little, and Maureen snapped him up, her blue eyes flashing. "Go on, Professor. 'Ever since that mad day!' 'Strike up the band, *Kapellmeister,* my regiment leaves at dawn!' Romance and stuff! Look. Do you have any quaint idea that I was doing anything but trying to get Polly out of a damage suit? Out with it. What's on your learned mind?"

The silence of offended dignity emanated from Drew Furness. Wordlessly he picked up his bag and started for the door. A sudden shadow of disappointment crossed Maureen's face. She started to speak, uncertain herself of what she would say.

The doorbell rang.

Maureen pushed past Mr. Furness, swung open the door with a bang, and said, "Yes!" with several extra s's.

"Package for O'Breen."

"I must beg your pardon, Miss O'Breen," Furness was saying as she signed for the package and started to unwrap it. "I realized that it was presumptuous of me to . . . That is, I . . . After all, my life, I fear, is a poor and cloistered thing, hardly fitting me to . . . My word!" he broke off. "What on earth is that?"

Maureen wondered too for a moment. It took her a little while to realize that what looked like an exceedingly modernistic kitchen gadget was actually a chromium-plated parody of a brassière, in an unflatteringly small size, and remembered her gag threat before Worth to bill the studio for damages incurred in the line of duty.

She read the card:

Not that you'll need it among the deductionists.

Love,
WORTH

"No," she observed to no one in particular, "I'm afraid I won't."

Chapter 4

THE WORKING press—a strange expression, that; it calls up a picture of a horde of other pressmen lolling about Hollywood on sumptuous divans, smothered by bevies of attendant odalisques, and thinking scornfully of their colleagues of the *working* press—the working press took kindly to the reception for the Baker Street Irregulars. The working press, in fact, always takes kindly to any function sponsored by F. X. Weinberg, who is noted, double takes and all, as the best host in the film colony. He never indulges in fancifully quaint invitations (there are members of the press who will never recall without a shudder the morning they received their bids to the *première* of *Robin Hood)* nor in coyly conceived souvenirs; but he sets a magnificent table, furnishes a resplendent bar, and generally provides guests who are newsworthy for much more than mere cinematographic importance.

Maureen suffered, in fact, from a certain professional worry as she circulated among the party. No one was paying much attention to *The Speckled Band.* Each correspondent (or columnist or whatever name he bore to distinguish himself from a common, or garden, reporter) was sounding out his victim along the lines of that individual's personal fame, and doing very nicely without a thought for Metropolis Pictures.

"Socialized medicine," Dr. Rufus Bottomley was declaiming with wags of his lively imperial, "is at once a golden goal and an abyss of horror. The medical profession cannot survive much longer without it, and yet may well be destroyed by it. The point is that reform, imperative though it is, must come from within the profession and not be totalitarianly imposed from without by an arbitrarily constituted bureaucratic authority. Mrmfk. I hear that an experiment along these lines is being made now in California. Could you tell me how close to success it has come?"

"I'm afraid," his columnist admitted, "I haven't heard about that."

"Hell and death!" Dr. Bottomley exclaimed, with three rhythmic thumps on the arm of his chair. "Does a man have to come from Waterloo, Iowa, via New York to tell you Californians that an experiment of vital importance to our whole social structure is going on in your very midst? Is this the vaunted omniscience of the press? Why, man—"

Maureen wandered to the table near the bar, where Harrison Ridgly III sat with a bottle of scotch and an interviewer, obviously considered in that order of importance.

"A campaign for clean literature?" he was saying. "Why, well and good. But why should that affect me?"

"I've heard, Mr. Ridgly, that they're trying to ban *Sirrah* from all the stands in this country.

Ridgly laughed. "To the pure, my dear man, all things are impure. I have a rankling suspicion that that paraphrase has been made often before, which might seem to invalidate its claim to truth; but I assure you that I believe it implicitly. *Sirrah* is modern. *Sirrah* is honest. Worst of all, *Sirrah* is amusing and popular. Therefore *Sirrah* must be a hot breath of corruption sweeping over the fair face of the land. Which inspires me with a rather pleasing slogan; *Sirrah*—Hotter than the Sirocco."

"But they say," the interviewer persisted, "that your stories, and especially your drawings, have an erotic effect on the minds of degenerates. Do you have any statement to make on that?"

"Of course they have an erotic effect. Why do you think I pay Denny such outrageous sums for his drawings? But the normal man, however he may delight in the erotic, controls his impulses for fear of society, and the degenerate's uncontrolled impulses scarcely need my aid to arouse them. Look here." He calmly reached out a lithe hand and seized Maureen by the wrist as indifferently as though she were an article of furniture. "Here is a damned attractive wench. Look well upon her. Now: Do you want to ravish her? Of course you do. So do I. So would any normal man. But we don't. Whereas a degenerate would pounce upon her with logical unrestraint, whether he had ever seen a Denny drawing or not."

Maureen shook her hand free. "Mr. Ridgly," she said, "the fear of society keeps us from a lot of things. Right now it's keeping me from landing a good sound kick right in your masculine modernity."

The interviewer took another drink and settled back. This looked as though it might be good.

"Tush," said Harrison Ridgly III. "Please don't play the insulted heroine. You simply came up appositely to serve as an illustration, and surely you must realize that you are a damned attractive wench."

"I've heard that before when I liked it better."

"I have no doubt. The chivalric approach is generally far more effective, I admit. But I no longer find it easy to assume my

Galahad rags. You see, I once respected a woman deeply. Only he who has done that can know you for what you are. I might," he smiled, "tell you a little story. There was once a shepherdess, named Phillida, who lived—it might not be inappropriate to say dwelt—in a vine-covered bower with her brother, the poet Corrodon. One day—the Fates had smirkingly ordained that it should be in the merriest of months—"

Maureen tossed her black hair impatiently. "Modernity, hell, Mr. Ridgly. You're pulling a line that nobody's got away with since Oscar. And strictly confidentially, it creaks."

She left Mr. Ridgly staring at the fifth of scotch with a strange grin of morbid contentment.

"I'm sorry," Drew Furness was explaining, "but I really haven't any idea."

Maureen smiled in passing. The columnist who had chosen the English professor was a onetime sports reporter, who was now anxious to learn how many of U.C.L.A.'s 1938 first-string men had showed up for spring football practice.

"Then tell me, Professor," he went on undaunted, "what do you think are the odds that Kenny Washington'll rate All-American recognition this fall?"

Furness cast an appealing look at Maureen, begging for deliverance from this inquisition; but she feigned not to see him, and passed on to where Otto Federhut was holding forth to the more politically aware of the correspondents.

"Battle is not the word," the Austrian was saying. "Nor yet is it struggle. Fight perhaps—and no, not that either. One thing must we say for our paper-hanging madman—he has given into your language one of our noblest words: *Kampf.* '*Mein Kampf,*' he has said in his blind arrogance. But we take his word, and to you we give it. This is *unser Kampf, unser aller Kampf.* It is of all of us the *Kampf*, even of you, too."

His heavy resonant voice sank a little. "When Austria was Austria, I knew it and loved it for its gaiety and charm. But I was not of those who made its charm. I was not the Austrian you see in your minds—the dashing young *Leutnant* who drank wine at the *Heuriger* and whirled the *süsse Mädels* to the waltzes of Strauss, while on his wine-moistened lips lingered a jest from Nestroy. No, I was not gay; but I gave to Austria that without which there is no gaiety under the sun; I gave to her justice. I used to call my justice the justice of Mozart; for as in him classical purity was tempered by beauty and the warmth of human melody, so in me my scholarship, my logic, was softened by mercy and human understanding. But now is no longer the time for mercy, my friends. They know no mercy, nor can we now afford to know it. It is justice only that we seek, and justice that we shall obtain."

"I'm not so sure," said a voice beside Maureen.

It was such a very small voice—almost like that of the Gnat which sighed in Alice's ear in the railway carriage—that Maureen instinctively looked down, though the elderly man was nearly as tall as she was.

"I beg your pardon," she said.

"I suppose," said Jonadab Evans, "that a vernacular translation of that would be, 'Just who the devil are you?'"

Maureen smiled. "It's true that I can't quite place you . . ."

"We have met, though. At the station with Ridgly and Dr. Bottomley—you remember? I imagine I was rather lost; I usually am."

"Oh. Then you're—"

"John O'Dab. Yes. Creator of that stalwart and spectacular

adventurer, the Honorable Derring Drew. At that," he went on, "I sometimes think that spirit writing is the safest of all—you know, like *Revelations by Shakespeare's Spirit.* Then no one can ever meet the author in the flesh and be disappointed. After all, one should be logical enough to realize that if a man were a splendid and romantic hero, he'd hardly waste his time writing about splendid and romantic heroes."

"I think you're sweet," Maureen said unexpectedly.

Mr. Evans beamed. "Could I get you a drink?" he said. The words were ordinary; the phrase was one that Maureen had heard and often welcomed at endless dozens of parties. But Mr. Evans managed to invest it with such a delightful Edwardian gallantry that you almost thought he had said, "May I bring an ice to you in the conservatory?"

"No thanks," she said regretfully. "I'm on duty, so to speak. But what did you mean about not being so sure?"

He frowned. "I'm not so sure about Herr Federhut's merciless justice. Modern politics, and particularly the politics of foreign nations, is not in my line, save when I find it necessary to bring about the encounter of Derring Drew with a dastardly international spy. Then, of course, it is safest to make my villain an agent of the totalitarian powers; American literature has declared an open season on them at present.

"But ignorant though I am, I cannot help thinking and feeling and worrying. And it seems to me, Miss O'Breen, that to forswear mercy is to forswear humanity. If to destroy evil we take up its very weapons, we shall learn in time that all we have destroyed is the best in ourselves."

Federhut's heavy voice, which had served as ground bass to this dialogue, now paused briefly, just as F. X. Weinberg joined the group around him. "Fine, Mr. Federhut, fine!" the producer exclaimed, quite as though he had heard the whole discourse. "You are an inspiration to us here in Hollywood. You show us the paths that we must follow along."

"I am pleased that you recognize the truth, Mr. Weinberg. In the hands of you and your industry the destiny of struggling mankind may lie. You have not forgotten those meetings of which you spoke, at which you will introduce me to my exiled compatriots?"

"So I should forget that, Mr. Federhut? What do you take me for? But I will do more than that. I'll tell you: Metropolis will produce an anti-Nazi picture that will stir the world. You think there have been anti-Nazi pictures maybe? Ha! Wait till you see this one. We'll put all the best resources of Metropolis into it, just as we are doing with *The Speckled Band,* that stirring Sherlock Holmes adventure which all America is waiting for."

Having got in a plug at last, Mr. Weinberg sighed contentedly and relapsed into silence.

In a corner of the room, hidden behind an elaborate floral decoration in the shape of a Persian slipper (a fanciful idea suggested by Dr. Rufus Bottomley), sat Detective Lieutenant A. Jackson of the Los Angeles Police Department. (What that *A.* stood for was a deep mystery never solved by all the professional skill of his fellow workers, who had long since given up the riddle and decided to call him, with inevitable logic, Andy.)

Lieutenant Jackson was at the moment an exceedingly unhappy man. He had little interest in the film industry or in the arcana of Holmes research, although the Doyle tales were among his happiest childhood memories. He had come to this reception principally because it was his day off and the invitation had come from his brother Paul. When two brothers are engaged in such irregular activities as detective work and film acting, they are naturally fated to see little of each other, and any opportunity is welcome. But Paul Jackson, at the last moment, had been recalled to the studio for retakes on the last *Derring Drew* film—a couple of scenes had drawn misplaced laughs at the sneak preview in Pomona.

The Lieutenant knew none of those present except Maureen, with whose brother Fergus he had collaborated on an extraordinary case last January.* And she was so busy with other guests that he had retired quietly into a corner to watch the goings-on with a somewhat numb interest and to wave away the occasional reporters who mistook him for his celebrated brother. This not unnatural mistake occurred with monotonous regularity, varied only by one gentleman, fresh from the bar, who insisted that the Lieutenant was Gary Cooper.

This, Jackson thought, was certainly no busman's holiday. Nothing farther from a routine of crime could be imagined than this gay gathering of the eminent and their parasitic recorders. It was a complete change from his usual routine and in addition, he realized, it was extremely boring. The hour was growing late; there was no longer much chance of Paul's dropping in. He was ready to grope his way through the mob to the nearest exit when a fluttersome female in a print of an incredible green descended upon him.

"I know you!" she exclaimed, something in the manner of Archimedes crying *Eureka!* "You're Paul Jackson!"

And Detective Lieutenant A. Jackson of the Los Angeles Police Department did one of the few absurd things in his efficiently ordered life. "Of course," he said, "And what can I do for you?"

---

*   *The Case of the Crumpled Knave.* Simon and Schuster, 1939.

"Tell me," said the eager damsel, "is it true that you and Rita La Marr—"

It would, of course, have been Paul Jackson's own fault for luring his brother to such a party. The Lieutenant was fully prepared to launch into a magnificent and all but unprintable explanation of the affair Jackson-La Marr which would have trebled the circulation of the fan magazine lucky enough to receive it—and probably would have caused that magazine's writers to be barred for good and all from the Metropolis lot.

But before Lieutenant Jackson had time to blast his brother's reputation irretrievably, both his attention and that of the green flutter were distracted by the first interesting event of the evening.

The prelude was the sudden entrance of Mrs. Hudson. The rimless spectacles were missing, and the once so forbiddingly kempt hair was streaming like Ophelia's. Her efficient speech was reduced to a series of plaintive yelps, among which the name of Mr. Weinberg and Miss O'Breen could barely be distinguished.

Before anyone could learn the source of her distress, that source loomed in person on the threshold. One look at Stephen Worth, and no one needed to ask why any female should scream and run away and even yelp.

Worth's ability to carry vast quantities of liquor without showing it was a notorious fact of Hollywood gossip. The quantities he had consumed this evening must have been far more than vast; for there was no denying that he showed it, and in a major manner.

But this was no jolly uproarious drunk. He looked belligerent and mean and damned nasty. His clothes were messed as though he had already been in a lesser fight or two along the way; but his eyes glistened as though those had been just practice for the really dirty work to come. In complete incongruity to his rough appearance, he dangled a neatly strapped brief case from his left hand.

Writers are influential and often colorful figures of the Hollywood scene; but their faces, naturally, are not part of the public consciousness. One or two of the columnists present, however, did know the novelist ex-detective, and murmurs of "Stephen Worth!" began to ripple over the room. The cathedral pronouncements of the interviewed Irregulars dwindled into silence, and strong men turned from the bar. Some even set down their drinks.

"Hiyah!" said Stephen Worth.

His tone was expansive but venomous. The women among the correspondents looked about for stalwart protection (the one in green clutched Jackson's arm with coy terror), and the men began to remember the rougher days of their apprenticeship.

"Isn't this pretty?" Worth demanded of the universe. "Isn't this just too ca-yute? A whole room full of whimsy-wholmesy!"

F. X. Weinberg stepped forward pigeonlike. "Mr. Worth—!"

"Easy does it, F. X. Remember the legal department. I'm just here to tell these lads and lassies a thing or three. Let 'em know what they're celebrating. They might think it's funny there's a big party for *The Speckled Band* with everybody there but me—and I'm just the guy that's writing it. They might get the wrong idea. You see, ladies and gentlemen of the press, Polly doesn't trust me on this picture. They're afraid I might put a little guts in the damn thing; and Holmes and Metropolis must be purer than the lily—purer than the Hays office even."

He staggered and recovered by grasping a table. "You think this is something petty. Just another studio squabble and so what? But it's more than that, and you're going to get the story. Sure, I know—this is all supposed to be a guarantee of classical fidelity; but I know better. I know it's a plot to get me out of the way. And I don't mean just off the script either. I've had threats lately—threats against my life—and I know where they came from. I'm not taking them to the police—I can take care of myself; but I just want to give you a little idea how goddamned real this setup is."

Dr. Rufus Bottomley's laugh was loud in the silence of the room. "Come now, sir, are we supposed to take all this seriously? At least, Worth, I never suspected you of being a neurotic. I thought if anything you were too infernally unrepressed."

"Interesting persecution complex," Harrison Ridgly agreed. "In his state—which, I may add abstractly, I envy—one might expect tales of little men with green beards and purple nose rings. Instead we find ourselves cast in the roles of his persecutors. Picturesque."

Stephen Worth twisted his face into an ugly grin. "Almost as picturesque as being a bereaved brother, isn't it, Ridgly? Of course you've all of you spotted that ducky little arm band—what the well-dressed mourner will wear according to *Sirrah?*"

Lieutenant Jackson was edging warily through the crowd. This situation was loaded with dynamite, and it was up to him, even though he wasn't on duty, to see that nothing too regrettable occurred.

"Gather around," Worth went on, "and you'll get the real low-down why they've got to get me out of the way. For one thing, I know a little too much about Mr. Weinberg's political activities. Anti-Nazism is a pretty mask for a lot of very unpretty things; and the Dies Committee might like to know a few things about good old F. X. and his Russian buddies."

Mr. Weinberg snorted. "Nonsense, gentlemen! So because I hate Hitler I'm a Communist yet? For twenty years I vote the straight Republican ticket. In the Sinclair campaign I'm at Mayer's right hand. And now this . . . this . . ."

"Sure he denies it. Who wouldn't, if he thought I didn't have any proofs? He forgets how much his little side-kick here knows, and how talkative she is under a nice warm blanket."

Then everything happened at once. Without a word Maureen advanced, her face calm with the stern exaltation of Saint Agnes in the brothel, and struck Worth a coldly vicious backhand blow across the mouth. Her ring cut his puffy lip. The blood flowed unnoticed as he coolly placed his open palm against her face and shoved her flat on her back.

"You see, boys?" he inquired callously. "A pushover!"

It was in the middle of the word that Drew Furness swung at him. It was a futile, amateurish swing, that left the swinger hopelessly wide open for a return attack. But in delivering that return, Worth's uncertain foot slipped. His hard left missed its goal, swung all the way round, and landed full in the eye of Detective Lieutenant Jackson.

The answer was an efficient professional one-two to Worth's whisky-gutted belly.

Lieutenant Jackson slapped imaginary filth from his hands. "He's out cold," he announced. "Anybody want to prefer charges?"

Silence.

"Then I think, Mr. Weinberg, you'd better break up the party."

But that was hardly necessary. At least half the guests has already streamed off in search of telephones.

Chapter 5

LIEUTENANT JACKSON heard the noise only vaguely, and did not even bother to notice the time. He had more than once been professionally furious with a witness who had heard the crucial shot and thought it simply an automobile's backfire or some such familiarly civilized sound; but after this case he was more understanding. To a policeman looking at matters afterward, with full knowledge that murder has been done, it seems impossible that anyone could have disregarded a sharp *crack* in the night; but when you are present yourself, deeply engrossed in the solid pleasures of conversation and (in this case) cryptanalysis, it seems equally impossible that anything more sinister than an ugly mechanical noise could be going on in your neighborhood.

The party had broken up quickly. Even the caterer's men seemed to go about their cleaning-up with unusual dispatch, prompted by the thought of getting home and telling the strange things that happen at Hollywood parties. Very soon only a handful was left in the flower-bedizened room: the five Irregulars, Maureen, and the Lieutenant, who felt a certain responsibility for seeing things through smoothly. F. X. was outside on the phone, using desperately every power that he possessed to induce the newspapers to kill the Worth story and seemingly, from the frantic rising of his voice, enjoying very little success.

Stephen Worth and his brief case had been carried into a spare bedroom upstairs and dumped respectively on the bed and on the floor. The surprisingly heavy brief case seemed to have stood up well under the strain of the evening. It still looked trim and efficient; but its master obviously needed several hours of oblivion before he could even be argued with. Just what was to be done when he did recover consciousness, no one knew; but this problem had been tacitly shelved until it had to be dealt with.

Even this small remaining group broke up in its turn. Harrison Ridgly III, who had been rapidly approaching the state which he had claimed to envy in Worth, announced that he would take a walk in the cool night air, and departed, with warnings from Maureen concerning the ease of getting lost on Romualdo Drive and its fellow angle-worms. Dr. Bottomley retired to his room for a quiet pipe. Jonadab Evans simply disappeared, and no one seemed to notice his absence. The remaining four conversed feebly (Jackson had never before realized fully the meaning of the word *desultory)* until Maureen rose abruptly.

"Look," she said. "I'm a working girl, and if I know reporters it's going to be a busy day at Polly tomorrow. I'm going home."

Jackson looked at his watch. "Could I drive you, Miss O'Breen?"

"That's all right. I can walk down to Highland, if I don't run into our pet cynic in the night air, and catch a red car there. That takes me practically home."

"Miss O'Breen . . ." Drew Furness offered diffidently. "I—it is my habit to have a breath of air in the evening. I was, in fact, about to take my car out. If I could combine health and service by offering you a lift—" He wondered what his Aunt Belle, who religiously ragged him for not getting out enough, would say to this freshly discovered habit.

Maureen smiled quizzically. "All right. Never let it be said that an O'Breen didn't try anything once. I'll go get my coat and powder my nose."

"I assure you, Miss O'Breen, that your nose is not in the least shiny."

Maureen caught Jackson's eye and grinned. "Sometime, Mr. Furness, I'm going to give you a brief introductory course in idiomatic English. You go bring the car around; I'll be right down." She ran off lightly to the stairs.

"Good evening, gentlemen," said Furness. "I'll see you later, I presume—or possibly in the morning."

"So long," Jackson waved, and Otto Federhut grunted, "'*n Abend.*"

"I suppose," observed Jackson, left alone with the *émigré*, "that in your judicial work in Vienna you had a great deal of contact with European police methods?"

Federhut nodded his shaggy white head. "*Jawohl, Herr Leutnant.* And I hope that you do not feel tonight that you must at once depart. I should like to hold with you a little conversation about the police."

"I'm off duty till noon tomorrow. There isn't much reason why I should hustle off to bed." Jackson was pacing idly about the room. "Shoot."

"Shoot?"

"I mean—go right ahead."

"When even a professor of your language," Federhut smiled, "has difficulties with your idioms, who is to blame a poor foreign scholar such as I? I make a note here in my mind: *shoot* does not always mean *bang!*"

Bang! came the noise from somewhere outside the room.

Otto Federhut started. "Does this house echo me," he exclaimed, "or was that—?"

Jackson shook his head. "Automobile, probably. Just Furness bringing his car around."

The jurist sank back relieved. "Sometimes I forget that I am in America, where a loud noise means only the pleasures of life and not a sudden end to those pleasures. But what I had wished to ask you is this: Is it not true—I have heard the rumor—that here in Los Angeles you have what is much like Herr Himmler's *Gestapo?*"

"Gestapo?"

"Once more an echo, *Herr Leutnant?* The *Gestapo* is the *geheime Staats-Polizei*—the secret State Police, which out-ferrets the Communists and the Jews. Have you not here some similar band for persecution?"

"Oh, you mean the Red Squad. Yes, we did have. The new city administration has pretty much broken it up; but it did get away with some damned raw stuff. I've always been glad I was on something as relatively decent as homicide. I'd hate like hell to be out for some poor bastard's blood just because he—" Jackson halted abruptly.

"Yes?"

"Look. What the devil's this? Seems to be some stuff of Worth's."

He picked up the white envelope—it rattled gently as he did so—with the typewritten address:

Stephen Worth, Esq.
Tender c/o Baker Street Irregulars
221B Romualdo Drive

and the penciled inscription:

> *Mr. Worth—*
> *A man called—foreign voice—said to tell*
> *you it was "concerned with Amy Gray."*

Otto Federhut looked at the envelope incuriously. "I admit that it is odd that Mr. Worth should receive messages here where he was not expected; but I do not concern myself with it."

"That's not what interests me so much," said Jackson. "But take a look at this." He held up the visiting card.

Federhut contemplated it in silence, while Mr. Weinberg's excited voice shrilled at the hall telephone. "It is strange," he said at last. "Ricoletti. That brings something to my mind, but it is too absurd to mention."

"I never heard of an Italian named Talipes," Jackson observed. "Sounds more nearly Greek if anything. But it's this picture drawing that interests me."

He set the card down again on the table. The two men bent over it, staring at the fantastic line of little figures:

This, of course, is an enlargement. The original was so finely drawn, as it had to be to fit the back of a visiting card, that Lieutenant Jackson took out a small magnifying glass—the only conventional detective's tool which he habitually carried, even off duty.

"It's a code of some sort," he explained. "Now that's not regularly in my line—we turn all such things over to a staff that specializes in them—but I've always been more or less interested in codes, as sort of a professional amateur."

"Then at least, *Herr Leutnant,*" Federhut snorted, "you should have sufficient knowledge not to call a cipher a code. So much of your language even I know."

"You're right," the Lieutenant admitted. "Sorry. With all your experience, you probably know much more about these things than I do. But let me make a stab at some rudimentary cryptanalysis. I'd guess offhand that the guys that hold flags mark the end of words—seem plausible to you?"

"Yes."

"All right. That gives us a six-word message—more likely five and a signature. It's too short to be sure of anything as far as frequency goes; but the one standing on his head occurs so often that we could tentatively say that was E. The one-armed squatter, the sprawl, and the spread eagle—all next in frequency—could be T, N, S, or the common vowels—maybe H or L. That doesn't help much."

"No," Federhut agreed, with a half-smile which seemed to indicate something up his sleeve.

"There's another approach, though. Notice the fifth word—a sign followed by another doubled. That is, the form 122. Now I'd venture that the commonest word in that form is *too.* That gives us tentatively two more letters, T and O. Also you'll notice that the man with no legs holds the flag twice—that is, that letter ends two out of these six words. It's probably S. To be sure, the one doing a jig holds two flags too, but one of these is the last word—probably the signature and not so likely to be a plural or a verb."

The Austrian nodded. "I am not so familiar with the frequencies of English, but this seem plausible. What does it give you?"

Jackson took out a pencil and scratched on the white envelope:

- E -- S -- --- ES -- TES - T - - - - - TOO --- E - T - E -

"I don't know just what to make of that," he confessed. "But it is a start, and no violent implausibilities yet. Now if you—"

Otto Federhut laughed. "I am afraid, *Herr Leutnant,* I have been only curious to see how you American detectives attack a cryptic problem. I believe indeed that you mean well, but it is the shortness of the message that must defeat the logic of your approach."

"OK, then." Jackson sounded a bit resentful. "You tackle it."

"Very well. This, it is apparent, is some joke played upon Mr. Worth because of his hatred of Holmes; for this cipher, as you may recall, is that employed in the Holmes adventure, because of it, called *The Dancing Men.* Now let me see . . ."

He glanced around the room until he espied the volume of the complete Sherlock Holmes stories which had occupied a place of honor in the reception. Deftly he leafed through it until he found *The Adventure of the Dancing Men.*

"I have always thought," he said as he set to work with pencil and paper, "that the great Holmes solved this cipher with an ease too complete. He approached it as you did, and with but little more to go on, and solved it; whereas in all likelihood he should have been as confounded and mired in a mass of insufficient probabilities as were you. But if our oddly named friend of the visiting card used the same cipher as in the story, our task should now be simple. Aha, already it comes! S—T—E—V—H—E—N: STEVHEN, that is Mr. Worth's name."

"Look," Jackson objected. "STEPHEN could maybe be with a V, or it could—in this case I'm pretty sure it is—with a PH; but it just can't be VH."

Federhut snapped his fingers with irritation. "But of course. It is strange—in my monograph have I mentioned it—that in this cipher the same man, the one with no arms and the walk of Charles Chaplin, may stand for either V or P. A slip, no doubt, from the pen of that most careless of chroniclers, Dr. Watson. The next symbol I do not find here. It must be that of a letter which is not in the original, though still I seem to have seen it before."

Drew Furness stuck his lean face into the room. "I beg your pardon, gentlemen, but have you seen Miss O'Breen?"

Federhut remained preoccupied with his problem. Jackson thought back. "No—matter of fact, I haven't. I just took for granted you were both gone by now."

"I've been waiting in the car for almost a quarter of an hour. Do you think—?"

What Lieutenant Jackson thought was that this was a deliberate joke. It had probably pleased the girl's malice to sneak out of the house the back way and slip down to the Highland car, leaving her unwelcome escort very thoroughly stood up. But he said nothing of this. He merely observed, "You never can tell how long it takes a woman to powder her nose, Furness."

"This is too long. Something might have happened. Remember

that Worth is upstairs there." Genuine worry sounded in his dry voice. "Have you heard anything?"

"Not a thing. There's been a deathly 'ush except for Weinberg on the phone and your car backfiring."

"My car didn't backfire. I'm going upstairs."

Before the full significance of this remark reached Jackson, Furness had left the room and Federhut was jubilantly waving his scrap of paper. "It is magnificent," he cried. "How shall I rejoice when I see that Worth read this! The letter I did not know, it must be a W. And the rest—behold!"

Lieutenant Jackson looked at the paper and read:

STEPHEN WORTH
DEATH CANCELS ALL CONTRACTS

Chapter 6

"I'll be damned," said Lieutenant Jackson softly. "I start in by simply being curious about a screwy code—I beg your pardon, cipher—and I end up with a death threat on my hands. Is this some sort of a rib?"

"'Rib'?"

"Joke. Gag. Hoax. Skip it. What I mean is, do you think anyone was serious in this threat?"

Federhut shrugged. "It would not surprise me. From the little that I have seen of Mr. Worth, the desire to kill him would seem to me almost an automatic reflex."

Jackson smiled and rubbed his purpling eye. "I see what you mean. But if every loudmouthed low-life was rubbed out automatically, it'd play hell with the population."

"Herr Furness!" Federhut exclaimed loudly.

Jackson's back was toward the door into the hall. At this cry, he whirled around and saw the lean young professor standing in the doorway, bearing in his arms the unmoving body of Maureen O'Breen.

"Brandy," Furness said quietly. Almost tenderly he carried her across the room and laid her down on the soft.

Jackson hurriedly cast an eye over the half-empty bottles on the bar. "You'll have to make do with whisky, I'm afraid."

Quickly he poured a stiff jolt and brought glass and bottle to the sofa. Questions, he decided, could wait until later.

Drew Furness was bending over the girl, holding her hand in his and rubbing it in what he hoped was the way you were supposed to in such cases. Jackson waved him away. "Open a window," he said sharply, then realized that two windows were already open. The room seemed terribly silent. He wondered why; then realized it was because the sound of Weinberg's voice on the telephone had stopped.

The little producer stood in the doorway through which Furness had entered. "Fifteen years of advertising I pour into the newspapers," he was moaning. "So now I need them and what happens? Nothing. And now this. What," he groaned, "happens here?"

"I do not know," Federhut said. "Mr. Furness comes into the room bearing this young lady, and else we know nothing."

"Maureen!" There was genuine sympathy in Weinberg's voice, but Jackson gestured him away.

"Give her time to come around. This whisky should do it. It doesn't look like anything worse than a faint."

"Is there anything I can do?" This was Jonadab Evans. When or whence he had entered the room no one could say; but there the inconspicuous little man was, with an intense desire to be of some use glowing on his dry face.

"Yes. You can run upstairs and ask Dr. Bottomley to come down here. We might need him."

"Thank you," Mr. Evans nodded, and disappeared again.

Jackson had forced the whisky through Maureen's lips. Her body stirred a bit; she seemed to be slowly coming back to consciousness. The Lieutenant turned to Furness.

"Where did you find her?"

"In the hallway upstairs. Just outside the door of the room where we left Worth. I missed her when I went past the first time. I looked in—in the other places where she might have been, and then as I was coming back, I—I almost fell over her."

"Was Worth conscious yet?"

"I didn't look in his room. All I wanted to do was to get her down here and help her. But I think I remember that his room was still dark."

A disturbing thought continued to nag at Lieutenant Jackson. "And you're sure your car didn't backfire?"

The question seemed to amaze Furness. "Quite sure, Lieutenant. But what on earth—"

"Nothing . . . I hope."

Dr. Rufus Bottomley came in just then, with a large calabash in his hands and a small *Derring Drew* writer trailing behind him. With no needless words he crossed to the couch. "She's quite all right," he pronounced after a brief examination. "Just give her time to come around."

"It's merely a faint then?"

"Can't say, Lieutenant. There's a bruise on the back of her head—maybe from the fall. Maybe not. Mrmfk. What happened?"

"I'm afraid," said Jackson, "she's the only one who can tell us that. Notice anything wrong on the upper floor?"

"Not a thing."

"You didn't happen to look into the room where we left Worth?"

"No, I didn't But why—?"

"She's regaining consciousness!" said Drew Furness, jubilantly if pedantically.

Maureen sat up a little and gazed at the six anxious men. "I am," she articulated slowly, "in the living room of the temporary home of the Baker Street Irregulars at 221B Romualdo Drive courtesy of Metropolis Pictures produced by F. X. Weinberg. There! See—I did *not* need to say where am I."

"The poor child is delirious," Mr. Evans murmured sympathetically.

"But," she added, "I would like to know why am I."

"So would we," said Jackson.

"Oh my." She looked at him. "You're the police lieutenant, aren't you? Fergus' friend?"

"Yes," he smiled.

"Now I begin to remember. . . ." She shuddered. "Lieutenant Jackson, I'm afraid you're going to have to act as though you were on duty after all."

"So what has happened?" Mr. Weinberg groaned. "In the papers is already a scandal, and now you bring us something new yet? Maureen, to me you should do this!"

Jackson disregarded him. "What do you mean, Miss O'Breen?"

"Seems to me I remember some understanding soul pouring whisky into me. I think if you let me have another go at that, I might manage better."

Drew Furness filled the glass and handed it to her. Dr. Bottomley considerately passed over the bottle as well.

She sipped a moment and gave a little jerk as though to coordinate her distraught memories. "There. All right, Lieutenant, here's your assignment: I saw Stephen Worth murdered."

She made the statement calmly enough, but her voice trembled despite herself. The men reacted variously. Mr. Weinberg executed a moaning double take; you could hear him thinking on scandalous headlines. Jonadab Evans seemed to wish that he had a tortoise shell to draw his timid head into. Drew Furness turned and made as though to hasten upstairs to investigate.

Lieutenant Jackson stopped him. "Let's hear the story first," he said.

Dr. Bottomley nodded. "Not that we distrust you, Miss O'Breen—"

Maureen grinned. "I know. You think I'm crazy with the heat, and you don't want to start a ruckus till you hear if my yarn makes any sense. I don't blame you."

"Now tell us, Miss O'Breen, just what happened. Then," Jackson assured her, "I'll take whatever steps seem necessary."

"Sure. Humor me. I get it. Well, you remember I went upstairs to powder my nose."

"What time was that?" Dr. Bottomley asked.

"I don't know. Ask the Lieutenant—he was here."

"Lieutenant?"

"I'm afraid, Doctor, I don't know. I'm beginning to understand now why witnesses are so uncertain. It was some time around eleven."

"Well," Maureen resumed, "whenever it was, I went upstairs. To go to the bathroom, I had to pass all the bedrooms. They were all dark, including the one Stephen Worth was in, except for yours, Doctor. I noticed a light under your door. When I came out, I got my coat and started down the hall again. Only this time there was light pouring out of the room where you left Worth. I tried to slip past it as quietly as I could; but he was standing in the doorway and he saw me."

She paused and sought fresh strength in the whisky. "Go on, Maureen," said Furness.

She seemed not to notice his first use of her given name. "He still looked sodden and bleary-eyed and vicious. He just stood there for a moment, sort of swaying, and I thought maybe I could get by. But all of a sudden he called to me and I stopped. I don't know why. It was partly to humor him, I suppose—keep him from starting another scene. But besides there was something in his voice—kind of a rough authority. I don't know. I hated him and I wanted to get away and still I stopped there.

"Then he began talking. His voice was low and persistent and just went on—saying things. You can guess what he wanted; I don't have to tell you that. But it wasn't only that. It was the things he kept saying about me and about Mr. Weinberg and about Drew. It was foul.

"And as he went on I began to get stronger. I lost this funny feeling of compulsion that I'd had at first. I knew he didn't even have the strength and virility he boasted about so much—he was just a stupid weakling, trying to cover it up with a lot of ranting obscenity. So I started to go.

"As I said, he was kind of weaving about. Just then he had staggered back a couple of steps into the room, but when he saw me leaving, he reached out into the air—just grabbing emptiness about a yard away from me. His face was awful. It was the way it was that morning in the publicity office or later that day in your office, Mr. Weinberg—remember? And just when he was grabbing at me like that, the shot came."

Dr. Bottomley thumped his chair. "Hell and death! Then it *was* a shot I heard."

Jackson nodded. "We heard it too, and like bright little boys thought it was Furness' car. What time did you make it?"

"For my own amusement, Lieutenant, I often observe the

exact time of backfires. There is always the flattering chance that I might be a witness to something significant. And I clocked this one at 11:08."

"Seems plausible, though I didn't check it myself. Go on, Miss O'Breen. Where did this shot come from?"

"I wasn't sure then, but now I think I know. All I noticed then was Worth grabbing at his heart, and the blood beginning to drip. He was really staggering now, different from before, somehow. He just looked at me, and he said . . ." She hesitated.

"You'll have to say it sometime, Miss O'Breen," Jackson reminded her.

"I'm not being maidenly, Lieutenant. It's just that it's all so . . . Well, what he said was, 'You bitch! So you did have the guts!' And then he crumpled up all in a heap and the blood began to ooze over the floor."

"You fainted then?"

"No. I damned near did, but I managed to get a grip on myself. After all, no matter what I thought of Stephen Worth, here was a man who'd just been shot. I had to do something for him. I never stopped to think that there must be somebody else in that room—somebody who'd just shot him in cold blood."

"So then you—"

"I don't think I even cried out. I might have though, I'm not sure."

"I heard nothing," Dr. Bottomley contributed parenthetically.

"I went over to him and knelt beside him and—look!" she exclaimed. "There's a splotch of blood on my skirt where I knelt." She shuddered. "And while I was kneeling there, I thought I heard a noise. All of a sudden I realized that I wasn't alone—I couldn't be alone. Whoever shot him had to be there with me. I jumped up and started to run out of the room. I didn't even have sense enough to scream. I just wanted to get to one of you for help. But before I could reach the doorway, something hit me on the back of the head. That's the last I remember until I was here on the sofa."

"Are you sure that he was dead?" Otto Federhut asked.

"I'm afraid I'm not qualified to give medical evidence," said Maureen. "But he was awfully still and he was bleeding from here," and she laid her hand over her heart.

"I'm going upstairs," said Jackson. "Somebody will probably remind me pretty soon that I've got no official standing at the moment; but just the same, with your permission, I'm taking charge. As soon as we find out just what's happened, I'll phone headquarters. One of you come along with me—you, Furness. You're young and active, even if I'd hate to have to rely on your fists in a pinch after this evening's little set-to. I think I can trust the rest of you to stay together here."

Dr. Bottomley acted as spokesman. "Go ahead, Lieutenant. We shall jointly guard each other."

"Come on, Furness."

"Who—who found me?" Maureen asked, as the two younger men left on their investigation.

"Herr Professor Furness. He was agitated because you were so long in returning to the car, and when the *Herr Leutnant* and I knew nothing of your whereabouts, he went in search of you. Then he came back carrying you unconscious."

"Carrying me? I calls that downright touching."

"Miss O'Breen," Jonadab Evans ventured hesitantly, "you said that you deduced later where the—the murderer must have been. Could you tell us?

She nodded. "Get a piece of paper? I think I could draw it easier than tell it. At first I thought he must have been standing behind me to hit Worth in the heart like that, but then Worth must have seen him; and I don't think he was so drunk he wouldn't notice a man with a gun. Then I remembered where the noise seemed to come from, and I think it must have been like this." She completed her hasty sketch and showed it to the others:

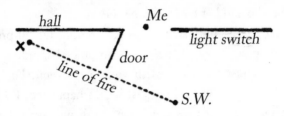

"You see, the murderer must have come into the room when it was dark, switched on the light, and ducked behind the open door. The light woke Worth up. He got up and was just looking around when he saw me in the hall. He couldn't see X behind the door. And all X had to do was to wait until Worth, with all his staggering, would weave into a good line of fire."

"But why should he shoot when he knew you were there?"

"Why not? I hadn't seen him, and before I could raise any kind of an alarm he knocked me out. He knew I couldn't give any testimony against him."

Federhut seemed to be considering the testimony as a trial judge. "It could be," he delivered as his opinion.

"Why don't they come back?" F. X. Weinberg plaintively wanted to know. "I should know the worst yet."

"They've been gone only a couple of minutes," Dr. Bottomley reminded him. "You don't know how long the Lieutenant might want for a preliminary examination."

But just then the two men returned. Furness went straight

to the sofa in answer to a surprising smile from Maureen; but Jackson remained near the door and faced the group.

"You might as well make up your minds," he said, "that you're in for a night of it. You're going to be questioned till you're blue in the face and probably elsewhere. The police will take over 221B and there'll be no rest for anybody. So you're warned."

A dreadful inarticulate noise came from Mr. Weinberg.

"Not the best publicity, is it? But you're up against the fact that a serious crime has been committed in this house. There's no doubt of that any longer. There's a damned sight more than Miss O'Breen's story to go on now. There's more blood in that room than any man could lose and live. The room itself, is to coin a phrase, a shambles. The only thing that's lacking for a perfect murder case is a corpse."

"A corpse!" Maureen cried incredulously.

"Exactly. There is no trace in this house of the body of Stephen Worth."

Chapter 7

TIME: One A.M., Tuesday, July 18, 1939
PLACE: Still 221B Romualdo Drive

TWO HOURS earlier they had been simply a group of people, of assorted trades and professions, quietly recuperating from a somewhat disastrous party. Now they were unified as The Suspects in the Worth Case. There they sat in the flower-decked room—Maureen, Mr. Weinberg, the Irregulars (all five of them, for Harrison Ridgly III had been picked up by a squad car on one of the intertwining streets near Romualdo Drive, as hopelessly lost as Maureen had prophesied), and even Mrs. Hudson, now restored to a worthy semblance of efficiency. Lieutenant Jackson was in the room, too; and near the door sat a stolid police sergeant, silently and relentlessly consuming a vari-colored package of Lifesavers.

"This," said Jonadab Evans wistfully, "is very different from what the Writings have taught us to expect of a police investigation." It was the first remark anyone had made in almost a quarter of an hour.

"How so?" asked Maureen.

"We have come to believe that a few policemen arrive at the scene of the crime, trample about ruthlessly for a half-hour or so, ask some obvious questions, and end by (*a*) making a patently wrong arrest, or (*b*) finding themselves completely baffled. Then they depart, leaving the field clear to the ingenuity of the cultivated amateur. But here we find none of this heedless trampling. The police descend on us in great numbers, but organized with supreme efficiency. They take over the house and set to work with insufflators and cameras and every imaginable mechanism. The Master himself could no more expect to find a disregarded clue left behind them than he could hope to find a grain of wheat left in the wake of a storm of locusts."

"And the questioning," Dr. Bottomley added. "Hell and death, sirs, Gregson or Lestrade or Athelney Jones would have had our stories by now in the fullest detail. Already they would have been leaping blithely from crag to crag of erroneous conjecture, while this Lieutenant Flinch has heard nothing but Jackson's brief résumé."

"Finch," said Jackson.

"Finch? I beg your pardon. But Finch or Flinch, why should the man keep us waiting around here like this?"

"Effect on the nerves. I don't think I'm giving away any trade secrets. Point is: if there's a murderer among you, which, as clear-minded men, you must admit seems a logical conclusion for Finch to draw, that murderer had a nice pretty story all ready at eleven thirty; and the first thing he wanted to do, as soon as the police arrived, was to tell it. The longer he waits around here, the more he's going to wonder whether it's as good a story as he thought it was. He's going to try to plug up the holes and give it a bit more polish. And the final result will be a yarn that Finch can spot as a phony on first hearing."

"But wouldn't he be afraid that we'd take the chance to go over things among ourselves for our own protection?"

"With me and the Sergeant here? Not so likely."

"Look," said Maureen. "What kind of a guy is this Lieutenant Finch?"

"A good detective," Jackson said with sincere admiration. "A sound, shrewd man. Nothing spectacular—he isn't brutal and he isn't brilliant; but he knows his job. He's lousy at guessing games on paper, so he's never passed a promotional examination since he got to be a lieutenant years and years ago; but he's just about as good a man as we've got on the force."

"Horse feathers," said the Sergeant unexpectedly, and guffawed.

Jackson smiled at their surprised faces. "Don't worry. That is not insubordinate contempt of a superior officer. The Sergeant is just warning you, in his own cryptic way, about one peculiarity of Finch's speech. For some reason, his slang is exclusively of the twenties; but don't laugh at it. It mightn't be wise."

"Curious form of retarded development," Bottomley observed. "I'd like to see what a psychiatrist might make of it."

"Nothing, I hope. Finch has a swell wife and six children."

"So this isn't your case, Lieutenant?" Mr. Weinberg put in. "It's this Finch we've got to worry about?"

"As I told you before, Mr. Weinberg, I'm off duty. Officially, I'm just another guest at this party."

"But you can get—oh, a transfer of duty or whatever they call it—something like that, can't you?" Maureen suggested.

"I don't know. That's up to Finch."

"So look, Lieutenant." F. X. Weinberg lowered his voice a little. "A scandal we mustn't have. Don't get me wrong; I don't ask you to do anything but be a good detective. But if you could incidentally watch out for the reputation of Metropolis Pictures . . ." He ended with a slight upward inflection which suggested the pleasant crackling of bills.

"Yes?" Jackson's voice was hard and sharp.

"It's not like you were a stranger, Lieutenant. In our studios your own brother works. So if you could—"

Jackson stood up. "Look here, Weinberg. Sure, I know, they've pulled that stuff in Los Angeles and got away with it. The captain of our late-lamented Red Squad, that Federhut was so interested in, used to pull down a pretty penny as 'labor consultant' for the big companies, and he earned it whenever a strike came up. But I wasn't made for rackets like that. If I work on this case, Metropolis will get all the breaks it deserves—no more, no less. But I'll be working to get the murderer, and I'm not having any strings tied on me."

The Sergeant answered a rap on the door and conferred a moment with somebody outside. He turned back to Jackson. "Finch wants to see you first," he said.

"One parting word of advice," Jackson announced to the company. "I've asked questions long enough to know that the truth, no matter how screwy it sounds, is always the safest answer. Not that you'll pay any attention to the advice, but there it is. So long."

Lieutenant Herman Finch, middle-aged, wiry, and half an inch over the police minimum height, was waiting in the library, surrounded by walls of books apparently chosen by an illiterate interior decorator. As Jackson came in, he was filling a corncob.

"Sit down, young man," he said, "and light up."

Jackson obeyed.

Finch frowned. "How do you expect to think on a cigarette? Might as well try to dig ditches on a meal from a tea shop." He struck a large kitchen match on the underside of the oak desk. "My wife's good training," he explained. "No polish under there to scratch up, and if there was nobody'd see it." He lingered unduly over the lighting ceremony.

"Let's start in, Herman," said Jackson impatiently.

Slowly Finch shook the match out. "OKMNX," he said. "Now don't go touchy on me, Andy."

"Not much danger."

"'Cause there's some men on the force might be a little peeved about what I've got to tell you." He puffed hard at the pipe. "It's this way, Andy: as far as this case is concerned, you're on the other side of the fence."

"I was afraid of that."

"As well you might be. I just wanted it clearly understood."

"It's understood all right. Worth's murder is your baby. But there's no reason why we shouldn't work together, is there? In eleven hours I'll be back on duty, and I'm pretty sure I can get assigned to help you. So if I string along with you up till then—"

"Uh uh. You're young, Andy; your hearing ought to be better than that. I said you were on the other side of the fence."

Jackson half rose. "You mean—"

"I mean that this very evening you had a fight with the vanishing corpse. You've got a black eye now as a result. Put it this way: if two geezers are out for each other's blood at nine o'clock and one of 'em is murdered at eleven, you don't put the other in charge of the investigation at one."

"It's funny, Herman," Jackson said slowly. "We're equal in rank, the two of us; but I still remember when you had your commission and I was a rooky fresh out of college. And what you say's gospel to me. I can't say as I like being on the other side of the fence, but if you say so—" He managed a sort of smile. "Want to question me about my movements?"

Lieutenant Finch was relaxing from his momentary stiffness.

"Horse feathers, Andy," he said. "I've got your statement here, and this German ought to cover you for the time of the shooting; but I just wanted to get things straight."

"Purely for the sake of the record," Jackson corrected, "Federhut's an Austrian."

"Austrian. All right. And now that we've got things settled, you want to sit in with me while I talk to these people? You know 'em—might give me a lead here and there—unofficially, of course."

Jackson grinned, "You're a good joe, Herman."

"Don't think I'm getting softhearted; I'll see you make yourself useful. Hinkle!" His quiet voice rose to surprising volume. "Tell Watson to bring in the girl. Want a little advice, Andy?" he added as the Sergeant left.

"No harm done."

"It's this. You're due for a vacation later this month. Why not try and get it switched to now? Then you can stick around— keep in touch with things. Otherwise you'll get assigned to some other work and I'll have a hard time finding you when I need you. Besides, this way the department'll be spared the embarrassment of having one of its own active men as a material witness in a murder case."

Jackson thought a moment and nodded. "Can do," he said.

"Miss O'Breen," said Lieutenant Finch, "it looks to me as though you know more about this case than anybody else except the murderer and Worth's ghost. So I want you to tell me, in your own words, everything that has happened."

"Starting when?" she asked helplessly.

Finch puffed his corncob. "Give me a little background first. Worth at the studio—his relation with these people—all that.

Then start in and go straight through everything that took place since you got to this house today."

"Remember my advice," Jackson said quietly.

"Can I smoke, too?" Maureen asked. "All right. I'll tell the whole truth, and I'll feel like a rat doing it. I'll get everybody in trouble, and I'll have no consolation but knowing that I'm doing my duty and following the Lieutenant's advice. So I might as well start by saying that everybody here hates Stephen Worth's guts—and that goes for me double and with knobs on."

"Hmm. You mean that each of the people in this house had a motive for killing Worth?"

"What is a motive?" Maureen countered. "I read a case once, in one of my brother's books, about a woman who was murdered for a pretty engraved advertisement, because her servant was dumb enough to think it was a Bank of England note. A motive's whatever you think is a motive."

Lieutenant Finch had a pleasant, drily crinkling smile. "That, young lady, is a shrewd observation. But you just tell me the facts, and let me judge what might or might not be a motive. Now who at the studio had any special grievance against Worth?"

"The girls in the commissary, the three secretaries he fired, the seven who quit, all the other writers he'd worked with, Mr. Weinberg, and me. That's just a rough start."

"We'll leave the others for a while. How about you and Mr. Weinberg?"

"Here's where the truth begins to sound like being a rat." She sighed. "It's this way: F. X. wanted to get him off the script of *The Speckled Band;* but Worth produced a trick clause in his contract, according to which either he wrote that picture or nobody did. There were a lot of protests about his doing it because he was notoriously anti-Holmes; that's why the Irregulars were brought out here to supervise. But life will be a lot simpler for F. X. without him."

"And yourself?"

"The good old motive, Lieutenant. Honor is dearer than life. You know."

"You mean that Worth had—"

"No. He hadn't. But he'd tried enough, and I was getting pretty tired of it. I'm afraid I can't say I'm sorry he's dead. I know that sounds heartless, but heartless is the only thing you could be about Stephen Worth."

"I see. Now, Miss O'Breen, besides yourself and Mr. Weinberg and Lieutenant Jackson, we have in this house the five members of these Irregulars and the housekeeper. How would you link each of these with Worth?"

Maureen did not answer at once. She was staring at Jackson. "My goodness, Lieutenant, are you a suspect, too?"

Jackson pointed at his eye. "The general feeling seems to be that I can't have been too fond of Worth myself."

"My!" was all she could say. "When my brother hears this— Why, Lieutenant, you're blushing!"

"Miss O'Breen," said Finch sharply. "Please come back to the point and spare our young friend. His being mixed up in this case is just an accident, I know; but officially—Now as to these others—"

"Well, with them it isn't quite so personal. It's just that Worth had ridiculed them and everything they stand for. Naturally they didn't like him. I suppose Lieutenant Jackson has told you about the ruckus this evening?"

"He has."

"Then you can see how there'd be bad blood."

"Of course. But," Finch added meditatively, "I can't see anybody shooting a man just because of a little ridicule. At the time, maybe yes; but hours later, in cold blood—banana oil! Wasn't there anything more personal in Worth's relations with these people?"

"He did make some sort of a crack to Mr. Ridgly about his sister. Ridgly's sister, I mean. She died a month or so ago, and Ridgly's in mourning for her. It seemed to cut pretty deep."

"That, I admit, is a little more personal. Anything about the housekeeper?"

"Only that Worth apparently mauled even her. Every time he was alone with a woman, any woman, you'd think he just got back from a desert island. She probably didn't like it very much—like the Chinaman."

Jackson laughed, but Finch looked hurt. "Do you know that story, Miss O'Breen? I never get over being amazed by what girls know nowadays. Only last night I discovered what my daughter meant by her collections of limericks. In my day limericks meant Edward Lear and the 'Old Man with a Beard.'"

"That *is* a good one," Maureen agreed gleefully.

> "Who said, 'It is just as I feared.
> Two owls and a wren,
> Three . . .'

I never can get that middle part straight. I always leave something out."

"That isn't surprising." There was suddenly nothing at all friendly about Finch's voice. "It's probably the same thing that makes you leave Drew Furness out of your story."

Maureen sat up amazed. "Why, Lieutenant!" she gasped. "I thought you were being so nice and sweet and you were just Leading Me On. I'll never trust a policeman again."

"And why should you—any more than I should trust a witness? Now tell me about Furness and Worth."

"After all that, there really isn't much to tell. Just that Mr. Furness came out to the studio to see F. X. about firing Worth and Worth was drunk and ugly and knocked him out. Then he hired Vernon Crews to play a very stupid trick on him. And today, when Worth was going good, Drew tried to stop him, and that's why the Lieutenant has a black eye."

Fince shook his head despairingly. "Would you mind going over that again? Who played a stupid trick on who?"

"It was in the commissary. I took Mr. Furness there for a drink to pick him up, but he doesn't drink, so I did and he had iced tea. Your brother was at a table near us, Lieutenant, and Rita La Marr was with him. Now you'd never think it to look at him, but Drew Furness has a crush on Our Rita. He kept sneaking a glance at her and hoping I wouldn't see him. Then a fat man with a big black beard stopped at the Jackson-La Marr table and came over to us. He said he was Doktor Friedrich Vronnagel of the University of Jena and was a great admirer of Mr. Furness' work on the Ireland problem, whatever that is. Oh, he buttered Drew up one side and down the other, and you should have seen him glow. Finally he said that Miss La Marr, too, was a great Furness admirer. That was too much for me, but Drew swallowed even that. So the *Herr Doktor* produced a beautiful red rose and said Miss La Marr sent this as a tribute. He held out the rose and pfssh! Right out of the middle of it shot a stream of smelly stuff—

hydrogen sulphide, I guess—all over Mr. Furness' good blue suit. Vronnagel vanished right away, but I knew then who he was. It was Vernon Crews."

"And who is this Crews?"

"It's funny, nobody seems to know about Crews outside of the industry. He's a bit actor, a very good one too sometimes, but mostly he's the colony's official ribber. He's terribly good at make-up and he can use all sorts of accents and voices. I remember once we hired a man who said he was a British major to be technical advisor on a picture from the Mulvaney stories. Somebody—I think, Lieutenant, it was your brother—had an idea he was a phony and hired Crews to be a maharaja. He came on the set and began to talk to the major in a funny gibberish until finally the major broke down and confessed that he didn't know a word of Hindustani, had been in India one week on a round-the-world cruise, and had never worn a British uniform except as a movie extra. The nice part was that Crews doesn't know any Hindustani either, but it sounded so convincing that it worked."

"Quite a guy," said Finch drily.

"Oh, Vernon Crews can do anything and be anybody. You simply can't recognize him. The same people have been had two or three times. In fact—" She stopped suddenly.

"Yes, Miss O'Breen?"

"A funny idea. I don't know. I'll tell you later where it fits in. But I think that's all about Drew Furness. I really wasn't trying to hide anything; it just didn't seem very important."

"I hope it isn't. Now if you'll tell us what happened today—"

Maureen took a fresh cigarette and thought back. "It seems so awfully long ago. I got here around three. Everything was in an awful mess because Mrs. Hudson hadn't come. I was run ragged for a while—but that hasn't anything to do with you. What you want to know is the things about Worth. Let's see. . . . There were five—you could call them Worth manifestations. And there was so much else going on. I just can't tell you what order they came in. Worth phoned himself—Drew Furness took that call."

"Furness was here that early?"

"Yes, damn him. It was just a mix-up about time."

"What did Worth have to say?"

"Drew wouldn't tell me most of it. I think it was pretty vile, in good Worth style; but the main point was that he was coming to the reception even though he wasn't invited. I think he was already drunk then."

"Did you or Furness tell the others about this?"

"I told F. X. I suppose he or Furness could have told the rest."

Jackson put in a word. "I overheard Dr. Bottomley mentioning the possibility to one of the others—maybe Ridgly."

"Then any one of you could have been expecting Worth to show up here tonight?"

"If you want to put it that way—yes, I guess so."

"And what were the other 'manifestations'?"

"There was another phone call—a funny foreign voice that wanted to speak to Mr. Worth. There wasn't any message—just to tell him it was about Miss Amy Gray."

"Amy Gray?"

"Yes."

"Do you know anyone of that name?"

"Never heard it before. Then right after there was a tall man with a beard. I couldn't see his face well; he had a soft felt pulled down over it. And it was a hot day, but he had on a heavy fur-trimmed coat. All he did was hand me a visiting card and say, 'For Mr. Worth.' It had funny squiggles on it."

"Is this the card?"

"Yes."

"Do you know anything about a man named Talipes Ricoletti?"

"I don't know. That's why I hesitated a little while back. The idea just hit me that this man with the beard might have been Vernon Crews. I couldn't swear to it; it's just a possibility. That'd mean that somebody else had hired him for a rib on Worth."

"That will be easy to check." Finch made a note.

"I'm not so sure," Maureen objected. "A ribber has his own quaint kind of professional ethics—he wouldn't ever tell who hired him for a job."

"He would," Finch said flatly, "if he was mixed up in a murder. Now would any of these people, aside from you and Weinberg, know about Crews and his profession?"

"Drew Furness would," Maureen admitted. "I explained to him after he was ribbed."

"I'm not so sure, Miss O'Breen, that this appearance of Talipes Ricoletti, even if it was your Crews, is only a rib. Did you know that Federhut and Lieutenant Jackson managed to decipher that message in, as you say, squiggles?"

"No! How? And what does it say?"

"It was written in a cipher alphabet taken from one of the Holmes stories—"

"And it says," Jackson broke in, "'Stephen Worth: Death cancels all contracts.'"

Maureen thought a minute. "But that's silly. If you're going to kill a man, you don't tell him about it beforehand. And if you do want to tell him you don't use squiggles."

"Murderers do funny things," Finch observed drily. "Any other manifestations?"

"He sent me a present, a foolish gag present, and there was a note for him by messenger. At least, it looked like a note; but it rattled and I don't think there was any paper in it."

"There wasn't. Do you want to see what was in it?"

"Indeed I do."

Lieutenant Finch picked up the white envelope and shook its rattling contents out on the table. There they lay in meaningless innocence—five dried orange seeds.

Chapter 8

In a way the orange seeds helped. They were the final touch of unreality. No one could feel the actual tragedy of death in a world where people drew dancing men for murder threats and sent dried orange seeds by special messenger. Maureen could now recite to the Lieutenants the whole terror of her experience as calmly as though she were telling an odd dream she'd had the other night.

The story was much as she had first told it on coming back to consciousness. Finch's most dexterous questioning could not produce any significant new details. At last she was released and returned under a sergeant's guidance to the living room, where she sat patiently until after three o'clock.

Those two hours were hell. The presence of the Sergeant— that solid, Lifesaver-munching symbol of the suspicion which hung over them all—was a painful restrainer of conversation. One by one the Irregulars, Mr. Weinberg, and even Mrs. Hudson were led off to Finch. One by one they returned—Mrs. Hudson in tears, Mr. Weinberg emitting racial groans, Harrison Ridgly in a state of jitters like a hangover setting in prematurely, Drew Furness somewhat shaken, and the three older Irregulars imperturbable and evincing only a certain abstracted interest in the crime *qua* crime.

Jonadab Evans was the only one to comment on his interview. "I like our Lieutenant Finch," he announced. "It may be simply that the pipe reminds me of a good friend in Missouri, but I swear that man is salt of the earth. I think we're in good hands."

The silence that followed his remark might have meant anything.

At last, around ten after three, Finch himself came into the room with Jackson. "We're calling it a night," he said. "I've got to sleep on this before I begin to get anyplace. You all realize, of course, that you're sticking around."

"Here?" cried Mr. Weinberg.

"Why not?"

"Why not? he asks me! Why not? One day without me, and where is Metropolis Pictures? *Kaput!*"

"He's right, Lieutenant," Maureen put in. "We've got to be back at the studio tomorrow, though Lord knows what sort of shape we'll be in."

"If I tried to stop you," Lieutenant Finch reflected, "Mr. Weinberg's legal department would be quick enough to point out that I haven't any right to. You're material witnesses, yes; but as things stand I'd have a hard time to prove in court just what you're witnesses to. That's where somebody was smart— maybe not too smart, but this isn't the time to point out where the slip was. All right, you two can go; but you understand, of course, that you'll be watched. You others all live here, don't you? That simplifies matters. I'm leaving Sergeant Watson here in the house."

A ripple of pure enjoyment spread over the group. It never quite broke into laughter, but the amusement would have been evident to a much more obtuse man than Lieutenant Finch. "What's the joke?" he demanded.

Dr. Bottomley at last let out the laugh he had been restraining. "It's too good, Lieutenant. Here are all of us, amateurs of criminology and devoted worshipers of the Master Holmes. Each of us doubtless fancies that he can solve this crime; and his chief need will be a confidant, a Watson. And hell and death, sir, what do you do but thoughtfully provide us with one!"

Finch shook his head. "It isn't so funny as all that. He's here for a very real purpose, and don't forget it. You'll probably all see me tomorrow, so a good night to you now—what's left of it."

He turned in the doorway. "By the way, Miss O'Breen, I finally got that limerick straight. It goes:

> 'There was an Old Man with a beard,
> Who said, "It is just as I feared!—
> Two Owls and a Hen, four Larks and a Wren,
> Have all built their nests in my beard."'

Good night!"

Lieutenant Jackson lingered. "Are you sure you all want to go to bed?" he asked.

Dr. Bottomley acted as spokesman. "If you mean what I think you mean, Lieutenant—that is, if you want to discuss the case with us—the answer is that we're yours till the dawn in russet mantle clad walks o'er the dew of yon high eastern hill. In short, go ahead."

"Mrs. Hudson," Maureen begged, "pretty please could you rustle up some coffee and maybe some sandwiches and things? Don't bother about dietetics; just get us something to keep us going."

"My standing in this case," Jackson explained as they waited for the refreshments, "is a damned contrary one. Officially, I'm nothing—just another one of you. Actually, Finch has taken me more or less into his confidence. Now I'm not going to violate that confidence; but I do want to do a little work on my own. I'm going to ask you a few questions, and in return for your information, I'll give you as much of the straight dope on the case as I legitimately can. Is it a deal?"

"Shall I call for a show of hands?" asked Dr. Bottomley. "No, I think it is hardly necessary. Behold these eager faces glistening at the thought of getting the straight dope. Mrmfk. You may fire when ready, Jackson."

"All right. First question's this: Do any of you know anything about a woman named Amy Gray? No? Well, do you know anything about a woman named Rachel?"

This seemingly serious question provoked an amusement almost equal to that occasioned by Sergeant Watson's name.

"Forgive us, Lieutenant," Dr. Bottomley chortled, "but we can't help thinking. I suppose next thing you'll tell us that her uncompleted name was found written on the wall in the victim's blood."

Jackson's usually pleasant face was drawn into tight lines. "I'm damned if I see what's so funny. That is exactly what I was about to tell you."

There was an awkward moment. "It is hard to say," Bottomley observed, "whether that makes it serious or just all the funnier. Come now, Lieutenant, don't you remember *A Study in Scarlet?*"

Jackson's face began to clear and then to redden. "I knew," he murmured, "that there was something about that. Something clicked back in my mind, and I couldn't—"

Jonadab Evans was leafing through *The Complete Sherlock Holmes.* "For most of my life," he said, "I have treasured these adventures, and now I invoke the blessings of all appropriate gods upon the Messrs. Doubleday and Doran for making them so conveniently available in one volume. Now at last the traditional problem of the desert island is solved. Who would think of taking with him Shakespeare or the Bible when in this one book—Ah," he broke off. "Here we are. 'Across this bare space there was scrawled in blood-red letters a single word—RACHE.' Then Lestrade explains, '"Why, it means that the writer was going to put the female name Rachel, but was disturbed before he or she had time to finish. You mark my words, when this case comes to be cleared up, you will find that a woman named Rachel has something to do with it."'"

"'"It's all very well for you to laugh, Mr. Sherlock Holmes,"'" Harrison Ridgly quoted from memory. "'"You may be very smart and clever, but the old hound is the best, when all is said and done."'" There was a relish, a freshness, almost a naïveté in his manner as he quoted, a surprising change from his usual weary cynicism.

"And you remember the result, of course, Lieutenant," Dr. Bottomley concluded. "'"One other thing, Lestrade . . . 'Rache' is the German for 'revenge'; so don't lose your time looking for Miss Rachel."'"

Jackson nodded. "I was right," he said. "That's what I told Finch: this case is all bound up with Holmes. It can't help but be. And if I put all these little details up to this board of experts, they'll give us leads we wouldn't ever think of by ourselves. He wasn't so strong for the idea, but he told me to go ahead with it on my own time and let him know whatever I found out."

Sergeant Watson now spoke for the first time in this session. "It's a German word, is it? Well, there's only one German here."

"My dear Watson." Otto Federhut smiled; his was the first chance to use the phrase which had been lingering temptingly on five tongues since they had learned the Sergeant's name. "It is elementary. That I am the only—I shall not say German in despite of the *Anschluss*, but German-speaking I am. That only I speak German means that I of all am least apt so to incriminate myself. Moreover, this is obviously a parody of the celebrated passage in *A Study in Scarlet;* and everyone here, as you have already observed from their quotations, is most familiar with the word from that source. By the way, Watson," he could not resist adding, "does your heart still give you trouble since you have stopped smoking?"

"Naw," said the Sergeant, "not a—hey! What goes on here? How do you know about my heart?"

"Allow me," Ridgly interrupted languidly. "The Sergeant's right hand shows extensive but almost completely faded cigarette stains. He devours an abnormal amount of sweets. In a man of his age, build, and profession, heart trouble is the most likely reasons for swearing off. Do I follow your deductions correctly, Federhut?"

"You do, Herr Ridgly."

The two bowed with mock courtesy, while Dr. Bottomley applauded lightly and the Sergeant took confused refuge in another Lifesaver.

At this point, the coffee and sandwiches arrived. "Won't you sit down with us, Mrs. Hudson?" Maureen asked. "After all, you're in on this too, you know."

"I hardly think I should, thank you, Miss O'Breen. After all, the knowledge of how to keep one's place is the keystone, one might say, of domestic success."

"As the departed Lieutenant might say," Dr. Bottomley rumbled, " 'Horse feathers!' Mrmfk. For there is neither East nor West, Border nor breed nor birth, When one strong man's been done to death, And of suspects there's no dearth. Last line's weak, but I like the third. Sit down, Mrs. Hudson; and you, Lieutenant, get on with the questions."

"Innaminna," Jackson mumbled through a ham sandwich. "Now," he said more clearly after a swallow of coffee (which did wonders for Mrs. Hudson in his estimation). "Now, I want to show you some of our other clues and see if they tie into the Holmes saga, too. Sergeant! Finch," he explained as Watson picked up what they all recognized as Worth's brief case and laid out its contents on the table, "Finch consented to leave these here in Watson's care. My position doesn't quite extend to such trust as that."

The clues lay there in orderly array—one white envelope, five orange seeds, a visiting card with squiggles, a tiny fragment of glass, a narrow length of black cloth, and a series of photographs.

First Jackson picked up the visiting card. "This I know a little about. Herr Federhut tells me that it is composed in the cipher employed in the story of *The Dancing Men*, and that it reads, 'Stephen Worth: Death cancels all contracts.'"

"*Momént*," said the Austrian. "May I once more see that card? I thank you." He contemplated the dancing men for a moment. "Yes," he said reflectively. "I thought that a chord of memory was stirred, and I find myself correct."

"What is it? Did you make a mistake in the deciphering?"

"No. It is not that. It is only," he turned to the group, "that you will recall that in the original cipher of the dancing men is no W to be encountered. With the name Worth it was needful that such a letter be found. This new symbol is a man halfway through a somersault and on one hand resting. Does that bring to your mind—?"

"Indeed it does," Dr. Bottomley replied promptly. "That's Derring Drew's signature."

"Derring Drew?" Lieutenant Jackson was puzzled.

"Your brother," Maureen prompted. "Paul's great starring role."

"My hero," Jonadab Evans explained hesitantly. "You see, whenever the Honorable Derring accomplishes some truly exceptional exploit, he always leaves a scribbling at the scene of the crime for Sergeant Inspector Pipsqueak to find. He draws a little man and writes a pun on his name beside it—like this." John O'Dab reached for a sheet of paper and hastily penciled:

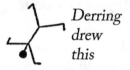

"Hm." Jackson compared this with the card. "That is the same as the W in the message all right. I suppose that a man trying to think of a new squiggle figure would most readily—"

"Stuff and nonsense, Lieutenant," Bottomley broke in. "If you're trying to implicate Evans, it's bosh. Any one of us might have thought of that figure—we're all Derring Drew readers. So is every other customer in every lending library, to say nothing of the flocks who've seen your brother play him on the screen."

"Maybe," Jackson admitted. "But I've seen Paul in the part, and I don't remember the somersaulting stick man."

"In the adaptation a few revisions were necessary," said Mr. Weinberg, and tried not to look at John O'Dab.

"I get it. But to come back to the card—Federhut, you were also going to tell me something about this name. Does Talipes Ricoletti mean anything to you?"

A half-puzzled enlightenment showed on the five faces. "The

Ricoletti part, yes," said Federhut. "You know, *Herr Leutnant,*
how many stories Watson alluded to which he never told. *The
Adventure of the Second Stain,* I believe, is the only episode
mentioned in advance and later written."

"Though at that," Dr. Bottomley complained, "with a curious
confusion of time and complete omission of the roles promised for
Monsieur Dubuque of the Paris police and Fritz von Waldbaum,
the well-known specialist of Dantzig."

"Still, *Herr Doktor,* at least it was written, while the others
remain to the world mysteries; and of these none is more
fascinating than that mentioned in *The Musgrave Ritual:* 'a
full account of Ricoletti of the club-foot, and his abominable
wife.'"

"Come now," Mrs. Evans protested, "how about 'the
politician, the lighthouse and the trained cormorant'?"

"And Isidora Persano," Drew Furness added dreamily, "who
was found stark staring mad before a matchbox containing a
variety of worm hitherto unknown to science."

"Hardly a verbatim quotation," Ridgly objected. "It actually
reads—"

"Gentlemen!" Jackson protested. "You can argue these fine
points later. Is there anything more definite in Holmes about
this Ricoletti?"

Federhut answered. "Nothing, *Herr Leutnant,* beyond that
one allusion—as regrettable a lacuna as exists in all literature."

"Not even his first name?"

"Not even that."

"Then what does this Talipes mean?"

"That, sir," said Dr. Bottomley, "is simplicity itself. 'Talipes'
is the Neo-Latin word used in surgery to describe the deformity
known as clubfoot."

"Which brings us right back where we were. Unless it could indicate medical knowledge?"

"Lieutenant! This is the same as the German word and the Derring Drew squiggle. As Federhut pointed out, no man is going to sign a crime with a fragment of his specialized knowledge. Besides, what proof have we that the dancing men and the visiting card have anything to do with the murder?"

"None," Jackson admitted. "But coincidence can be carried too far. Now as to these—" He pointed to the dry seeds.

"The five orange pips!" the Irregulars exclaimed like a well-trained *a capella* chorus.

"I suppose," said Jackson patiently, "this is another quotation. Go ahead."

"In the year 1887," said Drew Furness reflectively, "that same year in which Holmes solved the episode of 'the Amateur Mendicant Society, who held a luxurious club in the lower vault of a furniture warehouse'—is that sufficiently accurate, Mr. Ridgly?"

"Quite. I have often wondered if that Society included among its members that exceptionally skillful amateur mendicant, Mr. Neville St. Clair, who was to attain fame two years later as *The Man with the Twisted Lip.*"

"A possibility," said Dr. Bottomley gravely. "As Tantalus of this learned organization, might I suggest a brief monograph on the subject for some later meeting?"

"Come back to the pips," Jackson prompted.

"Yes, Lieutenant. In that year," Drew Furness resumed, "which was further distinguished by 'the singular adventures of the Grice Patersons in the island of Uffa,' and other notable cases, occurred the extraordinary tragedy of *The Five Orange Pips,* one of the few cases which Holmes did not succeed in bringing to a satisfactory neat conclusion."

"All right. But are these seeds pips? I thought pips were the markings on playing cards?"

"It is an odd use of the word, I admit. You sometimes speak of apple seeds as pips, but *orange pips* does sound strange. It may be British usage, or simply a quaint specimen of Watsonese. Yes, these seeds are pips; and according to the American Encyclopaedia consulted by Holmes, they were once a death warning of the Ku-Klux Klan."

Jackson looked down at what he still thought of as the seeds. "Of course we can disregard the Klan angle. That's no more significant than a German word or a medical term. The main point is that this is a Holmesian warning, which, like the message of the dancing men, Worth never received. If he had . . . Well, there's no use going into that.

"Now these," he held them up as he spoke, "are photographs of the room. They show you the position of the body as indicated by the bloodstains—that checks perfectly with Miss O'Breen's story. No footprints except hers, you'll notice. Whoever else was in that room was careful not to step in the blood. Fingerprints are no use either. Any one of us could have been in the room innocently earlier in the evening, and most of us were there when we tucked Worth away. The only place where prints might help—the walls in the corner where the murderer must have stood—is perfectly blank.

"But there are a couple of points of interest in these pictures. Here is the word RACHE. Above it, you'll notice, is a small chip in the plaster, apparently fresh. There's a similar chip in the corner we spoke of. Probably something that happened while the decorators were freshening up the house; but I'm giving you all

THE CASE OF THE BAKER STREET IRREGULARS · 107

the details. And here on the window is a fresh-looking dent in the wood.

"Now as to the brief case that Worth had with him: what would you say was in it?"

"I don't think it was empty," Maureen ventured. "Of course, it's a silly idea to carry around an empty brief case, but I'm getting where nothing would surprise me. Still, it didn't just dangle from his hand; he held it as though it had some weight."

"It did have," Dr. Bottomley added. "I carried it upstairs. I'd hate to estimate it to the pound, but I'd say it was as heavy as though it had four or five ordinary-sized books in it."

"I thought so," said Jackson. "I picked it up myself at one point, but I wanted corroboration. Well, when we found it, it was still strapped up nice and neat; but all that was in it was this piece of paper."

This was a sheet from a note pad, of the size technically known as a P-slip. On it was neatly typed a list of figures:

20518
25414
25723
20974
25191
25585
22394
25237

"Now is that," Jackson wanted to know, "another quotation from Holmes?"

"Lieutenant!" Jonadab Evans exclaimed excitedly, "There are bushes under Worth's window, aren't there?"

"I think so. Why?"

"Were they searched by the police?"

"They must have been."

"But then they were hunting for a body, weren't they? They mightn't have noticed . . . I'll be right back," he said hastily, heading for the door.

"Oh no you don't!" Sergeant Watson looked resolute.

"Please, I—"

"You could go with him, Sergeant," Jackson suggested.

"And leave all of you here?"

"After all," said Jackson, "unless you're convinced that I—"

"OK, Lieutenant. But I don't like it."

Sergeant Watson's heavy tread followed Mr. Evans' light footsteps down the hall and out of the house.

"What bit your little friend?" Jackson asked of the room at large.

"If I'm guessing right," drawled Harrison Ridgly III, "an extremely logical and utterly mad idea, which will turn this case quite upside down."

"I don't think I'd notice the change, Ridgly. This case is like a modernist painting—there just isn't any right-side up. But about this list of numbers—is there any Holmes echo here?"

"There might be," Otto Federhut decided slowly. "To me one of the greatest interests in Holmes is his use of codes and ciphers. There is one in *The Valley of Fear*—a code this time, *Herr Leutnant*—which has its points of similarity to this, at least in so far as that the same method of solution might possibly be applied. If you will give me time—"

But at the moment all attention was distracted by the reappearance of Jonadab Evans and Sergeant Watson. The Sergeant was scratching his head in the manner of one who knows that the woman wasn't really sawed in two, but *still* . . .

Mr. Evans advanced to the table and added his find to the set of clues.

It was a small and exceedingly pretty pearl-handled automatic. Stout twine was wrapped tautly about its handle, and at the end of a two-yard length of twine hung a ponderous volume.

"A woman's gun," Jackson observed bemusedly. "And this book—*Aynidge Bemmer* . . ."

Otto Federhut peered over his shoulder. "Einige Bemerkungen . . . It means: A few remarks upon the Ireland-Problem, with special reference to the theories of Drew Furness."

"'A few remarks'!" Jackson repeated scornfully, hefting the huge volume in his hand. "So they write books about you, do they, Furness? I suppose you own a copy of this? But why should you, or any other sane man, go around tying it onto pretty little pistols?"

Jonadab Evans was surveying his trove and beaming contentedly. "Thor Bridge," he said, as though that explained everything.

Chapter 9

"THOR BRIDGE?" Lieutenant Jackson echoed.

"As you might guess, Lieutenant," Harrison Ridgly observed, "that is the title of a Holmes adventure."

"But how—"

"I hope," said Jonadab Evans apologetically, "that my friends here will forgive my going into detail. Doubtless they had already reached the same conclusions as I. The nick on the window sill was irresistible."

"Look," said Jackson. "Put it in words of one syllable."

"Very well, Lieutenant. In *The Problem of Thor Bridge,* a woman is found shot with no weapon near at hand. The crime is, of course, thought to be murder. Actually, she had affixed a heavy stone to the end of a cord tied to the pistol. This stone dangled over the parapet of the bridge upon which the act took place. When her hand released the pistol after she had shot herself, the stone carried the weapon over the parapet into the water. All this Holmes reconstructed from noticing a chip on the stone parapet where the gun had struck against it in passing."

Jackson frowned. "That sounds familiar, but not from Holmes. Isn't it—?"

"You are probably thinking," Dr. Bottomley interrupted, "of *The Greene Murder Case*. Out of charity to the dead, let us say that it is an unfortunate example of coincidence in plot device. There snow served in place of water for the concealing agent; here it is bushes."

Jackson was examining the tiny weapon carefully, keeping a handkerchief between it and his fingers. "Not," he murmured, "that I've any hope of prints. One shot fired—fairly recently, I'd say. No help from ballistics with the body gone." Suddenly he stood erect and his eyes gleamed. "Look here," he said. "This indicates a damned sight more than just another Holmes quotation. Can't you see that? According to your *Thor Bridge* and my *Greene Murder Case* this is a device for concealing the fact that a wound was self-inflicted. What must that mean here?"

Ridgly smiled scornfully. "It must mean, Lieutenant, that Stephen Worth killed himself just to be nasty and then carried away his own corpse just to be confusing."

"Don't be so damned clever, Ridgly. What proof have we that he was really dead? He could have given himself a superficial wound by this method, just enough to account for the blood found, and then disappeared in the confusion."

Sergeant Watson re-entered the discussion. "Why?" he asked simply.

"What do we know of Worth's private affairs? How do we know what reasons he might have had for wanting to disappear after being thought dead?"

"What private griefs he had, alas, we know not, that made him do it," said Dr. Bottomley—possibly merely to show that he could quote more than Holmes.

Maureen made a noise which, coming from a man, would be called a snort. "So I'm a liar, Lieutenant?"

"You could have been fooled, Miss O'Breen. If it were a trick he would want a witness to—"

"Remember," she said with strained patience, "what I told you. I can't ever forget it myself. I saw his hands, both of them, groping at me in the air at the very moment that he was shot. And it was no superficial wound. I saw the blood ooze out from right over his heart. It's a nice idea, Lieutenant, but it just won't work."

"Here is a possibility," Ridgly suggested. "The murderer had intended that we should think this a suicide in the *Thor Bridge* manner. The inadvertent arrival of Miss O'Breen changed his plans and caused him to knock her out and, for reasons which we cannot as yet understand, to abscond with the body. But he had already planted this evidence in the shrubbery, and forgot it in his flight. How is that?"

"It won't wash," Jackson grunted. "He'd have to plant the same gun he used in the shooting."

"That was not the case," Jonadab Evans recalled, "in the original *Thor Bridge* problem. There two guns were used—one as a weapon and one as a plant."

"Which was long before ballistics. Anybody with any sense would know now that we'd check that point first thing. Well, that's two bright ideas that don't work. Any others? No? Then we file this away with the rest of our clues and get on to more of our choice little collection. Here. Can any of you tell me the Holmesian meaning of this?"

This was a tiny fragment, roughly triangular in shape, of very thin and somewhat cloudy glass. On it could be made out the letters OV, with a segment of an arc above them.

In turn all five Irregulars examined the fragment and shook their heads. "No," said Dr. Bottomley, "that means nothing to us. Where did you encounter this curious object?"

"In the metal wastebasket in the corner where the murderer must have stood. We thought the basket was empty; but one of our men, just to be thorough, turned it over. That bit of glass fell out. And you mean to say that it is not a Holmes clue?"

"I'm afraid not."

Jackson now took up the piece of black cloth. "It's obvious enough what this is," and he looked significantly at Ridgly. "But can you tell me any more abstruse meaning which it might have."

Ridgly himself answered. "I see what you mean. It is, I believe, the exact duplicate of my arm band." He compared it with the one he was wearing. "Yes, identical. The implication, I suppose, is that I dropped it at the scene of the crime?"

Jackson smiled. "That's making it too easy, isn't it?"

"I sincerely hope so."

"And is this a quotation, too?"

Again all five Irregulars paused for reflection, and again the result was nothing.

"No arm bands in Holmes? That's something. Now let me go over all this again. Whoever planted all these quasi clues was damned careful to involve all five of you, and Miss O'Breen as well. Weinberg, you should feel hurt at being neglected. There's the German word for Federhut, the medical term for Bottomley, the arm band for Ridgly, the book for Furness, the signature squiggle for Evans, and the lady's weapon for Miss O'Breen—or could it be Mrs. Hudson? There is, of course, one point to notice: the arm band, the item involving Mr. Ridgly, is the only one which is not a Holmes quotation. I don't know what that might mean—"

"I know," Ridgly interrupted, "what you infer that it might mean. That the murderer carefully planted Holmes clues to involve all the others, and that the clue involving me, not being a part of the Holmesian structure, is accidental and therefore really indicative."

"A flight into death, Ridgly," said Dr. Bottomley. "You seem obstinately determined to make the worst of things. Does an electric chair—no, a lethal gas chamber here—call to you with so sweet a voice?"

"It's an old gambit," said Jackson wearily, "to make the case against yourself so black that the investigator will automatically disregard it. Trouble is, it doesn't work very often. But let's drop these clues for a minute."

"We couldn't," Maureen asked wistfully, "just drop the whole thing till morning? We're all simply dead."

"We couldn't," Jackson replied firmly. "The next thing I want is something nice and solid and not at all learned or deductive. I want a complete timetable of this evening, for each of you."

Maureen sighed. "Mrs. Hudson," she pled, "could we have some more coffee?"

Jackson seated himself at a table with pencil and paper while the others gathered around. "First off," he said, "let's get the topography straight. I'm no good at architectural drawing, but I'm going to make a rough sketch of the top floor as best I can. There's a hallway running the length of it, with three bedrooms and a bathroom on either side. That's a bedroom for each of you and the extra one we put Worth in. Mrs. Hudson has a room downstairs. Right?

"Now at the end of the hallway is a door leading onto a sun porch. This porch runs the whole width of the house. The wraps had been left originally in the empty bedroom, but when we put Worth in there, they were moved to the sun porch, and that's where Miss O'Breen went first on her trip upstairs."

"To be exact, Lieutenant," Maureen put it, "it's where I went second."

Jackson started to ask a question, then guessed the answer, and looked embarrassed. "From this sun porch," he resumed, "a flight of enclosed steps leads down to the ground. The door at the bottom has a spring lock. I think that this pretty much eliminates an outsider from our considerations. Although the murderer could leave with the body that way—in fact, he must have, since Mr. Weinberg was at the telephone at the foot of the front stairs all the time—he could not have entered there, unless of course he was of the household. The front-door key also opens that door. This is all a résumé of what you testified, among you, in front of Finch, and I'm just going over it for the record; but I want you to check me if anything's wrong."

"Very well then," said Dr. Bottomley. "Does that locked door eliminate an outsider so completely? Are you sure that it was locked?"

"I checked it at five this afternoon," Maureen explained. "I didn't want anybody crashing the party that way."

"And no one," the Lieutenant added, "admits to using that door, as entrance or exit, since then. It must have been locked unless it was deliberately left open from within, which brings us right back to the people in this house again. Now here is my rough sketch. To fill it in, will you tell me who occupied which room aside from Worth's?"

He penciled in the names as they gave them. When he had finished, this was the sketch which lay before him:

This task accomplished, Lieutenant Jackson drew another sheet of paper to him and wrote nine names down its edge. "I'm putting down all of us," he explained, "in alphabetical order, so there'll be no hard feelings. The crucial time we'll fix at from 11 to 11:20. Dr. Bottomley clocked the shot at 11:08, and that seems acceptable. It was about ten minutes later that Furness found Miss O'Breen."

"And in those ten minutes," Harrison Ridgly interrupted drawlingly, "the body disappeared? You make this, Lieutenant, a case not for Doyle of the Holmes days, but for the later Doyle of psychic research."

"I was going to add," said the nettled Lieutenant, "that the body might conceivably have been removed after Furness' discovery, while we were all listening to Miss O'Breen's story. One member of the group was still missing then."

Ridgly settled back with a smile.

"Even at that," Jackson resumed, "we have to presuppose an accomplice—somebody outside the house with a car. If the body had been left anywhere near this house tonight, it would have been found in the police search; and nobody here had time to drive any distance and return. But to get back to our timetable: during that twenty-minute period I can account for Herr Federhut, who was in this room with me working on the cipher of the dancing men, and for Mr. Weinberg, whose voice we could hear on the telephone. I'll admit we weren't listening to him carefully; but if that noise had stopped for any appreciable length of time, we would have noticed it. Now to take the rest of you in order: Dr. Bottomley?"

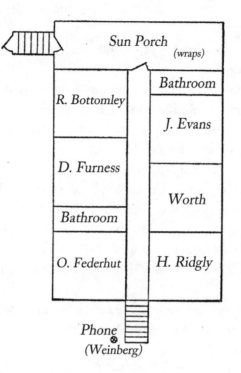

"As you know, I was sitting in my room reading the *Journal of the A. M. A.* That is, I was attempting to read it. Most of the time I was smoking my calabash; and those who know me well will tell you that I smoke a pipe only as an accompaniment to worry."

"Why were you worried?"

"Why? Because the absurd scene staged earlier by Mr. Worth seemed to indicate that what I had hoped would be merely a pleasant vacation might prove to be a damned ugly mess."

"Any corroboration?"

"I suppose you consider—and quite rightly, too—that the light which Miss O'Breen saw under my door is no corroboration whatsoever? Mrmfk. I thought so. Then I can offer you no other."

Jackson scribbled on his paper and went on. "Mr. Evans, I guess you're next."

"I am afraid, Lieutenant, that my story is a trifle less conclusive than even Dr. Bottomley's. I was merely wandering—upstairs and downstairs and even," he bowed courteously to Mrs. Hudson, "in my lady's chamber."

"Couldn't you be more specific?"

"I was restless. Like Dr. Bottomley, I was worried by Worth's scene. When our group broke up, I did not know what to do with myself; and I cannot seek consolation in a calabash. I did stop in at Dr. Bottomley's room for a brief visit—"

"Why didn't you mention that?" Jackson snapped at the doctor.

"Why? Because it was several minutes before I heard the shot; I thought that it would be meaningless for your chart."

"Go on, Evans."

"Then I came downstairs again—"

"By which stairs?"

"The front ones, of course."

"Did you see him, Mr. Weinberg?"

The executive roused himself from depths of melancholy preoccupation. "My world is crashing around me and you want I should see a little man on the stairs? Ha!"

But you told Finch you were sure that the murderer had not come down those stairs."

"Lieutenant Jackson! A man carrying the corpse of Stephen Worth I should notice if my own brother was dying before my eyes. But a little man like this doing nothing but walk downstairs—who can tell?"

"You're sure," Jackson turned back to Evans, "that it wasn't the stairs from the sun porch?"

"Quite sure," said Jonadab Evans unmoved.

"All right. And then?"

"I went out into the kitchen for a drink of water. Mrs. Hudson was there, and we chatted a bit. Her sister's girl, she tells me, is going to the University of Missouri, and we exchanged a bit of talk about Columbia."

Jackson looked over at the efficient housekeeper and was surprised to see an almost human smile on her face. "Is that correct, Mrs. Hudson?"

"Yes, Lieutenant."

"What time would you say that was?"

"I don't know. I never thought, of course, that anyone would ask. But I think it was about quarter after eleven. Yes, it must have been, because I remember after Mr. Evans left I looked at my watch and I said to myself, 'There's a good half-hour's work left to do and I won't get any sleep before midnight.'"

"And how long was he with you?"

"About five minutes, I'd say."

"Does that mean from 11:10 to 11:15, or from 11:15 to 11:20?"

"I really can't say. I hate to seem so inefficient, but heavens! one just can't go noticing all these things."

"That's all right, Mrs. Hudson. I didn't notice the time of the shot myself. And then, Mr. Evans?"

"I left the kitchen and walked around to the front of the house. I may have stood there a matter of minutes; I can't say for sure. Then I saw Mr. Furness go into the house rather excitedly, and after wondering for a bit just what was going on, I followed him."

"Thank you. Federhut I have, so this ties right onto the next name on the list. Furness?"

"A brief and uneventful story," said Drew Furness almost regretfully. "I left you gentlemen, got the car out, brought it to the front of the house, waited what seemed a very long time, and at last came into the house to see what had happened to Miss O'Breen. The rest you know."

"Just as a check—you saw no one enter the house during your waiting period?"

"No. And I'm certain I should have—naturally I was watching the front door for Miss O'Breen."

"And no one came in through the kitchen, Mrs. Hudson?"

"No one."

"You were in the kitchen during the whole time in question?"

"Yes."

Jackson entered further notes on his chart. "Your story, Miss O'Breen, we know well by now. That leaves us only Mr. Ridgly."

"As usual," Ridgly observed smugly.

"Mr. Ridgly," Jackson went right on, "is probably just panting for the chance to show me once more how all-fired guilty he must be, but I don't think we need to go into all that again. He was wandering in the streets and there's no way of checking it. So that's that." He scribbled again and folded the paper.

"May we see your notes, Lieutenant?" Bottomley requested.

Jackson thought a moment. "OK," he said at last. "What's the harm? But don't take that *Cleared?* column too seriously. That's just a tentative listing."

The schedule passed from hand to hand around the eagerly curious group and finally returned to Jackson. He refolded it, slipped it in his pocket, and rose. "The Sergeant here," he said, "will keep an eye on you tonight. Finch'll be back in the morning,

I imagine, and possibly I will, too. In the meantime, a very good night to you all. I haven't the heart to add pleasant dreams."

"Of course," said Mrs. Hudson nervously when Jackson had gone, "the Lieutenant must be wrong somewhere. It was a person from outside."

"Of course," Harrison Ridgly assured her. The assurance would have been more convincing without the wry half-smile which accompanied it.

Lieutenant Jackson's schedule of the movements in 221B Romualdo Drive.

Name	At time of murder	Corroboration	Cleared?
BOTTOMLEY	Reading in room	Evans & O'Breen—partial only	No
EVANS	"Wandering"	Bottomley & Hudson—but sufficient gap between them?	?
FEDERHUT	In living room working on cipher	Jackson	Yes
FURNESS	Waiting in car	Evans—but bare possibility on split-second schedule?	?
HUDSON	In kitchen	Evans—but time enough before?	?
JACKSON	In living room working on cipher	Federhut	Yes
O'BREEN	Present at scene of crime	Evidence checks with story—but if it was designed to?	?
RIDGLY	"Wandering"	None	No
WEINBERG	At telephone	Federhut, Jackson	Yes

Chapter 10

DREW FURNESS did finally drive Maureen home that night. When their ride was first proposed she had had ideas, half malicious and half—she would have been hard put to it to define that other half. But the carefree thoughts of that ride now seemed, not five hours old, but rather like something dating roughly from the Taft administration—to the celebration of whose fall by that loyal Democrat Terrence O'Breen, Maureen owed her existence. Neither malice nor that undefinable other half swayed her now. She was simply worn and weary; and she had no memories of the time between leaving 221B Romualdo Drive and being gently removed from Drew Furness' shoulder in front of 1233 Berendo. She murmured a sleepy good night, which she hoped later was not too rude, and wove uncertainly into the house.

She awoke in bright sunlight, to find beside the bed an alarm clock which had run down completely with as little effect on her as the wild ass had on Bahram, that great hunter. For hazy moments she lay in a vacuum. Reconstructing the past night was more difficult even than it had ever been on the morning of January 1. But the morning paper revived her memories in all their full horror, and gave her more than enough to think about while she rushed frantically to the office where she should have been hours earlier.

The day at the studio was frightful. Mr. Feinstein had been helpless in her absence, and she was hardly more efficient herself. It was too much to cope with. At one point she entertained a haphazard thought of calling out the National Guard to form a barricade. So harassed and besieged was she that she never even noticed when Mr. Feinstein turned from the phone and said, "A Mr. Furness to speak to you."

"Tell him I'm busy," she said hastily, and went back to disillusioning a too clever young man who was trying to maintain that this was all a Metropolis publicity stunt. Three minutes later she executed a double take worthy of F. X. himself, and wondered what on earth the Professor had wanted; but she had no time to ponder the question. A jaundiced individual was wanting her opinion on the theory that Worth had been murdered—justifiable homicide, he added—by a critic.

Her one bright idea of the day came when an eager reporter was asking, "Is Metropolis going to engage a private detective to solve this case?"

This thought had been in her own mind. It would have been a sweet job to wangle for her brother, if he hadn't been in Arizona on a case just then; but suddenly she had a better inspiration.

"Gentlemen," she said firmly, "with five of the greatest authorities on detection present at the scene of the crime, why should we engage outside help? Metropolis is doubling the salaries of these Baker Street advisors in return for their services in clearing up the case!"

So the afternoon's headlines were really good. They ranged from the somewhat unimaginative:

LITERARY EXPERTS TO TACKLE
REAL-LIFE CRIME

to the splendid banner head:

SHERLOCK HOLMES RIDES AGAIN!

And although Mr. Weinberg's compliments were tempered by woeful protestations at the promise of doubled salaries, even those protests ceased when Maureen convinced him, with pencil and paper, that a salary of zero could be doubled indefinitely without imposing any further strain on the budget.

Maureen's first thought when she got home was a shower. Under its needling caress, she could forget for the instant Metropolis and murders and Worth and . . . But inevitably, no sooner was she really wet than the phone rang.

Towel-draped and dripping (this is, regretfully, not the sort of book that will describe her further), she picked up the receiver.

"Miss O'Breen?"

"Yes."

"Rufus Bottomley speaking, as Tantalus. Can you come to 221B tonight, about 8:30?"

"Why yes. Is anything wrong?"

A Gargantuan sigh made the receiver tremble. "My dear young lady, if I were to tell you all that was wrong, you would never believe me. Neither should I. Not unless you had met Miss Belle Craven. Mrmfk. But you will come? We want to resume last night's conference."

"Of course," she told him.

It was, she assured herself, simply a draught that made her shiver.

The cast was almost the same as that of last night's conference. But the atmosphere was no longer tense and weary. A certain lively expectation, almost a festive quality was in the air.

The five Irregulars were in conference over papers at a table. Lieutenant Jackson sprawled in an armchair, reflecting on certain notes. Mrs. Hudson presided over the bar, a reluctant Hebe, for such duties had never been included in the course leading to her bachelor's degree. Sergeant Watson sat by the door, on a straight chair propped back at a parlous angle. Only F. X. Weinberg was missing; and Maureen, knowing the hysterical rush of business that day, was not in the least surprised.

She accepted a beer from Mrs. Hudson and wondered a little at some subtle change in that woman's appearance. She was as deliberately unattractive as ever, but something in her eyes was warmer. "She's been through something," she murmured as she sank into the chair next to the Lieutenant.

"They all have," he said. "Look at them."

"And are you here officially tonight?" she asked.

"No. Just one of the boys. I'm on vacation. You see—"

But now four of the Irregulars resumed their seats and Dr. Bottomley, still standing behind the table, rapped for order.

"Mrs. Hudson," he began, "Miss O'Breen, Lieutenant, and my dear Watson. You four have been signally honored tonight by being chosen to attend an extraordinary session of the Baker Street Irregulars. Wonderful and incredible things have befallen all of us today; and it has seemed best to call this conference, where each of us may tell his story. What these stories have to do with the death of Stephen Worth seems to be a matter for conjecture. My own adventure, for instance, demonstrates little more than that my poise and command of situation is not what I had thought it. However, Lieutenant Jackson, and you too, Sergeant, I hope that you will listen to these narratives with attentive ears, and that you will perhaps aid us in sifting the wheat from the chaff. After we hear your advice, we shall know definitely whether or not we have any evidence to lay before Lieutenant Finch. Mrmfk. Now without further preamble, I give you the first narrator: Professor Drew Furness."

Furness rose and went to the table. A typescript quivered aspenlike in his hands. As he looked over the audience, Maureen caught his eye, and deliberately winked.

This wink was intended as a gesture of confidence and encouragement. As such, it was a lamentable failure. Maureen's blue eyes, in repose or in action, had never made a man look quite so helpless and sheepish before.

But resolutely Drew Furness cleared his throat, gave an extra twitch to the collar which had left his Adam's apple in shameless nakedness, and began to read his narrative.

NOTE TO THE READER

Do not distrust these following narratives simply because they are told in the first person by the Irregulars rather than in the third by the author. Each adventure forms an integral part of the Worth case; and each took place, the author guarantees, exactly as its protagonist recounts it.

A. B.

Chapter 11

THE SINGULAR AFFAIR OF THE
ALUMINIUM CRUTCH

being the narrative of Drew Furness, M.A., Ph.D.

The scholar is inevitably, of all men, the least versed in recounting details of his own life. Every belletristic writer, be he poet, novelist, dramatist, or essayist, is to some however small extent an autobiographer. The writer in other professions, whether it be the surgeon relating a singular operation, the lawyer preparing a brief, or the chemist reporting his researches, is describing an event of his life in which, to his own mind at least, he is the protagonist. Even the popular biographer records himself in portraying his subject, as the image of the beholder may be seen mirrorwise in the glass before a portrait. But the scholar, that most rigidly self-effacing of individuals, must write nothing but the facts of others. Even his own critical judgment, his sense of balance, must be held in abeyance while he struggles to set down, with minute exactitude, what others have said and thought and done before him.

You may, then, readily imagine my difficulties in this situation. Events have befallen me which must be told; and such is their singular nature that I myself must seem the leading figure.

Already, as you see, I have transgressed against scholarly canons by the mere use of that one word—I; and having done so, I feel embarrassed and out of place.

But enough of this preamble. Let me simply try to tell what happened, and implore your patience with my ineptitude in so doing. I shall follow no literary formula save that of the King of Hearts—to begin at the beginning and go on till you come to the end: then stop. (Already, I may add, scholastic compunctions overwhelm me. It is with the greatest difficulty that I refrain from adding here an exact footnote indicating the source of my quotation.)

I was up early this morning—earlier, I believe, than any of the others, save Mrs. Hudson and Sergeant Watson, who had, I imagine, never slept at all. I am not perhaps by nature an early riser, but the combination of eight o'clock classes on most mornings and my aunt's belief in the soundness of old proverbs has perforce made me so.

Mrs. Hudson, whose household efficiency is a source to me of awe and wonder, was already busy in the kitchen. As soon as I had shaved and descended the stairs, the odor of fresh coffee called to me. I found the worthy Sergeant there also, enjoying a snack of sorts before being relieved from duty. It did not take the deductive ability of a Holmes follower to conclude, from the plates before the good Sergeant and the fragments remaining thereon, that he had already consumed an egg or two, some bacon, a dish of oatmeal, and what is, I believe known as "a stack o' wheats." At the moment he was tapering off with some streusel cake, more than tempting in appearance, which Mrs. Hudson informed me she had prepared especially for Herr Federhut.

I envy men who can eat in that manner, particularly at breakfast. Occasionally, after a rousing set of tennis, I can do likewise;

but on the whole my sedentary life has left me unfitted for such Gargantuan or, to employ a more autochthonous idiom, Bunyanesque—exploits. In the morning I want nothing but a small glass of tomato juice, one slice of very dry toast, and one cup of coffee.

Mrs. Hudson seemed torn in her allegiance. As a onetime student of dietetics, she admired the simplicity and restraint of my order; but as a woman, if I do not misinterpret her glances, she felt a certain respect for the virile voracity of Sergeant Watson.

The excitement of the previous evening, however, did lead me to exceed my usual regimen to the extent of a second cup of coffee. Sternly rejecting the temptation to order a third, I had left the kitchen (where the Sergeant was engaged in experiments with the various jams which Mr. Weinberg had imported from England) and had entered this room to conduct an experiment which had occurred to me in connection with that sheet of numbers in Stephen Worth's brief case, when the doorbell rang.

I am not sure whether that ring was audible in the kitchen. If so, it may easily have been disregarded, since the Sergeant was otherwise occupied and Mrs. Hudson was busy preparing a fresh batch of streusel cake. At all events, after the ringing had continued unheeded for a moment or so, I resolved to answer it myself.

I deeply regret that I cannot describe the young man who stood in the doorway. He was of about my own age or slightly younger, of medium height, with dark hair and completely unobtrusive clothes. The only remarkable thing about him was that he leaned on a crutch held in his left armpit, though his left leg seemed quite normal to the untutored eye.

"Two-two-one B?" he said.

"Yes," I answered.

For some reason he seemed a trifle crestfallen by this reply. "Thanks," he said, and turned as though to leave.

To me this seemed incomprehensible. The new number of the house, 221B, was clearly announced in fresh figures on the lintel of the door. What could be the conceivable purpose of ringing the doorbell to ask that number and then walking away upon receiving an affirmative reply?

Then the only possible explanation occurred to me. Obviously the remark was intended as a sign or password of sorts. I could not imagine why anyone should be sending a secret message to me; but neither could I imagine why, if secret messages were being sent to this house, I should not at least attempt to intercept them.

There seemed to be only one logical answer to "Two-two-one B" as a countersign, and I made it. "Baker Street," I said.

The young man instantly turned back to me, using the crutch as a pivot, and said, "'The dog did nothing in the nighttime.'"

"'That,'" I replied automatically, "'was the curious incident.'"

(And here at last scholastic training overwhelms me. For the benefit of those not of our group, I must add, as an oral footnote, that this bit of dialogue is a famous excerpt from the adventure of "Silver Blaze"—perhaps the most noted example of that form of verbal riposte which Father Knox has christened the Sherlockismus, though Sherlockution is an alternative form which I find even more suitable.)

The young man smiled, and with that smile his commonplace face came to life and became that of an individual. If I were to seem him smiling, I am sure that I should recognize him, whereas his face in repose might be that of anyone. For this was a smile which threw every feature slightly off balance, and made of his normal and unmemorable physiognomy a curious mask, half friendly and half terrible. "Come with me," he said.

Macbeth's realization of the compelling force of blood applies with the equal truth to any enterprise not in our quotidian sphere of activities. To embark upon any unusual act means eventual recognition of the fact that should we wade no more, returning were as tedious as go o'er. I had answered the sign with the countersign; and now I knew a strange compulsion to follow the messenger and learn the meaning of this curious episode. So, feeling yet but young in deed, I walked with him to the sidewalk.

There at the curb stood a yellow taxicab. The young man with the crutch walked up to it and opened the door. Even at the time I should have thought this strange; but taxicabs are not a usual phenomenon on an assistant professor's salary. It was not until later that I recalled that it is always the driver, never a passenger, who opens the door.

"Get in the auto," the young man said—or at least so I thought at the moment. Now I am not so sure.

I hesitated an instant, and he added urgently, "What are we waiting for? The Irish girl told me you'd be in a hurry to get there, and now you go stalling around. Get in!"

For some absurd reason, this remark decided me. I entered the taxi.

Its interior, in contrast to the bright sunlight without, seemed so dim and dark that for a brief interval I could distinguish nothing. I heard my companion enter, I heard the motor start, but it was not until we were in motion that I could actually see the interior of the cab.

What I then saw filled me with amazement. I was in a box, a close, tight box. There were no windows, no jump seats, no meter, no communication with the driver's compartment-nothing, in short, to suggest the interior of an actual taxicab. A minute and dusty electric-light globe in the ceiling provided the little light that I had to see by, and an indistinct whirring above me suggested a ventilating apparatus of some sort.

But even more astonishing than the nature of this vehicle was the fact that I was alone in it. My companion of the unnoticeable appearance and the unforgettable smile had quite vanished, although I could have sworn that I heard him enter. He had, however, left behind a souvenir of his presence—the crutch.

I cannot say what my first thoughts were upon realizing my predicament. A numbed confusion doubtless predominated. Fear, I may say with all modesty, never entered my mind. Fear must imply conviction and belief; this whole situation was too sudden, too fantastic to stimulate more than wonder and curiosity.

I could see nothing of the streets along which we traveled, but the constant lurchings of the machine told me that we were following a winding and devious course, even more devious than the twists of the streets in this neighborhood would naturally occasion. Quite probably, I thought, the driver was taking all possible precautions to shake off a conceivable tail, if I may be allowed a cant term.

At first I entertained some thoughts of jotting down a record of these turns, in case it should be necessary later to trace the course; but after a minute or two I realized the impracticability of this ruse. We had turned at least a dozen corners before I could commence my log; and if the starting place is completely unknown, what can be the use of the most accurate record from that point on?

Instead I turned my attention to the cab itself, after first noting down the exact time and, from that, the approximate time of our departure from 221B Romualdo Drive. It was then 8:18; we must have left this house somewhere in the neighborhood of 8:15. The gauging of minutes without a watch has never been one of my accomplishments. I am told that it can be done by counting chimpanzees; but the idea seems implausible.

At this point the car was stationary for almost half a minute—halted, presumably, by a traffic signal. This was an admirable chance to open the door—not that I had the remotest intention of obeying the promptings of my more sensible nature by leaving the cab; I wished merely to see where we were in order to resume my log with some hope of its efficacy.

But there was no door handle. That there was a door was an obvious fact; I was still a creature of flesh and blood, small though the odds might be which a rational person would place by now upon my long remaining so, and I could scarcely have entered this box through solid walls. But the door apparently opened only from the outside; here within I was cabined, cribbed, and confined far more securely than a rat in a trap.

I mused briefly on rats, and wondered how a psychologist, such as my friend of the faculty, Professor Giancarelli, would rate my I. Q. at the moment, since that of the lower animals seems to be estimated chiefly by their ability to escape from involved traps. The psychologist's trap, however, like a crossword puzzle or a mystery novel, must be based upon the premise that there is a possible solution; and the more I examined the utterly blank interior of that cab, the more I came to the conclusion that solving this problem would be on a par with squaring the circle.

The Honorable Derring Drew, who is accustomed to such situations, would doubtless have fumbled through his pockets until he came across an apposite tool by *means of* which he might free himself; but a brief search of my own pockets yielded nothing but a pen, a pencil, a comb, a handkerchief, a pocketbook, a bunch of keys, a few random notes on the case, and some loose change. Rebuking myself with the reminder that the keys and the automatic pencil would doubtless have sufficed for the Honorable Derring, I regretfully returned my meager trove to my pockets and turned to examine the one tangible object in the interior of that cab—the crutch.

My first impression, upon picking it up, was one of extraordinary lightness. It had looked as though it were fashioned of wood, but now that I held it in my hand, I could see that this was a delusion caused by an ingenious varnish. The crutch was of some light metal, seemingly, from what I could see in one place where the varnish had chipped, aluminum.

You will recall that in entitling this adventure I have referred to the "aluminium" crutch, for I could scarcely be expected to neglect the amazing coincidence of my own experience with the title of one of Watson's manifold untold tales. But to an American, "aluminium" is a difficult word to pronounce; and I hope I may be acquitted of any charge of inconsistency if I employ the shorter American form in the body of my narrative.

But even, to resume my story, if one granted that the crutch was of aluminum, it still seemed remarkably light—so much so, in fact, that I was forced to the conclusion that it must be hollow. A moment's investigation proved me correct. The rubber tip came off with ease, revealing below it a dark line running around the circumference of the cylinder. The end of the crutch unscrewed readily, revealing a hollow interior.

What I expected to find there, I cannot say. I believe that I had some thought of rubies and emeralds. What I did find was a slip of paper bearing the typed message:

HTR OWMOR FEVOL HTI WTEE RT SREKA
BOTST UN

◇ ◆ ◇ ◆ ◇

At this point the proceedings were interrupted by a loud groan from Lieutenant Jackson. The speaker coughed nervously and remarked, "I beg your pardon?"

"For the dear God's sake!" cried Jackson. "Another code! You don't want a detective—you want a guessing-contest expert."

"You have said, *Herr Leutnant*," Otto Federhut reminded him, "that you are an amateur cryptanalyst. Surely here is for you the opportunity."

"But this is going too far. Dancing men and lists of numbers and now—"

"Getting too much for you, Lieutenant?" Sergeant Watson grinned.

"That's enough out of you, Watson. If Finch ever hears about your early morning appetite while valuable witnesses are being spirited away in unbelievable taxicabs—"

The Sergeant subsided.

"Calm yourself, Lieutenant," Harrison Ridgly murmured. "After all, you yourself have observed that this entire case hinges upon a knowledge of Holmes; and you know the extraordinary number of those stories which involve a code or a cipher in one way or another. We must all have a little deciphering session later."

"Meanwhile," Dr. Bottomley advised as chairman, "let us

hear the rest of Furness' narrative. This crutch I find highly
suggestive; but in justice to the speaker, we must at least suspend
judgment until he has finished. Mrmfk. Go on, sir."

"Thank you." Drew Furness picked up his papers again and
continued.

◇ ◆ ◇ ◆ ◇

I thought it wise for the moment to replace this cryptic note
in its hiding place, to rescrew the cap of the crutch, and to slip
the rubber tip back on. No matter what was to happen, it might
be well if I seemed not to know too much. I am, however, the
possessor of an admirable photographic memory, and I devoted
the rest of the journey to contemplating that row of letters in my
mind's eye and seeking to discover their secret.

So absorbed was I in this process that I did not notice when
the cab stopped; but the sudden opening of the door roused me
from my analytical meditations. I first looked at my wrist watch.
The time was 8:46—exactly twenty-eight minutes since I had
last looked and approximately a half-hour since we had left 221B.
I waited, my eyes fixed on the open door and my hand grasping
the crutch as a possible if cumbersome weapon. Enough time
had passed to account for quite a troop of chimpanzees before I
finally realized that the next move must be up to me.

I stepped out of the cab into a darkness compared to which
the vehicle's interior was a world of light. I could discern the
sound of no movements save my own. The floor beneath my
feet was *hard and* slippery; the wall, *against* which I struck my
knuckles as I extended my hand, was of cement. I stooped
over, touched my *finger to* the slippery spot on which my feet
rested, and brought my hand into the light of the cab. I ob-

served, with a certain sense of relief, that my finger was coated with nothing more sinister than oil. It was apparent that I was in a small *garage*.

Some means of exit there must be. As I thought back, I could now recall hearing a heavy clank just before the cab door was opened. That must have marked the lowering of the garage door through which we had entered. But the driver had let me out after that; there must be some other door through which he had disappeared, unless—disquieting thought!—he was even now lurking in the darkness about me. I began, for the first time in my life, to regret the fact that I had never succumbed to the incomprehensible lure of tobacco. A victim of that passion is bound to carry with him matches, a lighter, or some such means of illumination. That striking a light would make me an easy target provided a partial consolation in my helplessness; but so great was my desire to know something of my surroundings that I should have chanced even that contingency.

My present situation called not for the abilities of a Derring Drew nor even for those of a Holmes, but rather for the astonishing extrasensory perceptions of Holmes' eminent contemporary, the blind Max Carrados. Tapping the crutch before me (like old Ped, I thought, and then thought likewise of the Blind Spot and wondered again as to the meaning of that typewritten line), I felt my way to the front of the cab.

There at my right was a thin, all but indistinguishable, line of light along the floor. I felt my way toward it and ran my hand along the wall. This time there was a handle on my side of the door. What lay beyond I could not surmise, but know I must. Gingerly I turned the knob.

Before me a long and narrow flight of stairs led upwards,

ending in a wooden door above which hung a single small light globe. Clasping the crutch in one hand and my courage in both, I mounted the stairs, first closing the garage door behind me so that at least the sound of its opening might apprise me of any attack from behind.

A keen-eared guard must have been waiting behind the upper door; for before I could even knock, the door was opened. The sentinel was masked by a square of black cloth which covered his entire face save for the eyeholes. His hand lingered significantly in his coat pocket.

"Two-two-one B?" he demanded.

This time I answered without hesitation. "Baker Street."

"'The dog did nothing in the nighttime.'"

"'That was the curious incident.'"

He stepped back from the doorway, indicating that I was to enter. As I did so, his glance lit on the aluminum crutch. "I must say," he observed, "you don't look much like what we expected, Altamont."

(Here Professor Furness, revealing a quite unexpected sense of theatrical maneuver, paused to let amazement ripple audibly over his audience.)

◇ ◆ ◇ ◆ ◇

Altamont! Nothing in the adventure up to this point had amazed me as did this name. Whoever I was supposed to be, whatever the enterprise which had caused me to bring to this shabby room an aluminum crutch from a windowless taxicab, I was known as Altamont—the very name adopted by Sherlock Holmes in "His Last Bow" when, emerging from

his bee-keeping retirement on the Sussex Downs, he had devoted two years to becoming one of the most trusted agents of
the Imperial German Government, only to foil its most vital
schemes in August, 1914.

That name lent me new strength. No matter to what uses
it was being put in this present imbroglio, to me it was a name
ringing with honor and high emprise. It was the mantle of Elijah
fallen from on high, and I the Elisha who would bear it worthily.

I looked about the room. It was bare of all decorations, even
of furniture, save for an excessively plain table and a few purely
utilitarian chairs. It looked like a room taken only for the specific purpose of a brief moment, and ready to be vacated at an
instant's notice.

My only companions were the black-masked guard and two
other individuals, similarly protected, who sat at the table playing chess. White, I could see at a glance, had the advantage; and
even as I observed the fact, the player of the white pieces spoke.

"Schach!" he said, in guttural glee.

Under other circumstances I should have regarded a chess
game, even one conducted in German, as a pleasant evidence of
cultural leisure. It is a game which I respect and admire, although
I cannot lay claim to any especial proficiency. But in view of all
that had gone before, I did not find chess at this moment a good
augury. All too forcefully I remembered the remark of Holmes
in "The Adventure of the Retired Colourman": "'Amberley ex-
celled at chess—one mark, Watson, of a scheming mind.'"

White's advantage was even more marked than I had noted,
for in an instant he spoke again.

"Matt!" he said in tones expressive of the triumphant smirk
which must lie hidden beneath the black cloth.

Black pushed back his chair. "Es geht doch immer so," he

sighed without any particular regret. "That's the way it always goes."

Throughout the time that I sat in this little room, the three men conversed in German, though I have here transcribed their remarks into English. My first thought was that this was a ruse to exclude me from knowledge of their conversation; but later developments have caused me to think differently. At all events the ruse, had it been one, would have failed of its purpose; for though I speak German indifferently at best, I can follow a conversation readily enough.

"Let the world go as it will," White laughed. "Whether the vile forces of international Jewry triumph or we lead the world to a new and nobler life, one thing will remain fixed: I shall beat you at chess."

"He has his uses, though," the guard gestured at Black. "Who else was it who thought how to get rid of the body?"

"True," White admitted. "It was a master stroke, that. And how fortunate that chance had brought us to this house where the window so conveniently overlooks a railroad track."

I looked instinctively at the window; but the blinds were drawn down tight.

Black laughed. "It will be miles from here that it rolls off the roof of the car. And when it does, with the clothes changed and the face battered, who will know it for what it is?" Black looked across at me, as though for approbation of his brilliance. The smile which I contrived to assume might, I fear, have been strictly classified as sickly; but it seemed to pass muster at the moment.

"Our friend Altamont here is a silent individual, is he not?" the guard asked rhetorically. "But no matter. He is not our guest for social diversions; he has brought the crutch, and that is what counts."

"It is funny, that crutch," observed Black, who seemed to have a sense of humor all his own. "It is indeed as though we took from a cripple his crutch when from this Jew-ridden democracy" (he pronounced the word with infinite scorn) "we take its submarine plans."

"They will be more useful to us by far," said White calmly. "Another game while we wait for word from Grossmann?"

"He should be here any minute with the Irish girl," the guard told them. "She may be useful if she does not resist too much."

"We can at least make a start," said White and Black whistled the phrase from "Tristan" which accompanies the words: "Mein Irisch Kind, wo weilest du?"

As they set up the men and commenced their game, I reflected upon the terrible situation which this careless conversation had revealed to me. Whoever Altamont was, he had been scheduled to be the means of conveying, through the use of the aluminum crutch, vital American submarine plans to this group of emissaries of the Nazi German government. What vital information could be conveyed in a message as brief as that I had found in the crutch, I could not imagine; but as the moments passed I realized more and more strongly that it was imperative that that message should never fall into their hands.

I found it hard to concentrate on my problem. For some ridiculous reason, the guard's words concerning "the Irish girl" forced themselves constantly into the path of constructive reasoning. The phrase from "Tristan" haunted my mind, and with it, in superb incongruity to my surroundings, that opening passage of "The Waste Land" in which it is quoted. But this paper is no place in which to indulge in the fascinating subject of the results of free association.

To obtain anything but free association from my mind was, however, a task of supreme difficulty. At last I had reduced the problem to these simple terms:

A. I should shortly be escorted into the presence of this Grossmann.

B. Grossmann would expect me to hand over the crutch, and he would expect to find in it a cipher message.

C. If the crutch were empty, I should stand in great peril—a peril which might possibly involve the Irish girl as well.

D. Simple destruction of the message was therefore out of the question—the one possibility was substitution. There was a bare chance that the cipher might be one which Grossmann could not read off at once, but would have to decipher later or deliver to one who could do so. In that case . . .

Among the notes in my pocket was a copy of the list of numbers found in Stephen Worth's brief case. If I could slip the submarine cipher out of the crutch and replace it with that list, I might gain time enough to make all good. I toyed with the crutch idly swinging and turning it, until finally it was reversed, with the armrest on the floor and the rubber tip in my hand. Twice, as I grasped the tip, I felt the guard's eyes on me.

Then Black's voice rose jubilant. "Schau mal hier!" he called. "Look at this! The world will never change, indeed! Tell this lout how he is to evade this trap!"

Now was my chance, now while the guard's attention was fixed on the chess game. The rubber tip came off easily. With that concealed in my palm, I unscrewed the metal end. My fingers touched the paper. I my other hand waited the list of figures, ready for instant substitution.

But at this moment a knock sounded in the next room. "Grossmann!" the guard exclaimed. "Komm, Altamont!" He had turned his eyes full upon me; I could not attempt the substitution now.

There was only one chance, and I took it. Rising calmly, I continued to swing the crutch carelessly as I had been doing. I still swung it as I walked with the guard to Grossmann's door. And as we passed under the electric light, I swung the crutch a little higher.

The bulb broke with a startling shotlike sound. In the instant darkness I heard the guard cursing me furiously, and realized as never before the truth of Holmes' remark to Von Bork, that "'though unmusical, German is the most expressive of all languages.'"

The darkness lasted only a moment. Then Grossmann's door was flung open and light streamed into the room. But by that time the crutch contained a list of numbers, and the submarine cipher was in my mouth.

Grossmann's name suited. He was not only large, in the German sense of the word, but also gross in the English sense. His mustache was unwaxed, to be sure, and his haircut was relatively American; but he looked as intolerably Prussian as the villain of a film of 1917 vintage.

He scarcely glanced at me. All that he had eyes for was the crutch. This he snatched from my hands with a curt "Dank' schön, Altamont," and eagerly unscrewed.

I trembled while he unfolded the paper. It was a tremor partly occasioned by fear lest he know instantly that this was a substitute message (for no matter how strong the German emphasis on the merits of ersatz, I doubt if their enthusiasm extends to

ersatz-naval secrets), but even more I trembled for purely phys-
iological reasons. Swallowing a piece of paper is not nearly so
simple a task as my reading had led me to expect. For one terrible
instant I feared that I was going to give away the whole show by
the exceedingly unheroic act of being sick all over Herr Grossmann's office.

He glanced at the numbers and nodded. "Later," he said
curtly, "Number 17 will decode this. In the meantime, Herr Altamont, our thanks. Your reward you will receive in due time
through the usual channels. Are there any questions?"

I had finally, as a compromise, lodged the fateful paper squir-
rel-like in my cheek. It seemed to produce no noticeable bulge,
nor did it interfere with my speech. "Yes," I replied, in what must
have seemed childishly simple German, "one question. Where is
the Irish girl?"

Grossmann appeared not to have heard me. "You will return
as you came," he growled. "Descend to the garage and enter the
car. The driver will shortly return you to your dwelling."

"Where is the Irish girl?" I repeated, advancing a step toward him.

"Underling!" he exclaimed. "Of me you ask that? Go to
the car!"

As I took another step forward, the scream rang out. It came
from a third room, opening off this. I turned toward it only to
find Grossmann blocking my way with a drawn revolver.

Even though recent events seem to have involved me in an
utterly unwonted number of physical combats, I have acquired
no ability to describe them. I cannot say, "He led with this. I
countered with that." All that I know of this encounter is simply
stated:

The crutch was close to my left hand. With one abrupt twist

I swung it through the air and brought it down on Grossmann's right, knocking the gun to the floor before he could fire. I closed with him. We exchanged blows. Then someone—possibly the guard had followed me into the room—struck a heavy blow on the back of my head. The scream sounded again as I lost consciousness.

When I recovered, it was to find a policeman bending over me. He helped me to my feet, and I said, "Thank you, officer." That bit of paper was still in my mouth, and I am afraid my speech sounded somewhat thick. He looked dubious, but his doubts disappeared as I added, looking along the palm-lined street where I had been lying, "Could you please tell me what part of town I am in?"

Without a word he led me to the squad car at the curb. "Can you beat it, Joe?" he demanded of the man at the wheel. "Drunk at ten o'clock in the morning—and a nice-looking guy, too. Hop in, buddy," he added to me.

As my indignant protesting seemed only to increase his suspicions, I reluctantly obeyed. "Where are you taking me?" I asked.

"Lincoln Heights jail," he said. "Sorry, buddy, but we ain't got much choice. Lying around like that don't pretty up the streets none. What do you want to go hitting the bottle so early for?"

I disregarded the question. "Shall I see Lieutenant Finch there?" I asked.

"Finch—what's Finch on now, Joe?" he turned to his companion.

"Headquarters—division of investigation," said Joe.

"What do you want Finch for?" the other demanded.

"I don't," I replied. "But I think perhaps he wants me. If you could get him on your radio—"

"This is a one-way." He thought a minute. "Look, Joe," he said. "Pull up at the next call box. I'll just check with Finch; there is something funny about this. What's your name, buddy?"

At the next call box he descended. While waiting, I looked carelessly into the back of the car. There, on the floor, lay my aluminum crutch.

The brief remainder of this narrative is merely explanations. Lieutenant Finch told the patrolman that indeed one Drew Furness was wanted until further notice at 221B Romualdo Drive, whither the squad car brought me. The crutch they had acquired in the following manner:

The policeman on the beat had noticed men leaving what he knew to be a deserted house. Fortunately the squad car cruised past at that moment; he flagged the car and they gave chase. But the quarry had a brief head start, enough to lose themselves quickly. The police returned to examine the house, where they found nothing save a little cheap furniture and this crutch, which the squad car was taking to headquarters for whatever curious information might be obtainable from it. The house in which it was found, Joe added, somewhat surprised by my asking the question, was nowhere near a railroad track.

You will probably ask me now what conclusions I draw from this strange adventure and what bearing it has on the Worth case. For the moment, I prefer to stop at facts and leave theories until after I have heard the details of the, I gather, equally curious adventures which have befallen our other members. This much I will say: that apparently someone in this house is engaged in nefarious espionage, and that it is a blessing to our nation that I chanced to take his place this morning.

I have only one clue to the identity of this individual—the

young man's remark, "Get in the auto." It is a most unlikely re-mark to make to one about to enter a taxicab. One might say, "Get in the cab," or "Get in the taxi," or, most likely, simply "Get in"—but hardly, "Get in the auto."

It would be natural enough, however, to say, "Get in," fol-lowed by a vocative. And the more I reflect upon the problem, the more I become convinced that the young man, knowing his fellow conspirator by name though not by sight, actually said, "Get in—Otto."

◇ ◆ ◇ ◆ ◇

Silence greeted the end of Drew Furness' extraordinary narra-tive—a silence broken by a loud burst of laughter from Otto Fe-derhut. The Austrian jurist's shock of white hair trembled with the rhythmic amusement which shook his body.

"It is too much!" he gasped. "All things have I been called. Jew dog they used to call me when my decision went in all justice against some powerful *Gauleiter*. Atheist they have called me and filthy red and whore of Moscow. To these names am I accustomed; they no longer even amuse me in their inaccuracy of hysteria. But that I should now be called a Nazi agent—Herr Professor, you are sublime!"

Dr. Bottomley smiled. "It does seem, to say the least, a peculiar accusation. It might be better, Furness, if we postpone specific finger-pointing until we have heard all the narratives of today's adventures."

Drew Furness looked sorely confused by this reaction. "So that," Maureen put in to console his bewilderment, "is why you called me at the studio today."

But mention of this only added to his embarrassment. "Ah—yes," he admitted hesitantly. "Naturally, I—that is, of course, I wished to check my experience from every angle, and it was naturally indicated, so to speak, that I should attempt to ascertain whether you— In other words, since no other Irish girl to my knowledge—"

"In short, Furness," Dr. Bottomley broke in, "you were worried as hell about the girl and you wanted to find out if she was all right."

"Must you force these tender confessions into the light, Doctor?" Harrison Ridgly drawled. "Let our professor hide his secret passion if he wishes; don't make the poor chap bare his soul."

"You will observe," Jonadab Evans began didactically, "a certain curious parallelism in this adventure which we have just heard recounted." Drew Furness cast him a grateful glance; that drily erudite voice was a welcome relief from the uncomfortable probing of Bottomley and Ridgly. "The Holmesianism of the experience runs even deeper than the aluminum crutch, the passwords, and the name Altamont. Combine the stolen secret of a submarine and the disposal of a body by placing it on top of a train and what do you have?"

"My word!" Furness exclaimed. "I hadn't thought of it like that. Of course! When you're close to it, you can't analyze so clearly; but it is an exact parallel."

"To what?" said Sergeant Watson practically.

"To *The Adventure of the Bruce-Partington Plans*," Furness explained excitedly. "The same details—different in their application here, of course, but in essence—"

"More Holmes?" asked Watson patiently.

"Yes."

"Oh," said the Sergeant, and was silent.

"And now, Lieutenant," Dr. Bottomley began, but broke off suddenly. "Where the devil is the Lieutenant?"

All turned to stare at the empty seat beside Maureen. "I don't know," she faltered. "He slipped out just as Drew was finishing his story. I—"

"Here I am," Jackson said from the doorway. "Don't worry— no melodrama about my disappearance. I just wanted to phone— not that I don't trust you, Furness; but it never does any harm to check."

"And you found—?" Bottomley asked.

"A squad car did pick up Furness just as he says, and the story of the men fleeing from the empty house and the crutch left there is all down in the records."

"Merely corroborative detail," murmured Dr. Bottomley, "though hardly, I trust, in the sense in which Pooh Bah used the phrase. And now, gentlemen, with your permission the chair will take the floor. I believe that, for proper chronological orders, my own story comes next. Mrmfk." With careful gestures he smoothed his imperial, straightened his coat, and lit one of his miniature torpedoes.

Chapter 12

THE ADVENTURE OF THE TIRED CAPTAIN

being the narrative of Rufus Bottomley, M.D.

I'm damned if I'm going to be hampered by a sheaf of papers to read from. If I am a scholar at all, I'm a talking scholar—the kind who settles down with his fellows of an evening, equipped with cigar and stein, and settles the literary, political, and medical problems of the world by means of the spoken word. I know I'm known as a man of letters ever since I published "G. P."—and how I came to write that overrated mass of reminiscent pap, sound enough medical food to start with but carefully predigested and regurgitated for the curious layman, I'm damned if I know. Still less do I understand the size of my royalty checks.

This is no mock humility. I'm as proud a cock as the next. I love to vaunt my knowledge of Holmes, my familiarity with Restoration lyrics (to say nothing of other lyrics not quite so conventional), and above all the curl of my imperial and its deep-brown richness. I shall never forget the kick I applied to the pants of the advertising man who wanted my testimonial for Stabrowne Hair Tint; for every hair of this fine frolicsome foliage, ladies and gentlemen, is natural in its beauty.

The expression on your faces reminds me that the man who

types his narrative beforehand is at least likely to stick to his subject. I accept your unspoken rebuke, and will try to check my wanderings. But hell and death, my friends! The letter killeth; and this fantastic case, moreover, has already become such a convolute maze of bypaths that nothing can properly be called irrelevant. It would not in the least amaze me if the fact that my lovely beard is natural in color were to prove the key that unlocked the whole rigmarolypoly mystery. Mrmfk! But I shall try to be straightforward:

I was, I believe, the second of our group to rise this morning. In fact, as I was descending the stairs, I saw Drew Furness leave by the front door and wondered. That was by no means the last time today that I wondered about Drew Furness.

Sounds sinister, doesn't it? Planting suspense and menace and stuff. But it serves Furness damned well right after he makes out our poor white-maned Federhut as a Nazi spy of positively oogy-boogy proportions.

I shan't detail my breakfast, except to take this opportunity of congratulating Mrs. Hudson on her streusel cake—a morsel at once so delicate and so substantial as to—Words fail me in my improvisation; I am unable to conclude that sentence either emotionally or grammatically. But accept, my dear Mrs. Hudson, my deepest gratitude. I strongly suspect that the kitchen skill of a good mother has triumphed in you over all the dietetic principles taught by the schools.

It was with no thought either of escaping from the watchfulness of this house or of embarking upon an adventure that I stepped out of the front door after breakfast. I did so only because the first cigar of the day always tastes best in the open air. But I had hardly taken three puffs before the adventure began.

Its beginning was quiet enough—so quiet that a far more sensitive spirit than mine might well have failed to scent adventure in the morning air. A man—a firm, heavy-set, well preserved fellow of roughly my own age—was walking along Romualdo Drive. When he saw me, he turned off the sidewalk and came up the path to the door.

As I said, he looked in good condition, but at the same time lamentably weary. His sturdy arms hung limply at his sides, and his feet dragged heavily along the path. "My friend," he said, "I observe that you smoke a cigar."

There is nothing like that first morning cigar for inducing a feeling of general friendliness toward all mankind. "I do," I said. "Do you care to join me?"

"No," he replied. "But your cigar gives me hope. A cigarette smoker is only a conventionalist; but the smoker of a pipe or a cigar is a lover of tobacco, and therefore a man of good will."

I liked the fellow. I felt at once that here was a man after my own heart. "I hope," I replied, "that you will not judge the extent of my good will by the size of my cigar. What can I do for you?"

He looked down woefully at his feet. "You can lead me," he said, "to a chair."

I brought him into this room without further ado and settled him in that luxuriously overlarge armchair now occupied by Herr Federhut. "Light up your pipe," I said, "and take off your shoes." These commands broke down the last barriers that might have existed between us. He obeyed gratefully, and for a full minute we simply sat smoking in that friendly and unconstrained silence which the abstainer like Professor Furness can never know.

"I'm lost," he said at last. "But don't tell me where I am. I don't even want to know at the moment. Here I am comfortable, and if I knew which direction my hotel lay in, I should feel obliged to set out for it. So leave me to my ignorance for a bit, and the pleasure of your company."

My only regret was that the hour was somewhat early to offer a drink, and said as much.

"I warn you," he replied, "I am quite apt to stay until time ripens to that point, if you can endure me. I dislike imposing myself on a stranger in this manner; but finding a friendly soul here in the wilds of Hollywood makes my heart rejoice like that of Stanley, or perhaps even appositely, like that of Livingstone."

"Have you been ashore long?" I ventured.

"It's two months now since I retired, and already I . . . I beg your pardon, sir; what do you know of my being on the sea?"

"But you are a ship's officer, aren't you? Weren't you, rather?"

"Captain Fairdale Agar, at your service. But if you'll pardon my natural curiosity?"

"If you sir," I answered, "will pardon my ostentation. The deductive diagnosis was simplicity itself. Your carriage, even in your present state of exhaustion, suggested a man of authority in one of the more regimented modes of life. Your dark-brown skin indicates outdoor activity. The scratches on the bowl of your pipe, almost certainly caused by the use of a metal lid, show that you are accustomed to smoking in a high wind. Add to this that I fancied a certain slight roll to be evident in your dragging walk, and you can see—"

"Hang it, sir," he exclaimed, "you're a regular Sherlock Holmes." (My heart warmed to him.) "Never could believe that sort of thing really worked myself—certainly never expected to have it worked on me."

"And so," I added, "life on shore has not proved quite so un-eventful as you had anticipated?"

He reflected a moment and then laughed. "Ha! See how you

do it this time—this cut on my cheek. Too fresh to have happened two months ago before I retired—right?"

I nodded. "An admirable disciple. You see how easy the trick is once you catch on?"

But he did not explain the cut. Instead he rambled on with adventurous narratives of his sea experiences—all fascinating and all worthy of record, but none, alas, the least bit helpful in this present session. Some other day I promise you these stories—you, in that sentence, being understood as a pronoun of strictly masculine gender. Mrmfk.

"You know," Captain Agar suddenly broke off, "think I might have a shot at this deductive diagnosis business myself. Mind if I tackle it?"

"Not at all. We should always encourage neophytes to join the charmed circle."

"Let's see." He knocked the bottle from his briar and refilled it. "This is a two-pipe problem, eh? Well, you're a medical man—right?"

I nodded, pleased and a trifle puzzled.

"You're retired, too. Retired about two years ago, I'd say. Gone in for writing a bit since then—quite an amount of success, too. Am I doing all right?"

I marveled, as agoggle as a clubwoman at a literary tea, and demanded his explanations. "For the fun of these tricks," I expounded, "lies in the footnotes. Any man can make a damned shrewd guess; it's the ineluctable chain of evidence that furnishes the sport."

He laughed. "I'm afraid, old man, if your powers of observation are all you claim, you'll notice that one of your legs is quite a stretch longer than the other. I've been pulling it for all I'm worth. Fact is, I just suddenly recognized you from your picture. Saw it in 'The New York Times' or some such. You're Rufus Bottomley, aren't you?"

I admitted the soft impeachment.

"Daresay you think now I'm a mere celebrity hound. Matter of fact, I'd no idea who you were till a minute ago—just flashed into my mind. But now that I do know . . ." His voice trailed off. With the passing minutes his body had lost its weariness; but now I saw, in startling contrast, how terribly tired his eyes still were and how dreadfully wearied a spirit looked out of them. "See here," he resumed. "You doctor chaps—understand, I'm not a religious man myself, though I've sailed with Irishmen and Spaniards and I've seen what it does for them. Confession, I mean. And you doctors—you'll do it too, won't you? Listen— like a priest?"

I took a fresh cigar. "It used to be the fashion," I said, "to ridicule the Roman Church for its confessionals; but the world seems to be coming back to the practice. It's a need of the race, I fear, and people will seek it—whether in psychoanalysis or in the Oxford Group. The Catholics may be wiser than a good materialistic agnostic like myself cares to admit."

He waved his hand, brushing away my words as casually as he did a cloud of smoke. "It isn't theory I want, Doctor; it's the practice itself. In short, I want to talk, and I want you to listen. You're used to that, aren't you?"

In contemplative fashion I drew the first puffs of the new cigar. "Why not?" I asked simply.

"Good." He fell silent again, and when he finally did speak his voice was different. It was at once softer and more tense. "It's an odd thing," he said. "A devilish odd thing. And I'm afraid I want more than just an ear—" At this phase he seemed to wince and broke off for an instant. "I want advice. But hear the whole story first; they you can judge for yourself what I want."

I prepared to listen, marveling meanwhile at the rigorous discipline to which a priest must submit. Not to eat throughout the long hours before a noonday Mass seems to me difficult, but feasible; not to smoke, however, while you listen to the long list of a penitent's woes is to me an act of superhuman sacrifice. But I digress again. I slap my figurative wrist and return to my muttons. This then, is the narrative of Captain Fairdale Agar, as nearly in his own words as I can recall them:

"I first knew Peter Black in Pnompenh. You may not have heard of the place—very few Americans have—but it's a sizable town in Indo-China, capital of Cambodia. I used to meet him in Red Harry's, which was the favorite hangout of those of us who preferred a pint of bitter or a slug of bourbon to a vermouth-cassis. This was some twenty years ago—just after the war. I never gathered then what Peter's nationality was—American possibly, I thought, or more likely some sort of colonial British—but I did get the impression that he was more or less an exile from his native land. Faced a charge of draft evasion if he went back—something of the sort.

"Myself, I don't like that in a man. I'm a man of action, or was, and I believe that your country has a right to demand your action in her own cause. But I knew nothing definite, and Peter was a pleasant drinking companion.

"Shortly after we met, Peter Black got into a nasty spot of trouble—little business of smuggling out Cambodian relics without government permission. Big to-do about it, and no consul to act in his defense against the French, since he'd never admitted what nation had jurisdiction over him. Final upshot was really funny—he managed to prove that his 'relics' were fakes. That left him in the clear as far as the French government was concerned; naturally they couldn't claim that he was infringing on government privileges by carrying on such a trade. And before the foreign dealers could take any civil action against him, he'd disappeared.

"I saw him only once again in the next ten years—that was at Mindanao, in the Philippines. He'd shifted from crooked business to shady politics—was tangled up in internal affairs in some way, trying, as best I could make out, to collect from both the Japanese and the insurrectos, and to pick up a little spare change by informing to the United States military authorities on either or both of them. When I saw him he was in jail, and glad to be there; he knew he was safer locked up than he would be out where either of the parties he had double-crossed could have a chance at him.

"I heard later that he'd been released and disappeared again—probably for good. And I never thought of him again until about six years ago. Remember that scare about spies in the Canal Zone? Secret plans to blow up the locks and such? Well, I was taking a cargo from New York down to the west coast of South America. We heard a lot about spies in Colón—got the crew pretty jittery, in fact. A couple of them quit the ship—seemed to think we were going to be blown right up boom! if we tried to go through the locks. I laughed at the whole thing. I trust our army, even the small contingent stationed in the Canal Zone, to protect us against worse threats than that. But I was interested to hear the name of Peter Black as one of the chief spies being held for trial.

"When we got to Panama, at the Pacific end of the Canal, we heard more. Peter Black had escaped—by some fabulous trick which suggested that the man, if his mind had had a single honest quirk in it, could have followed on in Houdini's footsteps. I was not surprised; Peter, as you may have gathered, had a way of landing on his feet. But I was surprised, when we were a day out of Panama, to hear the announcement that we had a stowaway on board.

"You, of course, can see the way the story is trending, and you can guess who that stowaway was. But you can also, perhaps, imagine the complete astonishment with which I looked up from the charts in my cabin straight into the lean and badly aged face of Peter Black.

"Perhaps I should, at this point, have put about instantly, steamed by to Colón, and delivered Peter to the army authorities from whom he had escaped. But a loss of at least two days and a double-extra payment of Canal tolls wouldn't have pleased the New York office of the line. It would be quite safe, I figured, to turn him over to the American consul at Guayaquil, which was our first port of call. A friendly government was then in power in Ecuador; extradition shouldn't offer any difficulties.

"At least that is how I soothed my conscience. The partial truth, I suppose, is that I was glad to see Peter again; for rascal though he was, he was also damned entertaining company. I made him my personal prisoner—kept him with me most of the time—even got magnificently drunk with him one night, with a guard posted outside the cabin just in case.

"It was that night that he told me the only details I ever hear of his earlier life. He had never been reticent about the shady latter portion of his career; but no one had ever heard a word of his doings before 1917 or thereabouts. Now the best Cuban rum accomplished what no Indo-Chinese potations had ever succeeded in doing, and Peter Black talked.

"He was an American, I learned from his bitter story. Came from a small town somewhere in Kansas. Happy early life—devotion to the soil—the sheer ecstasy of watching corn grow. Something I could never understand myself; even retired, I'd find Kansas too much for me. To live where you could never behold the sea—it's no life for a man. But the young Peter Black had been happy there. Then he went to the State University to study agriculture.

"I'll make the story short—he fell in love with the younger sister of the wife of one of his instructors. Alice Craven, her name was. The professor and his wife were a wonderfully happy couple with a small child; and Peter and Alice, constantly exposed to their domesticity, resolved to be married at once. Then the third sister came to town.

"What she did, it was hard for me to follow. There are unhealthy overtones to this part of the story. Perhaps with your experience you'll understand—I didn't. But the upshot was that this sister poisoned Alice's mind against him completely. On the very day set for their marriage, Alice left Kansas for good. She was killed in a train wreck two weeks later.

"It was this tragedy, more than any technical draft evasion, which drove Peter out of the country. Some men might have turned furiously to war as a release for their sorrow; but Peter wanted freedom and wild adventure. The peace and tranquility of Kansas which he had planned to share with Alice—now it was loathsome to him; he was unwilling even to do battle in its defense. And his hatred for this sister filled him with contempt and venom toward the whole race. Humanity was his fair prey from then on.

"I understood Peter a little better after that. I began almost to feel a stupid and sentimental regret at the thought of turning him back to the authorities, though I knew well that no sad personal history could justify his vicious treachery. But I cannot say that I was sorry the next evening when, as we were entering the Gulf of Guayaquil, Peter Black sprang overboard.

"I did what I could. We turned on the searchlights, lowered the boats, and did our damnedest to find him, but with no results. It was conceivable that a splendid swimmer might have made the coast in the darkness. It was unlikely; but knowing Peter and his fantastic turns of luck, I thought it possible. Indeed, I hoped it possible; and cursed myself for a fool for the thought."

Here—this is Rufus Bottomley speaking again, and damning this oral delivery; but what is a man to do, short of making a jerking jargon of his speech with "quote" and "unquote"?—here the tired Captain paused in his narrative. He filled his pipe with incredible slowness, finally set it aglow with his fourth match, and then simply sat in silence, letting one finger stroke the fresh cut on his cheek.

"And what," I asked, "made Black draw a knife on you when next you met? Fear that you'd turn him over to the army for his espionage?"

"Eh?" Captain Agar looked startled, then smiled. "I see. My touching the cut—yes, I am catching on to your methods, my dear Bottomley. No," he mused, "I don't think it was that. Or at least not entirely that. I rather think it was because I was the only man who knew about the Craven sisters. But do you think my story has lasted to the point of—?"

I consulted my watch. "The bawdy hand of the dial, Captain, is even upon the prick of ten. I think we might—"

A highball seemed to refresh him; some of the nervous weariness left his eyes. "It was just a week ago," he said, "and I've been carrying the damned thing about with me ever since."

"You could hardly expect a scar," I observed stupidly, "to heal up so quickly."

"I don't mean the scar. You'll see soon enough. It happened in—I suppose you might say in a dive on Main Street here. A sailors' hangout—colored swing band, floor show of sorts, percentage girls—you know the kind of place or at least know of it. I was sitting at the bar, drinking quietly and taking a certain sullen pride in the skill with which I evaded the demands of the B-girls, when I recognized a familiar face in the bar mirror. A few stools away from me sat Peter Black. He had aged twenty years since that night in the Gulf of Quayaquil, but I recognized him instantly. I had forgotten whatever slight ill will I might once have borne him; and I left my stool, though not my drink, and went over to him.

"He refused to recognize me—denied that he'd ever seen me before or ever heard of any man named Peter Black. I was almost convinced that I had made a mistake until his protestations became so insistent that I was sure they were false. If he'd been more casual, he might have succeeded in fooling me; but he went too far, and I simply became damned angry. My words grew more violent than his; and violent words, with men like us, can't go on for long without leading to blows.

"We already had an audience—a cluster of sailors heckling us on and eagerly waiting for action. When the action started, they all pitched in. Damned lucky for me they did, or Peter's knife might not have grazed so harmlessly off my cheek. The cut stung, but the next instant I had forgotten that and all but forgotten Peter as I let myself go, despite my age, in the finest lustiest free-for-all I'd known in a dozen years."

The captain paused to finish his drink. "When we were all being led to the station wagon," he resumed, "one of the sailors stuck something in my hand. 'You dropped this,' he said. 'Ought to be glad one of them bitches didn't find it. They'll hook onto anything.' Unthinking, I slipped the small object into my pocket, and had no time to examine it until later. We were all herded down to night court, where those of us who could pay our fines were released at once. I had no objection to the fine; that fight had been well worth the cost, and even the cut on the cheek. Peter, I should add, was not in the line-up. As usual, he'd been smart enough to beat the rap.

"Not until I reached my hotel room did I think to look at what I was said to have dropped. To my surprise, it was a small box which I had never seen before. It—But there's no use in describing it when I can show it to you. Here."

He reached into his breast pocket and produced a small cardboard box, roughly three inches by four, tied neatly with string. The knot was an odd one—nautically significant, perhaps, but such specialized knowledge lies outside my purlieu. Instead I read what was more suited to my understanding—a hand-printed label on its surface reading:

> Miss Belle Craven 11473
> Shenandoah Road
> West Los Angeles

(I beg your pardon, Mr. Furness; please be so kind as to wait till I come to an effective stopping place.)

"Well," I said—and I must confess somewhat indifferently—"why haven't you simply sent it on to Miss Craven? There's no return address, no stamps—but it's obviously meant to be delivered to her."

"Because," he answered, slowly, "I am afraid to."

"Afraid? Hell and death, man—"

"You see, Dr. Bottomley, Belle Craven was Alice's sister. The woman whom Peter Black hated beyond anything else in this world."

"You think he dropped this then?"

"What else am I to think?"

"And what do you think is in it—some nice little poison trap or infernal machine? Or have you opened it?"

"No," he said. "No, I haven't opened it." And I knew that he was lying.

"And now, Mr. Furness," Dr. Bottomley broke off from his platform manner, "you may make your objections. Forgive me for shushing you, but you must allow a narrator his curtain lines. Mrmfk."

Furness was on his feet. "But it's absurd," he protested. "It's fantastic—ridiculous—"

"Laughable," Harrison Ridgly added helpfully. "Preposterous. Unbelievable. Ah—anyone have a *Roget* around?"

Drew Furness glared at the speaker, then at Bottomley. "Belle Craven is a dear, sweet old woman. To make her into an insidious villainess, with some sort of vile implication of—"

"Please. Please." Dr. Bottomley waved a hand feebly. "You overwhelm me with your torrent of indignation. Please try to remember that I am merely telling what happened to me. And by the way, your father *was* at the University of Kansas in 1917?"

"Yes," said Furness grudgingly.

"And you did have another aunt—Alice?"

"I hardly remember her."

"Because she was killed in an accident when you were very young?"

"Hang it, yes. But simply because that much is true—"

"It seems," Dr. Bottomley observed, apparently to the waggling point of his imperial, "that everyone finds this case merely a fascinating problem in crime and deduction until he is personally dragged into it. Mrmfk. But if, gentlemen, now that Mr. Furness has registered his protest, I may resume the narrative—"

"But what's he so het up about?" came the practical voice of Sergeant Watson.

"Sorry if I'm not being elementary, my dear Watson, but truly it is obvious. Professor Furness' address is 11473 Shenandoah Road, and Miss Belle Craven is his aunt."

"Oh," said Sergeant Watson.

"Three guesses," Harrison Ridgly offered, "what's in that box."

Jonadab Evans looked at him quietly. "Don't spoil the story," he counseled. "Write it down on paper now; we'll see later if we're right."

Dr. Bottomley caught their glance of mutual agreement. "Hell and death," he thumped. "And I never thought of that!"

"Get on with your yarn," said Lieutenant Jackson.

To resume, then: I gave Captain Agar what I thought the best advice—to take the parcel to Miss Craven in person, to explain how he had come into possession of it, and to leave further developments in her hands.

He nodded thoughtfully. "Maybe so, Doctor. I may be worried about nothing, I suppose. But I would be glad, now that you've gone this far with me, if you'd see the thing through. Come along with me to Shenandoah Road."

I wavered. It was a tempting adventure, but damn it, I had an adventure of my own right here in 221B. And as I sat there undecided, I recognized the Shenandoah Road address. That resolved me. If, through some outrageous fluke of chance, one of the men in this very house was involved in Captain Agar's fabulous tale, it certainly behooved me to see things through.

"It's a bit difficult, however," I explained. "There's been a little trouble in this house," I added, making a mental note to send my remark to our fellow Irregular Alexander Woollcott for his collection of understatements, "and I'm under police sur-however-er-you-pronounce-it. I'm not sure I can just walk out."

Captain Agar thought for a moment, and when he spoke I knew that this had been no idle musing.

A moment later the sergeant—I don't know his name; the one who replaced Watson for day duty—was forced to eject a drunken curiosity hound with a bronzed face who was roaming noisily about the house. While Sergeant Whoozis was thus busily engaged in his duty, I slipped out of 221B, darted around the corner as agilely as a man of my dimensions can dart, and waited for the Captain. He arrived in an instant, delighted with the success of his drunk act and only regretful that our schedule had not allowed him a really rousing fight with the sergeant.

I can well understand the Captain's getting lost and Ridgly's wanderings last night. Reaching Hollywood Boulevard was not a simple task to us, however it might seem to that crow who's always flying between places. But once there, we caught a red car marked West Los Angeles, and at its terminus found a cab which promptly deposited us in front of 11473 Shenandoah Road.

It is a pleasing house, as some of you may know—small but

new and comfortable, dating, I should judge, from Mr. Furness'
promotion to assistant professor. We rang the doorbell and waited. Just as we heard footsteps, Captain Agar whispered, "Take
this!" and thrust the package into my hand.

There was no time to argue, for the door was opening.

"Miss Belle Craven?" I asked of the small old woman in the
somewhat antique house dress.

"Yes," she said sharply. "What do you want? It isn't about
Them, is it?"

"My friend here—" I began.

"What friend?"

I turned in astonishment. I was standing alone on the door-
step.

Pause for effect. There. End of pause.

"What do you want?" Miss Craven repeated.

"I-ah-mrmfk—I have a package for you," I managed to say,
while my eyes looked vainly up and down Shenandoah Road for
a sign of Captain Fairdale Agar.

"Hm!" said Miss Craven. "I never in all my born days saw a
messenger boy with a beard before."

"I am not a messenger boy," I tried to explain in what I hoped
was a dignified manner. "Not precisely, that is. I am, as a matter
of fact, entrusted with a commission—"

"Not by Them?" she interrupted hastily.

"By someone whom I believe to be unknown to you at whose
request I have undertaken to . . ." The elderly lady's eyes were
small but possessed of a certain gimlet quality. Under their fixed
gaze, I was floundering badly and knew it. Moreover, although I
know by heart every grammatical rule concerning relative clauses, I am always apt to bog down when I use them aloud. I bogged
now.

"Come on inside," said Miss Craven abruptly. "We can't have you standing there on the stoop all day. They'll see you, and there's no telling what They might do. Come in," she repeated peremptorily.

I followed her into a neat and trim little living room, furnished with a curious mixture of Roosevelt II Californian and Roosevelt I Kansan. The latter seemed as comfortable as it was dowdy; I chose a well-broken-in Morris chair and hesitated before it until my—should I say hostess?—had seated herself.

"Sit down, young man," she ordered, with complete disregard of the fact that I could not possibly be more than a year her junior. "Tell me all about it. And remember, They've tried to fool me before, and it can't be done."

I sat down, and enjoyed a delicious moment of realizing how exceedingly comfortable a Morris chair is. Whatever else may be said of that unbelievable tangler of the utilitarian and the quasi-esthetic, William Morris undeniably knew how a man likes to sit. But Miss Craven's reservedly hostile gaze quickly aroused me from any sense of bodily ease.

As always when trying to resolve how best to approach a situation, I moved my hand unconsciously to my breast pocket. As I touched the inestimable herb there concealed, I recalled that I am, roughly speaking, a gentleman, and broke off to ask, "May I?"

"Indeed you may not," Miss Craven replied quite as casually as I had asked. "Get on with your story."

"You may remember," I began more or less helplessly, "a certain Peter Black."

"I do not," Miss Craven snapped.

I tried to carry on. "He was, I believe, engaged to marry your sister Alice some time around 1917."

"Was he indeed? And I suppose you know more about my own sister than I do?"

This was not going at all well. "Surely you remember," I ventured, "why your sister left Kansas?"

Miss Craven's only answer to this question was to walk over to my chair, seize my beautiful beard firmly in both hands, and tug like all hell.

I think I squealed. Perhaps I screamed or shrieked. At any rate—another for Woollcott's collection—I made a noise; and a stronger and bolder man than I need not have been ashamed to quail under the purposeful vigor of that tug.

"It was smart of Them," she said, "to send a real beard this time. Go on, young man."

"With all due respect, madam, may I ask you just who the devil are They?"

"We do not use foul language in this house," she said.

"I beg your pardon. But do you mean to imply that I am an emissary of some—"

"I know what They want now," she went on. "They're trying to get revenge for the one of Them that was killed. Of course he deserved to die; I don't blame Drew in the least after all he did to him like beating him up like that and then insulting him. Maybe that's what should be done to all of Them—kill Them."

She said this calmly enough, but with conviction—a conviction that did not add to my comfort when I realized that I was, in her eyes, one of Them, whoever They might be. "About this box," I said.

"I never thought They'd be so bold as to send one of Them right into my own house here. Generally They just watch around corners and fences and when I look again They aren't there any more. But one of Them right in here. . . . Maybe this was meant."

"It has your name on it," I continued desperately, "and so we thought—"

"Well," She pounced on the word. "Then you admit—"

Frantically I pulled the box from my pocket and thrust it at her. "Here," I said.

She took it almost reluctantly and turned her back on me to open it. She fumbled with the complex knot, then rose. "I need my glasses for this," she said. "I never can find them. Now let me see . . ." She moved questingly toward the hall. With impolite eagerness, I rose and followed her. After all this, I was not going to be done out of seeing the contents of that box.

"I think I left them in my wool jacket," she was murmuring. "That would be in this closet here. . . . Oh, dear!" Her hand on the open door of the closet, she turned back to me with a surprising new friendliness. "You do look like a nice man, for one of Them. Won't you pick up that box for me? My sciatica does bother me so when I stoop over."

The box had fallen well inside the closet. I was leaning over to pick it up when I felt an abrupt thump on my exposed tilted rear. I was incredulous at the thought of even such an eccentric old lady yielding to the temptation to kick me; but I was even more incredulous to turn and behold that I had been struck by the sharp closing of the closet door. Even as I gazed unseeing in the blackness of the little room, I heard the click of the key in the lock.

Noisemaking, I quickly realized, could do me no good. There was presumably no one within earshot but the very person who had locked me in here. Uttering a brief prayer that Miss Craven did not add pyromania to her other peculiarities (for I failed to see how else she could harm me in my imprisonment), I calmly sat on the floor, leaned back against the wall, and lit a cigar.

I must confess that I took a certain luxurious pleasure in the thought of polluting with my blessedly filthy habit even so small a part of an abstaining household.

Outside the closet I could hear the dial clicks of a telephone and the excited voice of Miss Craven. Somehow I felt that those indistinguishable soprano yelps boded no good for me, but I cannot say I was worried. I was perfectly willing to sit there and see what happened, half certain that I should wake up before long.

And then I remembered the box. I felt around in the darkness until my fingers hit it. Then I struck a match—and incidentally I thank you, Mr. Furness, for your acknowledgment of this one advantage in the vice of smoking—and tried to untie the string.

Have you gentlemen ever tried untying a string with one hand while holding a match in the other? I finally surrendered to my helplessness, fished out my pocketknife, and solved the problem in the manner of the great Alexander.

Gingerly I lifted the lid. I might, if I chose, expatiate upon my thoughts at this moment. What could this box hold that so strangely intertwined the fates of Peter Black, Captain Fairdale Agar, Belle Craven, Drew Furness, and my fat self? Could it be—and so on. But I spare you. I simply tell you that in that box lay what, if I had been one half so astute as the Messrs. Ridgly and Evans, both of whom, I see, know the secret already—

I told you relative clauses bother me, and this one has me licked, which isn't helping my climax any. But the tag line is this:

In that cardboard box, tenderly imbedded in cotton, lay a neatly severed and duly dried human *ear*.

◇ ◆ ◇ ◆ ◇

Dr. Bottomley resumed his seat.

"That," said Lieutenant Jackson feelingly, "is a hell of a place to end a story. You leave yourself locked up in a closet with a human ear, while a madwoman is telephoning to God knows what. How did you get back here safe and sound?"

Dr. Bottomley frowned. "You can thank Professor Furness for the incomplete nature of my narrative. Its closing portion parallels his own story so closely as to ruin my effect. Damned unsporting of him, I call it."

"You mean—"

"I got back here the same way Furness did—in a police car, after invoking the patronage of Lieutenant Finch. It was the police that Miss Craven was phoning. I don't know what she told them, but they seemed to be under the impression that I was an elderly degenerate who went around molesting helpless old ladies. (Helpless! Mrmfk.) I gather that there's been a tidy wave of sex murders here in Los Angeles lately, and a nice shiny new suspect is needed every so often. It looked as though I was elected, until Finch explained who I was and that I was in New York when Anna Sosoyeva was killed—whoever she was. Very decent man, this Finch of yours, though I can't say I liked his parting shot. I said how grateful I was for his clearing me, and he up and replied, 'That's all right. You mightn't think it to read the papers, but there are other murders beside Sosoyeva's.'"

"Now just for the record, gentlemen," Jackson said hesitantly, "is this damned ear something more out of Holmes?"

"Not only the ear, Lieutenant," Jonadab Evans hastened to explain. "The box, the seafaring adventurer, the wicked sister—they're all straight out of *The Adventure of the Cardboard Box*."

"And something more else," Otto Federhut added. "Did

you observe, *Herr Doktor,* the name of your Captain? Are not Fairdale and Agar to you familiar names?"

"Hell and death!" Bottomley exclaimed. "I'm not being bright, am I? Of course. Elementary."

"Before the Lieutenant explodes," said Harrison Ridgly, "I might explain that my colleagues refer to two others of the unpublished reminiscences of John Watson, M.D. Mr. Fairdale Hobbs was a lodger with one Mrs. Warren for whom Holmes arranged an affair—'a simple matter.' Dr. Moore Agar was a Harley Street physician, 'whose dramatic introduction to Holmes,' Watson promised, 'I may some day recount.' The rogue of a chronicler, I need hardly add, lied in his teeth. I trust," he murmured, "that no one has encountered today a gentleman named Moore Hobbs?"

Drew Furness had risen to his feet. "Doctor," he requested, "may I have the floor for a moment?"

"Certainly."

"I wish to go on record as protesting this stupid calumny against my aunt. That we, a group of intelligent men, should sit here listening to such infamous—"

"I think," Harrison Ridgly III interrupted drawlingly, "that it is my turn next. Contain yourself in patience, Mr. Furness; you may soon have the opportunity of seeing how well the doctor likes to have his own nerves plucked."

And with this cheering preamble, the editor of *Sirrah* took his place before the company.

Chapter 13

COLONEL WARBURTON'S MADNESS

being the narrative of Harrison Ridgly III

I too prefer to speak my little piece. It is not that I seek the vigor of extemporaneous self-expression desired by our good Dr. Bottomley; it is merely that I am on an editorial vacation, and the thought of needlessly approaching a typewriter terrifies me.

I shall omit the details of breakfast so lovingly dwelt upon by our previous speakers. Mrs. Hudson, with all due respect, strikes me as being that most highly praised abomination, a "good plain cook," who bears somewhat the same relation to my Gustl as a U.P. news cameraman bears to Steichen or Weston. But Gustl is in New York, and there is a legend to the effect that man must eat to keep alive. Having always had a due regard for superstitious ritual, I ate, but I prefer to say no more on the subject.

I had slept late, and it was almost noon when I finished breakfast and settled down to an idle period of musing—for even reading is far too reminiscent of editorial duties. The matter of my musing is not germane to the narrative, though close kin to the narrator.

You will pardon an occasional cryptic turn to my speech? There was a time not long past when life was clear to me. A source of amusement, yes, but of good clean fun—as absurd, as obscene, and as obvious as the antics of a burlesque comedian. Now I know that I was a fool—that the performance I am watching is rather that of the Grand Guignol, where farce and terror follow so closely on each other's heels that horror congeals the spine still trembling with laughter. And from such charnel hysteria it is some partial escape to confuse one's listeners in the hope that one may oneself be confused, lest one see too clearly.

But let me interrupt this chain of maundering as my own thoughts were interrupted—by the sound of the telephone and the voice of Mrs. Hudson. My caller was a stranger to me, though one whose name and accomplishments were familiar, as doubtless they are to most of you. He was Gordon Withers, M.D., proprietor, to use a vulgar term, of the most highly esteemed rest home in this abode of dementia and neurosis. I was surprised by the call. I should be the last to deny my perchance even urgent need of Dr. Withers' services, but I failed to understand how he could have become aware of that need.

He quickly disillusioned me. It is too often a mistake to assume that an unusual event must have a personal significance. Instead of regarding me as a possible subject for the practice of his soothing arts, Dr. Withers wanted me rather as an instrument—a vulcanized-rubber pacifier for one of his patients, warranted not to split.

Teddy Fircombe is an odd little individual who was for many months a hanger-on of the "Sirrah" offices. I had never heard a word concerning Teddy's past, his family, or anything else about him save his firm conviction that he could run "Sirrah" single-handed. I don't even know how he came to affix himself to us—I think vaguely that Denny acquired him one night on a pubcrawl, and not knowing what to do with him upon awaking the next morning, simply took him along to the office. Teddy, to hear his own most candid self-analysis, could draw better than Denny, write better than any half dozen of our biggest names, and edit far better than I. Moreover, he Knew What the Public Wanted. He was such a bumptious little man, so cocksure of his talents, that we took him to our hearts. He was a fixed point in a world of flux. His vulgar assurance in the midst of our moody pallor made him seem like a Hogarth character who had wandered into a Thurber drawing, and he delighted us. And out of each gross of his fluent suggestions, we might find one which would prove useful.

His great value, however, developed when Denny invented Colonel Warbuton. Most of you, I trust, are familiar with that outrageous little gentleman who wanders through the pages of "Sirrah" with one beady eye fixed on the dread Red menace and the other stroking the rump of a lusty wench. (This metaphor, I realize, seems to give him the ocular stalk of a lobster; but I hope my meaning is nonetheless clear.) This sturdy little supporter of the status quo ante bellum ac post coitum—to whom, I believe, "Sirrah" owes more of its circulation than to any other single factor save the Denny Girl—this contemptibly delightful figure was an exact reproduction of most of the body and some of the mind of Teddy Fircombe.

And now Teddy, the fixed point, the immutable constant— Teddy, the Normal Man, who guffawed at the pale neuroses of civilization—Teddy Fircombe had come to Dr. Gordon Withers.

The story of Teddy's affliction Dr. Withers declined to tell over the phone. He would only say that Mr. Fircombe had heard that I was in town, and that he felt the need of some friend— some connection, he had said, with the old time when things were all right—to stand by him in this hour of peril. Dr. Withers had acceded to this request, and thought my presence might well simplify his own task of bringing the patient back to normality.

I resolved to go. Why, it is hard to tell you. I should be the first to protest that humanitarian motives are rare and implausible sources for my actions; and I am not given to sentimental regard for a figure of fun simply because his mock presentment has indirectly swelled my salary. I suppose, if I must analyze, that it was a gesture of escape. I had come here to 221B to escape what is, with all due respect, no concern of yours, only to find myself once more involved in a—in events of moment. The sad dilemma of Colonel Warburton-Fircombe could in no wise touch me. To leave this house for Dr. Withers' sanitarium was to step out of the twisted husk that is myself into a new impartial freedom—to be once more the spectator I was.

The whisky, please, Mrs. Hudson. Thank you.

Now I am not an addict of adventure, nor have I ever considered personal precariousness a satisfactory vehicle of escape. Escape must be attained in physical comfort and mental detachment. So I contrived no convolute plans or stratagems to elude police surveillance. I simply spoke to Sergeant Hinkle (the good Watson's understudy) and explained to him that a physician had requested my presence with his patient.

The Sergeant has that innate sense of disbelief which so often passes for shrewd skepticism among the unintelligent. He verified my story by calling Dr. Withers back, then secured authorization from Lieutenant Finch, and finally arranged for a police chauffeur to drive me to the sanitarium.

The drive was pleasant. The day by now had grown hot enough to justify me in wearing a new model of slack suit, contrived by a "Sirrah" designer after some of the more extreme theories of Elizabeth Hawes. The effect, though perhaps startling to the untutored eye of the official driver, brought to me a certain contentment. I was wearing a garment I had never before worn, driving with a man I had never before met, through streets I had never before seen, to a destination I had never before reached. I had escaped from everything save certain cardiac cicatrices, if I may apply the vocabulary of modern medicine—with your permission, Doctor—to the concepts of outworn romanticism.

The sanitarium lies somewhere to the west of here. I did not bother to follow our route closely; but I imagine that it is situated not far from the scene of Dr. Bottomley's incarceration in the closet. It is constructed in a bastard style—offspring of the rape of Our Lady of the Angels by a modern German theorist. Esthetically outrageous, but nonetheless—it was a *warm* day and I had escaped—faintly pleasing.

The police chauffeur accompanied me inside, but had the grace to wait in the outer office when I was shown into Dr. Withers' sanctum. What the doctor is like, I cannot say; I saw only his professional manner, which is astutely blended of one part self-confidence, one part human kindness, and one part acidulous arrogance. Add a dash of bitters and stir profoundly.

Much more noticeable in the room when I entered was a stenographer—a tall slim girl whose hair I would not demean by comparing it with honey. Even as she typed records from charts, she infused her each movement with a grace of a Danilova. My mental comment, I must confess, was a note which read: eminently stuprable. But the girl finished her last transcript almost as I entered, and left without looking at me, abandoning me to no greater visual consolation than that afforded by the chromium smoking gadgets on the doctor's desk.

I had expected to find Teddy there in all his Warburtonian vigor and vulgarity, and said as much to the doctor. He frowned and went on to explain the situation at as great and detailed length as though he were expounding a unique operation to a group of eminent but awed colleagues.

In mercifully fewer words, his account was this: Teddy was not, as I had hastily supposed, a patient at the sanitarium. He had simply come to the office that morning and asked to see Dr. Withers on an urgent matter—so urgent, he informed the nurse, that his sanity hung in the balance. The nurse was impressed by his manner, but even more deeply impressed (and in quite a different way) by his resemblance to Colonel Warburton. She had come half agiggle into Dr. Withers' office; and the physician, curious to see the fleshly facsimile of so famous a character, had agreed to listen to him.

When the story was told and Withers had sent for me, he had asked Teddy to wait outside while he attended to other patients. When I was announced, he had told the office nurse to show Teddy in at the same time—to which the surprised nurse replied that the funny little man had left the building as soon as Dr. Withers had shown him out of the office. Why Mr. Fircombe had demanded my presence so urgently and then disappeared once I had been summoned, Dr. Withers found himself unable to surmise.

At first he was reluctant to tell me what the dire matter was which had reduced the Normal Man to the verge of madness. But the entire situation was so unparalleled in his professional experience, so difficult to match with exact analogy from the code of ethics, that he finally told me Teddy's story, in the hope that I who knew the man might throw some light on the confused affair.

As I have said, I knew nothing of Teddy's private life. It did not surprise me, however, to learn that he had married some fifteen years ago and had a son of an age which indicated the strictest dispatch in the fulfillment of marital ritual. Nor was I surprised to learn that Teddy, upon becoming a widower two years ago, had promptly married a much younger and exceedingly beautiful woman, who had been equally punctual in perpetuating the Fircombe line.

Devotion to this resultant infant was, one gathered, the chief sport and occupation of the Fircombe household. Its mother adored it. Its father adored it. Its nurse adored it. Only its elder half brother was ever known to waver in this orgy of adoration; and even he, apparently, paid the infant its due respect most of the time.

Life for Teddy was blissful—in the sound and normal fashion which he would most approve—until the nurse reported to him an incredible episode. Furious in his disbelief, he fired the woman. But later he had the evidence of his own eyes. He beheld—

◇ ◆ ◇ ◆ ◇

Harrison Ridgly III suspended his narrative and paused with a twisted half-smile on his face. "Yes, Herr Federhut?" he said gently.

Federhut ran his hand through his shaggy white mane in a gesture of incredulity. "I know that it seems madness in me as well," he said. "But may I state what your Colonel Warburton told the doctor that he had seen?"

Ridgly nodded. "Go ahead. I am certain that your astuteness will delight and confound the Lieutenant."

"He told the doctor . . ." Federhut hesitated as though what he was about to say were too outrageous for utterance. "He said that his wife was a *Vampyr*—that he had with his very eyes seen her to suck the blood from the neck of her own small infant."

The silence in the room was broken by the sudden glurp of Sergeant Watson inadvertently swallowing a Lifesaver.

"Look here," Jackson expostulated. "This is too much even for Holmes—this is oogy-boogy from a Universal B."

"I beg your pardon, Lieutenant," Jonadab Evans said, "but Holmes did encounter more than one case which seemed on its surface to be of supernatural origin. One of these was the curious adventure of Robert Ferguson, who had been three-quarter for Richmond when Watson played Rugby for Blackheath. The same situation—adolescent son of first marriage, young second wife, mother accused of vampirism on her own child."

"The explanation," Federhut added, "is that the mother was sucking from her child's blood stream a poison by the jealous adolescent administered."

"For further details, *vide*," Drew Furness concluded, "*The Adventure of the Sussex Vampire*."

In reply there came from Jackson only a cryptic noise.

"And you, my dear Doctor," Ridgly observed to Bottomley, "have you no comment to add on this singular coincidence?"

Dr. Bottomley seemed to rouse himself with difficulty from an unwonted absorption. "I beg your pardon," he said. "I was thinking—but no matter. Mrmfk. That is all of your story, Ridgly?" He sounded almost eager.

"No," said Harrison Ridgly succinctly.

◇ ◆ ◇ ◆ ◇

By now, naturally, I had come to the conclusion that Teddy had been indulging in a peculiarly atrocious form of legpulling of which I had never imagined him capable. I was not annoyed; the episode, absurd though it was, had at least provided me with a respite from the very real mysteries of 221B. But there was no use in prolonging the farce. I resolved to close the subject and to depart as soon as I could.

Of course one could hardly tell the sincere doctor that he had been immeasurably behoaxed. He had evolved two beautiful alternative theories, one to explain Mrs. Fircombe's incredible behavior as fact and the other predicated on the notion that it was all a delusion of Teddy's. Both, I may add with cautious euphemism, involved a somewhat debatable analogy between blood and another almost equally vital fluid. I had not the heart to point out that the solution to this case history lay in a less austere authority than Havelock Ellis.

The re-entrance of the blonde secretary, who laid some papers on the desk and retired with ineffable silent grace, provided me with a cue. I brushed aside the doctor's apologies for having brought me in quest of the wild goose, and added that I should get in touch with him again shortly to learn what more he had heard of Teddy and also to obtain the address of his employment agency. If I was to be here long, I explained, I might need a secretary; and I was more than anxious to learn where one could obtain young ladies with such hair, such bodies, and above all such grace of movement.

It took a moment's hesitation before he could decide to treat my query as genuine. Then he hemmed a bit and finally confessed that the blonde was not, strictly speaking, an employee at all. She was a patient—rather a singular case. A girl who had suffered a severe physical shock, so terrible that for a time her sanity had been in doubt. She had slowly recovered her balance under Dr. Withers' care, but with complete oblivion of all that had gone before the shock. The work she did here was of the same nature as her employment before the disaster. Its purpose was therapeutic—to re-establish her, so to speak, in her former life; but so far the experiment had met with no success. She was in every respect sane and normal; but the amnesia persisted. She was unable even to recognize the closest friends of her former existence.

Whereupon the doctor went on to say that he knew a friend of mine—had in fact seen him quite recently. Dr. Rufus Bottomley, whose practice he had shared in long-dead days in Waterloo, Iowa. He hoped that I would give his regards to Dr. Bottomley.

He hedged and hesitated until I realized that what he truly wanted, beneath all this verbal subterfuge, was some inside information on our murder, of which he must have read newspaper accounts. Despite the freakish cases of abnormality which he handled as daily routine, despite his reputed knowledge of more inside scandal than any other six men in the film colony, he was as eager as a shopgirl for good fresh dirt.

I toyed with the temptation to invent certain tidbits to delight him, but I was afraid that Dr. Bottomley might inadvertently upset my wax-apple cart when next he saw his friend. So I confined myself to detailing a few of *our* more outlandish clues which have not received due newspaper attention, and ended by stating in all truth that I for one had not the remotest notion of who had killed Stephen Worth.

From the doorway behind me came a single sharp scream and a sliding thud. I turned to see the lovely blond patientsecretary lying like a shapeless lump on the floor, the papers she had been carrying now scattered about and over her like the leaves on the Babes in the Wood.

I stood by with the shrinking futility of the laymen while Dr. Withers and two nurses competently attended to the girl, and my police chauffeur, drawn by the scream, watched the scene dubiously.

The blonde delight recovered consciousness quickly. But consciousness was all that she had recovered. Her mind, Dr. Withers told me in tones of quite unprofessional shock, had fallen back to its state immediately after her tragedy.

And all, it would seem, because Colonel Warburton had staged a stupid hoax and I had mentioned Stephen Worth.

◇ ◆ ◇ ◆ ◇

Harrison Ridgly III concluded his narrative with an air of malicious languor, and resumed his seat. Almost before he was seated, Lieutenant Jackson had come to the table and was facing the group.

"My turn," he said curtly. "Now those first two stories were strange enough. They offer lots of possibilities for consideration, even aside from all those Holmes angles you're so bright at digging up. But they can't be checked. No independent observer saw Grossmann the nasty Nazi, or Captain Fairdale Agar, who found a human ear in a Main Street brawl. This one's different. I know Dr. Withers by reputation. He's tops in his profession and as reliable a witness as you could ask for. And, leaving the Colonel Warburton angle out of the question for the moment, when one of Dr. Withers' patients suffers a serious relapse on hearing the name of Stephen Worth, it's damned important. All right. Now does any of you know anything about a girl connected with Worth who could be this mysterious blonde?"

"One of his secretaries at the studio," Maureen said, "did have a nervous breakdown. But so many walked out on him that it's hard to remember just which one. No. Sorry, Lieutenant, but it's no help. She was short and dark—sort of cute in a way, but not the wonderful beauty that Mr. Ridgly got so excited about."

"Anybody else?" Jackson stared intently at the silent gathering.

At last it was Ridgly who spoke. "You might be more specific," he suggested quietly. "Ask Dr. Bottomley."

Dr. Rufus Bottomley bristled. All at once the eccentric dignity which was so much a part of him seemed merely a false and hollow pomposity, a pretentious coat of mail which its wearer knew to be only too vulnerable. "Why the devil should I—?" he began.

"I see what Mr. Ridgly means," Jackson interrupted. "According to his story, Dr. Withers said that the girl was unable to recognize her former friends, then added that he knew of a friend of Ridgly's—you. That doesn't sound like a random remark; there's an association there. He also said that he was having the girl carry on the work that she'd done before her disaster; apparently that was work in a doctor's office. Out with it, Dr. Bottomley—who is this girl and what is her connection with Worth?"

Dr. Bottomley's usually booming voice sounded uncertain of itself. "You have no right to ask me that, Lieutenant. You know that you have no more official position here than any of the rest of us; I am under no compulsion to answer you."

It was Drew Furness who took him up, and with unwonted vigor. "But you are under a compulsion to answer us," he said. "We're gathered tonight to thresh this thing out. Whatever comes up has to be probed to its fullest depth. If you know any relevant facts—"

"I assure you that they are not relevant."

"And what relevance was there to your ridiculous, fabulous scandals about my family? That was all right, wasn't it? That was in the spirit of the game. Pull all the rotten crawling things out into the light whether they'll help us or not. Let's have a good look. But when it's your—"

"He's right, you know, Bottomley," Jonadab Evans broke in. "Whatever it is that you know about Worth—"

"True, *Herr Doktor*. Our investigations must we make without regard to persons or personalities—"

Rufus Bottomley had risen. The proud imperial waggled with hopeless indignation, and his short, stout body swelled with fury. He opened his mouth, but he did not say, "Hell and death!" He simply said, "God damn it! I'm not a man to be hounded like this. I've told you that Ann's case has nothing to do with Worth—nothing whatsoever. If it had . . . But no matter. It's hell that Ridgly should have stumbled onto this. But that faint, I swear to you, is the merest coincidence; and if you want to twist it to something else, you can dive with my compliments down to the deepest lake in hell and twist yourself silly."

"Control yourself, Bottomley," said Mr. Evans mildly.

"Control myself? It isn't enough that I should have to sit here and listen to news that would tear a man's heart. It isn't enough that I should be plagued with questions and insinuations and vile innuendoes of some unbelievable complicity. But now I must be asked to control myself? Control, hell!" he shouted—having done which, he seemed suddenly to obey the injunction he had scorned. A semblance of muscular control at least he did attain. His body no longer shook, and his beard was stern and unwavering as he walked to the door.

"I am going to my room," he said with forcible restraint. "I might, if I chose, question even Lieutenant Finch's legal right to keep us in this house. Certainly no one has the official power to detain me in this room. I shall be curious to hear later what further little surprises you contrive among you. At the moment I desire only quiet. Good night."

He walked out of the room. Neither Jackson nor the Sergeant made a move to stop him.

"After which touching scene," said Harrison Ridgly, "I propose another drink all around. And then, if I may take over the chair in the absence of our perturbed Tantalus, we shall have the privilege of hearing from Otto Federhut. And whose toes," he wondered aloud, "will be crushed this time?"

Chapter 14

THE REMARKABLE CASE OF THE
VENOMOUS LIZARD

being the narrative of Otto Federhut

This story, meine Herren, I must with two apologies preface. One is for the order of my speech; for although I have typed this manuscript and reread it with all care, still am I not sure where words should go. Often have I heard the Americans and the English protest at the order of words in German; but our words fall at least by rule. To you that rule may seem strange; but to us there is never doubt where a word must be. In your order ("natural," as I believe you call it), I am lost.

The other apology is that I provide you with no change of scene. I offer to you no deserted houses filled with Nazi spies, no sanitoria with beautiful swooning attendants. I give to you for setting only this house, this 221B and can plead for the interest of my story only that I found my life in greater danger than ever it was from the followers of the Führer.

After lunch my story commences when I find at the front door in progress a disputation between Sergeant Hinkle and a strange young man. The young man, I gather, is striving to see any one of us—any Irregular, that is, save only Jonadab Evans—a fact which at the time seems to be most peculiar. The Sergeant is stubbornly convinced that the young man is the reporter of a newspaper and resolved that he shall not pass, but on the face I read an intensity of personal concern which is not that of a man trying to secure for his editor a story.

I interpose myself in the disputation. "Sergeant," I say, "if this young man wishes to see one of us, why should he not? It may be of importance."

The young man's face lit up and he attacked the Sergeant with fresh vigor until at last that worthy officer with a grudge yielded.

"I am Otto Federhut," I explained. "And I fear that I alone must serve you. I have seen today none of the others save Herr Evans, and whereto they may be gone, I do not know. But if you will come to my room, we can confer upon your problem."

On the first floor it was hot beneath the roof. (I beg your pardon; as I read I remember that you say second floor. If I am to be a good American, I must accustom myself to these things.) I opened the windows and we both removed our coats and were comfortable.

I wish that I could here add the touch of the romancer and describe to you the young man, though it has ever seemed to me that physical description was of little aid in determining thought and character. For were it not else a rule of legal procedure that in each appeal of a case should be furnished a complete description of all parties and witnesses? The day of Lombroso is past; and the day of Hooton, though it has dawned, is not yet all-convincing in its light. Moreover to me the young men of America, in their slim and muscular homeliness, seem sometimes as indistinguishable as so many Chinese. So I can say no more save that this was a young American, who from his many brothers differed only in that he carried what is in this land so rare, a walking stick, and that I found him seemingly honest and straightforward even before I owed to him my life. Besides, it is possible that Mr. Evans will give to you a more complete description when I have finished.

Jonadab Evans sat up with a jerk. "What do you mean, Federhut? I never even knew you had a caller today."

Federhut smiled and wagged his mane. "You shall see."

"But you said the fellow specifically did not want to see me—"

"Would a stranger say that?" Ridgly interposed lazily. "It would seem to me offhand that that fact alone demonstrates that he knew you. No slur intended, Evans—simple logical deduction."

"You are right, Herr Ridgly. But I resume the narration."

The young man found difficulty in coming to the point. He smoked three cigarettes, each from the other lit, while we spoke in fragments of the Worth case and he sought to resolve himself. At last he began, and the story was this:

His name he wished for the moment not to state. He was a wandering youth who traveled about the United States, working now as reporter, now as salesman, now as day laborer, and always enjoying himself and his life. Some years ago he had been in Los Angeles for a long period, working in the gubernatorial campaign of 1934, of which he spoke as though it was most significant and I should know of it, though I comprehended only that he had had his part in working for the United Front. (That term, amid all the confusions of your local politics, is one readily understandable to me, who strove for it in Vienna so hard and so fruitlessly.)

During his stay here he served on a coroner's jury in the case of a young girl who had died mysteriously. The verdict returned was death from natural causes, but the medical evidence was not clear; and as the years passed, the young man found himself thinking on this case back and wondering if all was right. There had been a stepfather who was a herpetologist—a reptile student—and who appeared to have some financial interest in the girl, although its exact nature was never brought out. The name of this stepfather was Dr. Royal Farncroft, and the name of the girl was Miss Amy Gray.

At this point was it that I became most interested; for Amy Gray, if I mistake not, was the name which a strange voice mentioned on the telephone to Miss O'Breen. Coincidence was possible, I knew; but it seemed also that some clue to the Worth case might be about to come to my hands.

The young man worried long over this case. He has a sense of his duty as a citizen, and it seemed to him terrible that in serving the state as juror he might have frustrated justice. What most disturbed him was that this Amy Gray had had a sister Florence; and if it had suited Dr. Royal Farncroft to be rid of the one stepdaughter, why not then of the other.

When he returned to Los Angeles a few weeks ago, he was determined to learn more of this case. He asked among people whom he knew, and at last he contrived to be introduced to a young architect who had been at the time of her death to Amy Gray affianced. This man too had his doubts, because he knew that certain funds of Miss Gray's upon her marriage would from Dr. Farncroft's control pass to her, and he had not trusted the scientist's handling of those funds. Now, moreover, he heard that Miss Florence Gray was also affianced; and my young friend conceived lively and (as we were too soon to learn) not ungrounded fears for her safety.

Already had I remarked the extraordinary similarity which beyond doubt one of you gentlemen is now eager to call to my attention; but it was the young man himself who first remarked on the coincidence. He had read in some article of cinema gossip that Rita La Marr was to play in "The Speckled Band," and being (as what male is not?) a devoted admirer of the charms of that woman, he looked up and read the story. There, to his amazement, was the parallel of his own problem—the two sisters, the stepfather, the financial involvement, the mysterious death. He was thunderstruck.

(He read, I may add, only the short-story version of "The Speckled Band." To those who know also the dramatic form, I need not to point out that there is a further parallelism in his own role, that of the suspicious coroner's juror. This whole problem of the interrelation of story and drama is one much neglected, in particular the suppression in the short story of the previous connection with the Stoner family of Dr. Watson. But all this belongs to another paper which I have been of late preparing.)

This coinciding of plot led him to action. He thought his story too thin with which to go to the police, in particular since his political activities had not made him friends among officials. But he had heard of us, the Irregulars, through a man whom he knew who is of us; and he thought that we, interested by the analogy, might use influence to aid him.

"Your problem does interest me," I told him. "My knowledge of law is however that of the Roman code in Europe prevalent, and of Anglo-Saxon usage I am ignorant—a fact which does not make me happy in continuing my career here as an émigré. Our influence, moreover, is now in great doubt and jeopardy. We ourselves, if you have followed the journals, are not what you would call 'in the clear' with the law. However, what I can do to help you, that I will."

The young man did not look oversatisfied with this statement, but he grinned and thanked me. "Now I suppose," he said, "you want to ask me questions. OK. Shoot."

Involuntarily I thought of last night, when first I learned that idiom "shoot" and heard a shot in echo. But I brought my mind back to the present problem and asked, "The first thing that disturbs me—why do you carry a cane? It is surely not common usage among Americans."

"It isn't a common cane, either," he said, in both hands weighing the stick. "It's good stout wood, and the handle's leaded. This, Mr. Federhut, is a weapon."

"But why?"

"Because I think I've seen Dr. Royal Farncroft at times and places where he shouldn't be. I've got an idea he knows what I'm up to and he doesn't like it. There's no harm in going armed, just in case."

"Then you really think that you are in danger of your life?"

"I do." Quite simply he said it, and one had to believe.

"Tell me now more," I said, "about this Dr. Royal Farncroft. Give me some idea—"

In the hallway was a loud noise, compounded in part of the protesting voice of Sergeant Hinkle and in part of another voice, harsh, gruff, and to me unfamiliar. The young man started to his feet. "Either I'm nuts," he said, "or you're about to get the answer to your question. That voice is Dr. Royal Farncroft's."

He and the Sergeant came at once together into the room. "This guy insists he's got to see you," said Hinkle. "Say the word though, and I'll throw him out." The Sergeant glared upon the herpetologist as though he wished indeed that I would say the word.

His instant dislike for the man I could understand. Dr. Farncroft was of medium height, I believe, but he gave the impression of a large and burly man. It was in part his black beard no doubt, and also in part the frown of cruelty on his brow. With a strange courtesy of repressed violence, he waited for me to speak, setting on the floor beside him the black bag which he carried.

"Leave him with me," I said to the Sergeant.

"OK, if that's the way you want it. But you just say the word—" The Sergeant retired with a look desirous of action at my visitor's back.

No sooner was the Sergeant gone than Dr. Farncroft burst out. "I know you!" he cried at the young man. "You were on the jury. Well, the verdict was natural causes, wasn't it? Wasn't it?" he loudly repeated.

The young man said nothing until Dr. Farncroft had a third time screamed his question. Then he simply replied, "And will it be again?"

Ignoring him, the reptile scholar turned to me. "And you, you meddling busybody, what is all this to you? Why do you sit here holding conferences on what is none of your affair?"

I felt that I could not do better than to emulate Holmes on the similar occasion when Dr. Grimesby Roylott invaded his office. "It is a little warm for the time of year," I said in paraphrase.

"What have you learned from this young idiot?" he demanded furiously.

"But," I continued imperturbably, "I have heard that the crocuses promise well."

Dr. Farncroft stepped forward in a manner which indicated

that his menacing was to go from the verbal to the physical. The young man interposed before me himself and held his weighted stick ready for action.

"You trifle with me!" Dr. Farncroft's voice was half a scream. He seized the stick, held it in his two hands, and thus in midair, not even against his knee striking it, he snapped that heavy stick in two pieces.

"There!" he cried. "See that I do not need to apply the same treatment to you." He bent over to pick up his bag, seemed to find some trouble with the handle, and remained stooped for many seconds, which destroyed alas the dramatic quality of his exit.

"There you have it," said the young man. "Sweet little number, isn't he?"

"He is not," I admitted, "an antagonist whom I should choose. He is a dangerous man. But dangerous men I have met before. There have been those who swore to have my life when they from prison emerged; yet here I am, as you see me."

"What do you think we should do?"

"If you will give me time, I shall think upon the matter and perchance confer with my colleagues and with the young detective Jackson, who seems sympathisch. If you will give me your name so that I may come again with you into contact—"

He grinned a very broad grin. "You might, if you like, call me John O'Dab."

"John O'Dab!" I started. "But that is—"

"Creator of that dashing gentleman adventurer, the Honorable Derring Drew. Sure. That's me, and if you want I can prove it. But it's pretty much of a secret for a lot of reasons; we won't go into that. Maybe you better just call me Larry Gargan."

"My friend Mr. Evans—" I commenced.

"I know. Skip it. It's a long story."

I managed with an effort to control my curiosity. "And where can I find you?"

"I don't rightly know. I'm pretty much on the loose now. Tell you what—I'll call you here tomorrow or the next day, if the dear doctor doesn't carry out his threats, and find out what you've decided. And I hope it's good. This Florence seems a sweet kid, and if we don't take steps pretty quick, Dr. Farncroft may try to pull a fast one."

He started toward the door. My eye, moving with him, saw a curious object on the floor. Now I am slightly myopic (short-sighted, I think you say), and to me it was but an indistinct thing of black and pinkish-orange.

"He is indeed a curious man, your Dr. Farncroft," I said. "See what he has left behind him—a strange sort of beaded bag, is it not? Who would suspect that vigorous man of carrying—"

I leaned over to examine the thing more carefully. It was some fifteen inches long and two or three inches wide, decorated with an odd beaded pattern like to American Indian work. As I stretched out my hand to pick it up, it moved.

At that instant Larry Gargan thrust me back. "You damned fool!" he cried. "Can't you see—!"

I indeed saw. What had seemed to me as a bag pretty struck me now with inexpressible revulsion when I knew that it lived and moved. And move it did, slowly, sluggishly, but inexorably across the floor from the door toward us. I knew not at that moment what it might be; but I did know as by some instinct that its painstaking movements were the laborious advance of death.

"The stick's too short now," my companion muttered. "That breaking had more point to it than just showing off. The damned fiend; that's probably how he—I should have carried a gun."

I was backing away from the thing helplessly, understanding almost the fable of the rabbit and the snake. Then my foot met a rug. The rug slipped. I sprawled headlong and found my open eyes staring into the unutterably ugly face of the thing, from my nose not two inches removed. It came on. I could not even speak. Upon me descended the paralysis of sheer terror.

Then came a thudding crash and before my face I saw two heavy shoes. With a leap Larry Gargan had descended on the thing, crushing from it its evil life.

He helped me to my feet and pushed me back into a chair. "Got a drink around here?" he demanded. "You need it. And God knows so do I."

I gestured, still speechless, at the proper drawer of the dresser. He handed me the bottle, and when I had a long and much-needed Schluck taken, he also drank.

"I don't suppose," he said, "you know just what that ducky little pet is that the dear doctor sicked on us?"

I shook my head.

"Heloderma suspectum, to use the doctor's own language. The nastiest beast ever bred by the hot sun out of the deserts of Arizona. The only poisonous lizard known to mankind—thank God! In short, Mr. Federhut, you have just escaped from a Gila monster."

He drank from the bottle one last gulp, waved off all my protestations of gratitude, and took his leave.

For minutes I sat in the chair incredulous. More even than the events of last night had this amazed me. I could not believe it. Again was the room quiet, the sun through the windows gave me warmth and comfort, in my hand was a bottle of my favorite Schnapps, all was as it should be.

But on the floor before me lay a broken walking stick and the crushed remains of a beaded bag which had lived and moved and all but killed.

◇ ◆ ◇ ◆ ◇

"Evidence first," said Lieutenant Jackson. "This is another story that can be fairly well checked. Hinkle's off duty now, but I can get descriptions of these men from him tomorrow. And the cane and the Gila—?"

"I appreciated, *Herr Leutnant,* their evidential value—though as evidence of what I know not unless I choose to place against the doctor a charge of attempted murder. I gave these articles into the care of Sergeant Hinkle."

Sergeant Watson spoke up. "And he turned 'em over to me, Lieutenant. They're locked up in the hall closet and I got the key here."

"Good. Now—"

"One moment, Lieutenant." It was Harrison Ridgly's drawling voice. "The picturesque horror of this murderous attempt is of course fascinating. But two other points interest me more. One is the connection of Amy Gray with Worth. Do you remember this Gray case?"

"No," said Jackson. "But that isn't surprising with a verdict of death from natural causes. I guess the department just let it go at that."

"But you can check up on the records?"

"I'll do that tomorrow. What's your other worry?"

"What would it be but this extraordinary assertion by the young man that he was John O'Dab? We may very well be harboring a murderer in our select little group here; but it is, esthetically, an even more dreadful thought to suspect that we are harboring an impostor."

Jonadab Evans had the center of the stage as he had never had it before in his life. The mild drab little man rose and faltered. "I am sure," he began hesitantly, "that you will all understand—"

"Say it out clearly, Mr. Evans," Federhut admonished him with judicial authority. "Was my friend right? Is he John O'Dab?"

"Well," said Jonadab Evans, "he . . . In a certain sense one might say . . . As a matter of fact—yes."

Ridgly laughed—a high-pitched and unpleasant noise. "The mouse turns," he gasped. "Who would have thought the old man to have had so much guts? Our dear meek little Milquetoast is a first-class fraud!"

"No, please. It isn't like that at all. It . . . Oh dear! I wonder, Mrs. Hudson, if you . . . Thank you." And Jonadab Evans amazingly gulped a jigger of straight whisky. His next sentence or two was hopelessly lost in a series of choking struggles. "You see," he resumed, "I knew Larry when he was the physical-ed instructor at dear old Sampson Military Academy—a school in which I taught. He showed me a novel which he had written. It was exciting, but oh my, it was bad! I took it and saved all his plot and his crucial situations, but I—I might say I translated it into English. We submitted it under 'John O'Dab' from my own name Jonadab, and we sold it. Then Larry wandered off again; he couldn't ever stay in one place. And wherever he is he keeps sending me novels and I take their bones and put new flesh on them. It works very well.

So in a sense I suppose he is John O'Dab just as much as I am. I have done a few stories without him, but they haven't been nearly so successful. And now you know." He hung his head and looked utterly abashed.

Maureen's laugh was sweet and sympathetic. "There," she said. "It isn't anything so dreadful."

He half smiled. "But I did so enjoy having people think that I made up all those exciting things that Derring does."

"And that," said Harrison Ridgly scornfully, "is the Dread Secret. Dear me!" he echoed Mr. Evans' wistful tones. "If you have sufficiently recovered from the shock of this terrible unmasking, Mr. O'Dab, you might now give us your contribution to the day's narratives. And then, if we can lure the insulted medico from his sulking retreat, we shall settle down to full discussion."

Chapter 15

THE ADVENTURE OF THE OLD
RUSSIAN WOMAN

being the narrative of Jonadab Evans

After a shockingly late breakfast (I say shockingly because the rigors of private-school life have accustomed me to hours more like those of a farm hand than those of a civilized man of letters), I retired to my room and spent several quiet hours in a vain attempt to decipher that series of numbers found in Stephen Worth's brief case. The chain of reasoning by which I arrived at what I thought to be its secret still seems to me flawless, and I should like to discuss this point with you more fully after this narrative sequence is concluded; but at the moment all that matters is that I got nowhere.

I was intensely absorbed in my problem. I did hear some disturbance in the hall, which I realize now must have been the irruption of Dr. Royal Farncroft; but I paid no attention to it. Nothing distracted me until I came to the sudden realization that I was hungry.

This household was so upset today that no fixed luncheon time had been scheduled; but I felt sure that a little rummaging about in the kitchen would provide me with something to stay my pangs until dinner. I entered the kitchen expecting to find it empty or at most tenanted only by Mrs. Hudson; but instead I saw before me the most beautiful head of brown hair which I had ever seen on a male.

This man was of medium height—that is, an inch or two taller than I—and dressed in a black suit which had been cheap and drab to start with and had become no more fetching with the obvious passage of many years. But these long Absalom-like locks of fine rich brown which poured luxuriantly and luxuriously down over his shoulders lent him an extraordinary distinction which no clothes could obscure. His face I could not see; but I felt at once that this man was a Presence—a forceful authority who must dominate the room in which he stood.

Mrs. Hudson was facing him. Her bright rubber kitchen apron, of a shade known, I believe, as crushed raspberry, seemed in his presence like the vestment of an acolyte. In her hand was an egg whisk, transformed, to carry on the illusion, into an aspergillum for sprinkling holy water. On a table beside her stood a bowl of partially beaten eggs, forgotten as she listened to the man in the shiny black suit. She caught sight of me over Absalom's shoulder. "Oh, Mr. Evans," she said. "Come in. Perhaps you can help us. Mr. Evans," she explained, "lives here in the house."

Absalom turned and regarded me. "That is not the man," he said slowly, in a heavy and almost unintelligible voice.

The front view of him was a surprise. The high forehead, the deep glowing eyes, the heavy almost beaked nose—all these I had expected; and the long beard, falling halfway to his waist, was in itself nothing unanticipated. But that beard was a pure white, as smooth and beautiful as the brown cascades of his hair but completely incongruous to them.

"Can I help you, sir?" I asked, in tones whose reverential nature astonished me.

"I do not know. I hope it."

"He came to the back door," Mrs. Hudson said. "I thought he . . . Well, after all, that suit . . . I offered him some food, but it seems he wants to know something about one of the men in this house."

"I am Russian priest," he rumbled. "Old Russian. They drive me from my country twenty years ago. I have here little church. White Russians come to me much, slava Bogu!" He paused as though to find words.

"If I can help you in any way—" I prompted.

"I live among my people. I know not your words. I try. Prikhozhanka moya—how do I say? One from women in my care—"

"Parishioner?" I ventured.

"It may be. My pah-rree-shonn-airr—so?—send me here. She have seen man in this house. She know too much from him. She must make known."

"Who is it?" I asked quickly. "Stephen Worth?" I was eager. Information on Worth, from however strange and unlikely a source, might well prove invaluable to us.

"She knows not name. She saw him as she goes by this house. She drives strange trade, my pah-rree-shonn-airr. You see? I learn." There was a touching simplicity in the childish pride with which he pronounced his new word. "Me please not this what she does. I tell her so, and she swears no more to do so. But now she lies in death pains. She remembers what she must tell from this man, but she knows not name. You help perhaps?"

"What does he look like, this man of yours?"

"He is tall. Clean face." (I assumed that he meant cleanshaven.) "Dark hair, black almost. Thin. He smiles too much."

My eyes met Mrs. Hudson's. "That Ridgly man," she said. "That describes him to a T. Especially smiling too much."

The priest was regarding me with fixed and plaintive eyes. "You come?"

"You want me to go to this woman?"

He nodded. "Radi Boga, you come and let her tell what she need."

I could see efficient mercy glistening in Mrs. Hudson's eyes. "Does she have a doctor?"

"No, gospozha."

"But you say she's dying. She must have somebody there to look after her."

"She knows of herbs. She says she can care for herself without doctor. She will not have one."

"Doesn't she even have another woman to care for her?"

"No one, gospozha."

"This is absurd. To think of a woman dying and no one there to look after her but an old man, even if you are a priest." With deft hands she was untying the crushed-raspberry apron. "I'm coming with you," she said decisively. "Are you ready, Mr. Evans?"

I must confess reluctantly that I invented no elaborate subterfuges to evade the police. Although I admire the little comedy by which Dr. Bottomley and Captain Agar eluded Sergeant Hinkle, I must modestly state that it is nothing beside the pranks (not all of them the fruits of Larry Gargan's inventiveness) which the Honorable Derring Drew has often played upon his ancient friend and enemy, Sergeant Inspector Pipsqueak. But instead of duplicating Derring's prowess, I simply, and in the most prosaic manner possible, followed Mrs. Hudson and Absalom out of the back door and down the street to the priest's automobile.

Please do not look so grim, Lieutenant. I fear from your expression that dire axes are being sharpened for the sturdy neck of Sergeant Hinkle. But it is probably at that very moment that Otto Federhut was showing him item, one loaded cane snapped in two, and item, one Gila monster crushed to a pulp. Small wonder, then, that his attention was distracted from the kitchen door, which, after all, he might think safely guarded by Mrs. Hudson herself.

I know next to nothing of automobiles. To me, they are strange and hideous monsters which occasionally, in the possession of one's friends, may be useful vehicles; more intimate acquaintance with them I shun. To me there is very little difference between a 1939 Packard and a 1929 Ford. But even I could see that the priest's car was an extraordinary museum piece. One's first thought on seeing it parked on a Hollywood street would be, "Ah, so they're shooting a period picture here!" I cannot describe the peculiarities of its internal mechanism nor imitate the noises which issued from it; but I can give you some indication of its vintage by saying that it possessed a raucous horn operated by squeezing a bulb by hand. So far back in time did the sight of this machine take me that I was tempted to ask Mrs. Hudson if she had brought her motoring veil.

The priest did not speak during the drive. This was just as well. The merry jouncing of the high seat on which we rode would have left us little breath with which to answer him. Unfamiliar as I am with this city, I cannot describe our route, save that it lay in a southeasterly direction and that the journey took more than a quarter of an hour even at our none too rapid rate of progress. The only landmark I can proffer is a white frame church with green trimmings surmounted by a miniature Oriental dome, which the priest, briefly breaking his silence, pointed out to us as his parish church.

The dwelling to which he brought us was a small garret over a garage. As we climbed the rickety wooden flight (which seemed the bastard offspring of a staircase and a ladder), I felt as though we were leaving the bright and sunny world without and entering into the narrow abode of evil and darkness. In my mind ran the immortal line of James Thurber, that phase at once so intensely comic and so pregnant with suggestions of unnameable terror: "Now we go up to the garrick and become warbs." We were going up to the garrick all right, and warbs suddenly seemed the least terrifying of the things we might become.

The sight of the garrick itself—I beg your pardon, of the garret—did not add to my comfort. One small window allowed a minimum of sunlight to filter through, hopelessly weakened by its losing battle with a heavy coating of dust. The only other illumination came from a red vigil light burning before the garish painting of a somewhat Byzantine saint—a bishop who held in one hand the toy model of a cathedral.

It was a moment before my eyes could make out, in a far corner of this cubicle of obscurity, a heaped bundle of rags, and another moment before I realized that these rags were a crude bed and that huddled in them lay a gaunt and agonized old woman. Mrs. Hudson had seen her before me and started toward her; but with timid precaution I took her arm and held her back. The fetid air of the room suggested unmentionable contagions. "Of what is she dying?" I whispered to the priest.

"It is her back," he said. "She was struck by automobile," (the u curiously became a v-avtomobile) "perhaps by chance. Perhaps also not by chance."

The old woman had heard the bass rumbling of the priest's voice. She stirred a little, half sat up, and addressed plaintive words to him in Russian.

"Po-angliskii, Anna Trepovna," he commanded. "It is need to talk English. They have come."

She uttered a long phrase with such rapturous intensity that I recognized it as a prayer of gratitude. She made the sign of the cross, concluding it by kissing her thumb, and smiled contentedly at the saint who had presumably contrived our coming. Then she beckoned us close to her and began to tell her story.

I shall not attempt to reproduce this verbatim. Her speech was even thicker and less intelligible than that of the priest, and her thoughts kept wandering to her approaching death and to some unnamed agency which, she feared, might at any moment enter and hasten that deathly approach. I shall simply retell the tale freed of her wanderings and her strange idioms, and you must picture us hanging on her every word, questioning her, interpreting her, securing occasionally from the priest the translation of an especially obscure passage, and, in short, finding ourselves so absorbed in her narrative that Mrs. Hudson even forgot the merciful attentions which she had come prepared to offer.

This, then, is the story which we heard from the old Russian woman in the dark garret, while a vivid and oddly proportioned saint balanced a church in his hand and watched us.

Anna Trepovna (even under the spell of that dark garrick the name pleased me. You will recall that another of the untold cases filed by Watson in the vaults of Cox & Company recounts Holmes' "summons to Odessa in the case of the Trepoff murder"; and I believe that a woman of the Trepoff family would be known as Trepovna)—Anna Trepovna, I say, came from New York, where she had long practiced the curious art of the herbalist. Her mother before her had been the combined midwife, general practitioner, and witch doctor of a small village in the Caucasus; and Anna had been taught from earliest childhood the secrets of her mother's craft.

Most of her trade was harmless and even beneficial—herb teas to cure or to ward off colds, poultices to heal the wounds following upon too vigorous a vodka bout. Some was of a shadier nature—love philters, potions to restore virility. And one branch of her activities was downright criminal—she had a varied and masterly collection of abortifacients. All of her trade save this last was carried on merely within the confines of the Russian colony, among the poorer and more ignorant immigrants who could bring themselves neither to trust an Americansky doctor nor to pay his bills. But the infallible efficacy of her abortives brought her many customers from other walks of life, who dreaded the pain and danger, but even more the possible scandal attendant upon an illegal operation.

She never asked names in these transactions; but she could tell from the clothes and the cars of her clients that many of them were of the highest social (or at least financial) standing. Had she chosen, she could doubtless have made a thriving business of blackmail; but she was content with her simple lot and went quietly about her business in her dreary little shop.

A few months ago (Anna Trepovna's time concept was of the vaguest, and we could place the episode no more definitely than that), an exceedingly lovely and smartly dressed girl—very young, Anna thought, not more than eighteen—began calling at the shop. She seemed at first only a curiosity seeker, delighting in the strange names and stranger purposes of the wares displayed. She made occasional small purchases of freakish items for which she could have no possible use, and chatted lightly with Anna Trepovna (as much as chattering was possible in the old woman's broken speech).

She was a lovely girl, this, Anna Trepovna told us: fresh and bright and utterly entrancing—like a little bird singing on the first flowering branch of spring, she said. So pure, so sweet did the child seem that the herbwoman was shocked beyond measure when she finally dropped the pretense of idle curiosity and found courage enough to reveal her real need. But business is business; Anna Trepovna conquered her shock and sold a packet of the requisite herbs with full instructions, and that night said a prayer for the girl and invoked a small curse on the man who had driven her to needing Anna's herbs.

The next day a man came into the shop. It was the man whom the priest had described to us—the man Anna had seen at 221B. He demanded to know if a girl had been there, and described the child whom Anna had come to think of as her ptenchik—her little bird. The old woman asked what business it was of his, and he replied that he was the girl's brother—it was his duty to watch over her.

Anna Trepovna discounted this reply—"brother" was easily said, but she had her own ideas of the relationship—but saw too late what a mistake she had made in her own answer. Simply to have said, "No," would have settled the matter then and there; to ask what business it was of his implied that his suspicions were true. She tried to remedy matters, but to no avail; the man departed with the ugly frown of knowledge on his brow.

For several days she thought no more of the affair. And then the ptenchik returned. She was afraid—perhaps it was too late— did Anna have anything stronger? Most reluctantly Anna gave her another packet. As the girl—not so fresh and bright now, but troubled and fearful—left the shop, the old woman saw a man leave a doorway across the street and follow her. It was the same man.

It was again a matter of days before she learned of the ptenchik's death, and then only because she saw the girl's photograph in a newspaper which she was using as wrapping paper. She asked a customer to read the caption to her, and learned that this was one of the most renowned debutantes of the season—she could not remember the name—who had been killed by a speeding automobile on the very evening when Anna Trepovna had last seen her. The driver was being held for manslaughter but was protesting that he had been helpless—the girl had seemed to jump or be thrown directly under his wheels. Anna Trepovna remembered the face of the "brother," and wondered. But as always she kept her thoughts to herself and said nothing.

The next day three gangsterish toughs entered her shop and told her that she was going to California. Her protestations were as fruitless as her clients after treatment. In the space of a few hours she found herself bundled onto a train with a ticket to Los Angeles and bags containing her few personal belongings and the cream of her stock. She was repeatedly warned that return to New York meant death. No reason was given, there were no specific commands of silence, but again Anna Trepovna had her own ideas.

For two months Anna had lived quietly here in Los Angeles. The priest had helped her to become established in a strange city and had even found clients for her, on the condition that she should restrict her trade to its more harmless aspects. Then yesterday, while hunting for the home of some relatively prosperous Russian exiles who like her herb teas, she passed 221B and saw The Man. She was not sure then that he had seen her, but later she was certain; for nothing could make her believe that the automobile struck her by chance. She knew The Man's secret, and even shipping her out of New York no longer seemed safe enough to him. She was not yet dead, but she knew that he would see to it that soon she was.

Mrs. Hudson and I looked at each other as the old voice trailed off. I could see in her eyes much the same thoughts which I knew must stand revealed in mine. What could we do? There was no doubting the old woman's sincerity; but her story was at best supposition, and even if one granted its truth, what was one to do? The accusation involved was too horrible to treat lightly, but too scantily supported to justify any serious action.

As we stood there meditating, before we could say a word, the course of our thoughts was abruptly halted. We heard footsteps on the ladder. Anna Trepovna heard them too, and huddled down fearfully into her rags until she seemed an inanimate part of them. The priest glanced at the painted saint as though to fortify himself, and then turned and resolutely faced the hole in the floor to which the ladder led.

Heavily the sound clumped up toward the garret. A head appeared above the floor level. A felt hat was pulled over the forehead, and a small black beard obscured the lower half of the face. Now the shoulders rose into view. On this hot day the man was waring an astrakhan-trimmed overcoat. A shudder of memory and recognition ran through me.

He stood beside the hole now and faced us. His right hand remained in his overcoat pocket—the attitude familiar to habitués of gangster films. He spoke quietly and without an accent.

"I can't see in this damned hole," he said. "Where is she?"

"She is not here," said the priest. "Friends sent her to hospital."

Obviously the man was not to be taken in so easily. I saw that his eyes had marked the bundle of rags, but he did not move toward it yet. "And who are these?" he asked.

"They are good friends from my church. Sometimes they help me to visit sick people."

"Why should I ask these questions?" the man demanded of no one in particular. "The lies aren't even good." He turned to us with quiet menace. "Get out of here," he said. "I've got work to do. It won't be pretty. God knows what the old woman's told you, but it doesn't matter. Judges don't like hearsay evidence. All the same, I'd advise you to keep quiet. Now get out."

Mrs. Hudson looked at him with contemptuous self-possession. Much though I admire her assurance, I must plead that it was most unwise; for in this calm arrogance she said what I had known ever since his entrance but sternly refrained from uttering. "And why should we obey you," she asked, "Mr. Ricoletti?"

The hand in his pocket twitched, and a nasty light glowed in his eyes. "Just a friend from the church!" he quoted in an ugly voice. "And how did you know about Ricoletti? You're pretty smart for your size, aren't you, sister? Maybe just a little bit too smart, huh?"

Throughout this muttered speech he had been drawing nearer to Mrs. Hudson. Now, on that final "huh?" he whipped his free left hand across her face.

Then I acted. It was not perhaps an action worthy of Derring, but I feel sure he would have appreciated my motives. I threw myself at Ricoletti's feet and pulled him on top of me, at the same time contriving to seize his right wrist as firmly as I could. We tossed and writhed on the floor. Twice I felt the metal rod dig through his pocket into my ribs, and each time I expected his finger to pull the trigger. I still do not know whether my grip on his wrist was paralyzing or whether I owe my life to some perverse compunction on his part. As we thrashed about, I could see Mrs. Hudson hopelessly searching the room. I cried to her to escape, but she seemed intent upon remaining and finding some weapon to aid me. In that bare garret, however, there was nothing—not even a stool with which to strike a blow.

At last I felt my hand tiring. In another moment his wrist would be free, and then I knew not what fate awaited us all. I had all but despaired when I looked up and saw the priest standing over us. In his hand was the flickering red vigil light. He leaned over. The flame licked Ricoletti's hand directly below my grip. My antagonist gave a sharp cry of pain, loosened his hold on the revolver. The priest seized; I heard a crack! as he brought it down on Ricoletti's skull.

At the same time a high scream rang out. The priest hastened to the ragged couch, bent over the still figure, and turned back to us with a woeful face which needed no words to make its meaning clear. "Go," he said simply. "I stay here with her. I must say prayers now."

"I'll send the police for this man," I promised. "But supposing he comes to while you're alone with him—"

"I have this." He touched the revolver. "And I am watched." His gaze went heaven-ward.

Reluctantly we left. As we descended the ladder-steps we were almost blinded; even the relative obscurity of the garage was dazzling to eyes that had stayed long in that garret. That is why I did not see the sack until it had descended over my head and shoulders.

And that, I regret to say, is all of our story. We never saw our captors nor, indeed, did we know who they were; for if they were accomplices of Ricoletti's, why did they not come to his aid when they heard the struggle overhead? All I know is that they released us from their car, still hooded, some two blocks from here. By the time we had freed ourselves from the sacks, the car was gone. Mrs. Hudson, whose admirable sense of direction was not in the least shaken by the episode, guided me back here. A phone call to Lieutenant Finch brought a squad car, with the aid of which I finally located the garret.

And here my story seems to duplicate that of Professor Furness. The garret was empty. Not only were the priest, Ricoletti, and the dead woman gone, but so were the few inanimate objects—the rag pallet, the saint, the vigil light. Only a few drops of fresh wax on the floor indicated what had happened there. The men in the squad car looked at me in none too flattering a manner.

It is with some misgivings that I close this narrative. The accusation embodied in it is far more serious than any other that has been made this evening. But I can only say, "This is what happened," and wait hopefully for an explanation that will make all clear.

◇　◆　◇　◆　◇

During this last narrative Harrison Ridgly had been drinking with a quiet persistence remarkable even in him; but he seemed sober enough when he rose to resume the chair—sober enough, that is, until you noticed the whiteness of his neck and the tense insistence with which his slim fingers clutched the table.

"Gentlemen," he said quietly, "we have been privileged to hear five extraordinary narratives this evening. I had thought that my own experience, embellished as it was with the grotesque, the macabre, and the beautiful, was a singularly colorful one; but I fear that it has grown pale indeed beside the other episodes which we have heard. I am certain that after the indignation of

Drew Furness, the huffing withdrawal of Rufus Bottomley, and the diffident confession of John O'Dab, you expect me to show some interesting reaction to the unusual accusation just hurled at me."

The expectancy was obvious without this comment from the chair. As Harrison Ridgly III coolly poured himself yet another straight shot, there was not a sound in the room. A sudden irrelevant and irreverent malice prompted Maureen to find a pin to drop; but Sergeant Watson chose that moment to crush his current Lifesaver, and the reverberation of that crunching crack was enough.

"The only observation possible," Ridgly resumed, "is that Jonadab Evans has fully redeemed himself in my critical eyes. The incredible young gentlemen who leaps on Gila monsters may indeed have furnished the plots of the Derring Drew novels; but there remains no doubt in my mind now that Mr. Evans is an exceedingly accomplished creator of imaginative crime fiction in his own right."

The little writer was not disconcerted. "It happened," he said simply.

"I was there," Mrs. Hudson broke in. "I heard all that poor old woman had to say. And the squad car saw the grease from that vigil light."

Ridgly indulged in his twisted smile. "A few drops of red grease are readily planted. I shall not speak of the suborning of housekeepers."

"It happened," Mr. Evans repeated stubbornly. "That's all I have to say."

"Which is as well, the laws of slander being what they are. Such scurrilous imaginings—"

"Scurrilous?" This adjective seemed really to offend the

novelist. "And the editor of *Sirrah* dares to complain of scurrility?"

"Just a minute, boys." Lieutenant Jackson rose to his full rangy height and placed himself between the disputants. With a gently forceful twist he wrenched the bottle from Ridgely's hand and set it on the farther end of the table. "We aren't here to talk personalities. I don't care if one of you is a ghost writer or another is a spy or another has all the Jukeses and the Kallikaks in his family tree. All I want to know is which one is a murderer—and I don't mean a murder that maybe happened months ago in New York either. I want to know—and the rest of you ought to be with me on this—who killed Stephen Worth, and I'm damned if I see where all these stories get us. With me, Sergeant?"

Sergeant Watson nodded.

"And the first question," Jackson went on, "is this: *where's the body?*"

Chapter 16

"Where's the body?" Lieutenant Jackson was still saying an hour later in the somewhat different surroundings of the beer garden known as the Rathskeller.

Judith (a trim little blonde whose sole connection with this story is that she lived halfway between 221B and the Rathskeller, a location the great convenience of which Jackson was just realizing) smiled. "It doesn't go with the waltz, darling. It jars."

Jackson frowned. "Worse things than murders have jarred with Viennese waltzes. So much worse that this Worth business seems clean and wholesome and refreshing."

"Don't go all-over earnest, Andy. I never can remember which Strauss waltz is which, but I do know this is one of my favorites. Wouldn't you sooner dance?"

Jackson shook his head. "Listen, Judith. I didn't drop by tonight just because I'm off duty and wanted some beer. I've got to talk this thing out, and I can't say the Irregulars were much help tonight. I'm on a spot because of my personal mix-up with Worth; but if I can dope this case out, it'll mean a lot to me. Now why," he clicked down the pewter lid of his stein, "should a murderer abscond with the body?"

"He might be a cannibal," said Judith helpfully. "Remember

that sweet little piece in the book you lent me about the family that lived in caves and dined off the bodies of the people they'd robbed?"

"A woman!" Jackson snapped. "Why can't you say things directly? If you mean Sawney Bean, why not say Sawney Bean—not 'that family in that book.'"

"Well, he might be," Judith went on unheeding. "And then there was that man Gene Fowler wrote about in Colorado."

"Sure," said Jackson. "He might be a cannibal. And he might be a ghoul or a werewolf or a necrophile."

"What's that?"

"Never mind. But," Jackson grinned to himself, "a necrophile with Stephen Worth's corpse would top any man-bites-dog story that I ever heard. He could be any of these things; but it seems to me a damned sight more likely that he's a shrewd and clever man who had a smart reason for carrying off that corpse; and it's my job to find out what that business was."

The earnestness of his voice impressed Judith. "All right, darling. Go ahead. I won't heckle any more. I'll just sit here and drink my scotch and you tell me the reasons why people carry off corpses."

"The trouble is," the Lieutenant frowned, "that there's a lot of reasons and they just don't fit this case. The chief reason for disposing of a corpse is to make it appear that no murder ever happened—make it seem like an ordinary disappearance. Crippen's probably your prime example—though I suppose the primest are the ones we don't know about because they got away with it. But that reason can't apply in this case because the O'Breen girl saw him shot, and the murderer knows it.

"Another reason might be to conceal the means of death. Supposing you killed a man with a peculiar poison which only you could get hold of, or with some strange weapon that only you could handle. You might want to get rid of the body, even if the fact of murder was known, because an autopsy would point straight at you. But that can't apply here either, because Worth was shot."

"How about ballistics?" Judith wondered (going with a detective teaches you a lot of things). "If the bullet could be traced directly to the murderer, mightn't he want to get rid of that evidence?"

"It'd be so much simpler to get rid of the gun than the corpse. Besides, unless the murderer was an outsider—which is just about incredible in view of Weinberg on the phone and that locked back door—the gun must have been disposed of, unless it was that fancy one under the window. The only weapon in the house, and we made a thorough search, was Harrison Ridgly's automatic."

"And isn't that suspicious?"

"All in order. He had a license to carry it and it hadn't been fired recently. No, that angle's no use. Now why else—You might dispose of a corpse to raise some doubt about identity."

"How?"

"Well—supposing A kills B and then makes off with the corpse. People hear a shot, find blood and signs of a row; but both A and B are missing. Maybe the stupid authorities—that's Finch and me—think B killed A and set out a dragnet for the wrong man while A gets away clear."

"It sounds too much like algebra. When you start calling people A and B, right away you expect them to divide up their apples."

"I thought you said no heckling. But that's no good either, because whoever A might be, Maureen knows who B was and

A knows that she knows. And that goes no matter how you figure it. You might run off with a body if you wanted to leave a confusion as to the time of death—it might be a question of survivorship; or if you wanted to make it appear that the murder had happened someplace else—someplace you couldn't possibly have been. But why? And, for the matter of that, how? How could any one of those people have had time to go wandering about with a corpse tucked underneath his arm? Except perhaps Ridgly—the boy that wants me to suspect him. Anybody else would have had to have an outside accomplice. And I don't," Jackson added plaintively, "I don't like accomplices."

"Andy!" Judith exclaimed suddenly. "I know I'm just supposed to be listening to you but I can't help it—I just had an idea myself. Supposing it wasn't a corpse?"

"Wasn't a corpse?" This inspiration hit Jackson in the midst of a swig of beer and resulted in some mildly spectacular gurgling.

"No. Supposing the shot didn't kill Worth—just stunned him. Shock, you know. So then the murderer—or A, if you must have it that way, though X has more menace to it—then the murderer carries him off to where he can finish the murder leisurely and efficiently."

Regretfully Jackson shook his head. "Sorry, Judith. Nice going, but two big objections. First the time element. If your X had that much leisure after the crime, he can't have been anyone in that house; and if so, how did he get in? Second, the girl saw the wound, and we've got to accept her story unless she's X herself. The bullet went straight into the heart. No, we come right back to the same thing: if you know there was a witness who saw who was killed, how he was killed, when he was killed, and where he was killed, why the sweet hell do you steal the body?"

"Maybe he didn't think there was a witness. Maybe he thought he'd killed the girl, too."

"If he'd meant to kill her, would he have stopped at a crack on the skull when he had a gun in his hand? And then carefully stolen one corpse while he left the other there for us to find? No. There's no sensible answer to this unless—" He finished his beer, licked the foam from his lips, and murmured "—unless"— again with a tensely rising inflection. Then suddenly he burst forth with most unwonted excitement. "Judith, my dear, you're marvelous. What would I do without you? What would the Los Angeles Police Department do without you?"

Judith recoiled slightly. She could hardly be blamed. "Why, what have I done?"

"I think," said Lieutenant Jackson—"mind you, I guarantee nothing—but I think that you've found Stephen Worth."

Sergeant Watson, at this moment, was making himself comfortable for the night. He dragged the most promising chair from the living room out into the hall and placed it between the stairs and the front door. On the telephone table, within easy reach, he set a package of Lifesavers, a copy of *Dread Stories,* and the thermos of black coffee which Mrs. Hudson had prepared for him. Two of his charges had left 221B (Finch had instructed him that they were to go as they pleased, but that anyone entering was to be held for questioning); but upstairs he could hear the everyday noises of the other three getting ready for bed.

The Sergeant didn't know quite why he was there. Murderers didn't repeat themselves so soon, not if they had any sense. The current issue of his favorite pulp promised to be much more exciting than anything that might happen at 221B that night. He cast an appreciative eye over the luscious blonde on the cover, who was about to be bloodily shredded by an apparatus suggesting the collaboration of the Marquis de Sade with Rube Goldberg, and opened to *Bride for the Seventh Zombie*.

"Sergeant!" It was the high voice of Harrison Ridgly. Clothed in the apogee of *Sirrah*-styled dressing gowns, he stood on the stairs, taut and nervous.

Reluctantly Sergeant Watson laid *Dread Stories* to one side. "What's the matter?"

"Will you please help me make a search? My automatic has disappeared."

"What a strange lot of men the Irregulars are!" Maureen observed to Drew Furness as they drove along Sunset.

"I suppose they are. I'd never thought of it before all this."

"Tell me, Drew. How on earth did you ever happen to—?"

He smiled. "You mean how did anyone as ordinary and prosaic as I am happen to be chosen in such a group?"

"You know I didn't mean it like that. But tell me."

"Even an academic man has his lighter side. English professors, in particular, grow weary of composing learned dissertations upon minutely insignificant points in order to make immortal contributions to human knowledge—and incidentally to assure themselves of a promotion in the department. In such a vein of weariness some two years ago, I amused myself by writing a short article clarifying, by the best research methods, the hitherto unsolved problem of the nomenclature of the brothers Moriarty. I wrote it, as you might say, with a dead pan, and sent it in to the *JEGPH*."

"To the which?"

"The *JEGPH*—*The Journal of English and Germanic Philology*—an invaluable scholarly publication which the layman, I fear, would find intolerably dreary. That feeling, I may add, is not necessarily confined to the layman. My ill-advised article was, of course, returned to me, and the head of the department delivered a gentle rebuke for my thoughtless irreverence. I redeemed myself with a monograph tracing the sources of William Ireland's pseudo-Shakespearean *Vortigern*, and thought no more of the matter. But in some way word of my hoax had reached Christopher Morley, who wrote asking for a copy of my article. I gladly submitted it to him, and shortly received an invitation to join the Irregulars."

"That sounds like fun. Could I read it sometime?"

"You mean you would really like to read my poor effort? Miss O'Breen . . ."

"Look. I called you Drew, didn't I? We might as well be consistent. Of course I'd like to read it; but what I'd really like now is some beer. And there, since the gods are benign, stands the Rathskeller. Pretty please, could we?"

Drew Furness looked sadly out of place in a beer garden—even more so than he had seemed in the commissary at Metropolis. "I must do something about that," Maureen thought, and was surprised at what she found herself thinking. She fished in her bag for a penny and tossed it in front of the abstracted academician.

He looked down with a start. "What is that?"

"For your thoughts."

"Oh— To be frank, Miss—"

She made a reproving noise.

"To be frank, Maureen, I was thinking about my aunt."

"You don't think anybody believed that wild story, do you?"

"No. No, I don't. But there is just enough nucleus of— You see, Maureen, the fact is that my aunt— Oh, I suppose one might call it simply mild senility or some such polite name; but more and more I fear that she is not quite sane. She does have this absurd delusion of persecution. Who 'They' are heaven only knows; I'm sure Aunt Belle doesn't. But her obsession with Them continues to grow. I'm afraid even that someday I may have to—to take steps. It isn't nice to think about. And to have it dragged out like this, even in such a ridiculously twisted form . . ."

The waiter came just then, with a vast foaming stein for Maureen (who was that rare wonder of her sex—a woman who truly likes beer) and a small glass of white wine recklessly ordered by her escort. Maureen said nothing; something inhibited the easy Irish words of sympathy which she would normally have found. She could see how Drew's nerves would have been twisted by Dr. Bottomley's story. She could see too how the rumor of a crazy relative would not help a man's standing in academic life. She wanted to do something to rouse him from the melancholy preoccupation into which she could see him sinking.

"Look," she said. "Here's a challenge for you as an Irregular. See that girl alone at the next table? Her man must have stepped in back for a minute. Now let's see you deduce him for me before he returns."

Drew Furness smiled, almost as though he realized the motive for her question. But he accepted the challenge eagerly and turned to survey the table.

In a moment he faced Maureen again, his lean face aglow with childlike pleasure. "There is nothing," he said, "so good for the soul as the influence of the Master. You would laugh, Maureen, if I told you how dearly I love those Writings."

"That's all very well. But tell me about the man."

"Oh, that." He was being devilishly offhand. "He is between forty and fifty, well and expensively dressed, of average height but much more than average weight, with a round bald spot on the back of his head."

Maureen gasped. "Are you fooling?"

"Of course not. That would be sacrilege. The description, I admit, is guesswork; but it follows from the deductions. Put together a blonde as pretty as that, wearing a large diamond which is manifestly not an engagement ring, and the band of a Corona Corona Corona in the ash tray; and you see that her escort must be an elderly and prosperous—ah—what I believe they call 'sugar-daddy.'"

"Nice," said Maureen. "That is really pretty."

"Elementary," said Drew Furness.

At this point the missing man returned to the next table. He was Detective Lieutenant A. Jackson.

Chapter 17

"So that," Maureen concluded chortling, as the two couples gathered at one larger table, "is the correct picture, according to Holmesian deduction, of you, Lieutenant."

Jackson laughed heartily. "Beautiful job, Furness."

"But good heavens, Lieutenant," Drew Furness protested, "you don't mean to tell me that you smoke Corona Corona Coronas?"

"On my salary? I should say not. The waiter forgot to empty the ash tray, that's all."

"And the young lady's diamond?"

Judith smiled. "From Woolworth's."

A mightily crestfallen Drew Furness sipped his wine. "What sort of an establishment is this?" he asked. "I've never been here before."

Jackson shrugged. "That's a question I wouldn't mind knowing the exact answer to. Some things about it you can see at a glance. It's got a pretty sort of fake arbor effect, the four-piece orchestra plays dull American fox trots and first-rate Viennese waltzes, the floor's small but good, and the beer is the best in town."

"It sounds pleasant."

"It is pleasant. But—"

"But what?"

"Mmm!" sighed Maureen. *"Count of Luxemburg* waltz. Want to try it, Drew?"

Furness was slipping back into his shell. "I'm afraid not. I am really exceedingly inept. Out of consideration for your shoes I should refrain."

"There!" She turned to Judith. "What do you do with a man like that?"

Judith grinned. "Andy used to pull that on me when I wanted to try a polka or something fancy. I just said, 'Yes, it is easier to get a new man than new shoes,' and he generally gave in."

"All right, I'll try." Maureen looked formally forbidding as she announced: "Mr. Furness, it is easier to get a new man than new shoes."

Drew Furness looked at her strangely—not at her so much as though he were looking in a mirror for the first time. Then he said, with a nearly successful attempt at a worldly swagger, "I fear, Miss O'Breen, that you'll have to be satisfied with the man you've got, and deuce take your shoes."

And off they went to the floor, as Maureen winked at Judith over her escort's shoulder.

"There's a sample," said Jackson resignedly. "You see the kind of suspects I've got in this case? A lot of overeducated screwballs. God knows I've taken some ribbing on the force because I'm a college man myself; but I'd sooner handle the crummiest drifters on Skid Row than this mob."

"Didn't you learn anything tonight?"

"I told you their stories—five of the goddamnedest I've ever heard in all the evidence I've listened to, and I don't see where we're any further ahead than we were last night. This is what it all adds up to: everybody's story digs up a piece of scandal about somebody else. Some of it—Furness' half-mad aunt and John O'Dab's ghostwriting—turns out to be true. Some of it—Federhut's spying and Ridgly's murdering his sister—is fantastic. The business about Bottomley and the nurse in the rest home I just don't get.

"And there's only two answers: either everybody took this opportunity to reveal 'accidentally' something about one of the others, which is pretty coincidental; or somebody planned the whole set of adventures. It must be that; they're too neat to be just a happenstance. Every story has two Holmes angles—a parallel to one of the written stories and a tie-in with the name of one of the unwritten."

"Double, double, Doyle, and trouble," Judith contributed.

"'And trouble' is right; everyone also gives away a secret, or pretends to. Now who would arrange a scheme like that? I've got a pretty good idea that there's only one possible . . ."

"Oof!" Maureen gasped as she and her partner returned to the table. "You may be right about men and shoes, Judith; but shoes go on the budget."

"Please forgive me," Furness ventured stiffly. "You will recall that I gave you fair warning—"

"Hush now. I didn't mean to hurt your feelings. But I'm going to give you some private lessons in slippers before we venture out again—which is taking a lot for granted, isn't it? Or is it?" she added pensively.

"You know," Furness replied, "I'm not sure that it is."

"I think I've just had a gallant speech made to me." She let her hand rest on the professor's for a moment, then turned to Jackson. "Guess who we saw?" She felt Furness' hand wince slightly at the *who* and instantly withdrew her own.

"How should I know? I don't know all your little friends."

"This is one of your friends, and not so little. Over there in the corner. He didn't see us."

Jackson craned his neck and saw the man. "I'll be damned," he said.

Judith craned too, but it didn't help. "Who is it?" she asked.

"Another of our menagerie. Otto Federhut."

"What's so surprising about that, Andy? He's a German, isn't he? Wouldn't he naturally come here?"

"I'm not so sure," said Jackson slowly. "Nowadays there are two kinds of Germans."

At 221B the blonde heroine had been reduced to one single last garment which barely covered her firm, high, rounded, quivering breasts. On the floor at her feet lay the mangled and desecrated body of the girl who had succumbed to the unearthly lust of the sixth zombie. No garment save the flowing red of blood covered her high, quivering, rounded, firm breasts.

With a sinister leer on his scarred face, Dr. Vladimir Radin pulled the switch which poured the vivifying current into the seventh zombie. The monster lurched awkwardly to its feet and stumbled across the laboratory. His clumsy hands tore the last thin garment from the heroine's rounded, firm, quivering, high breasts.

In agony the hero strained at his bonds, forced to watch this abominable creature defile with his slavering lips the quivering, rounded . . .

Sergeant Watson heard a rap at the door. In an instant his mind had left Dr. Radin's laboratory for the more prosaic setting of the hallway of 221B. The Sergeant might not be bright, but he was dutiful. He took his gun from the holster, pulled back the safety catch, and slowly advanced to the door. As he neared it, the rap was repeated—this time in a sort of rhythm.

Sergeant Watson smiled and relaxed, but he kept the door on the latch as he opened it.

"It's all right, Watson," came Lieutenant Finch's voice. "You can let me in."

Watson unlatched the door. "Anything wrong?"

"Not a thing, Sergeant. It's just that I—This sounds haywire, but I got a hunch. Something bothered me. I kept saying to myself, 'You'd better take a look at 221B.' 'Horse feathers!' I'd say right back at myself. But it went right on worrying me until I couldn't stand it. So I took the fifty thousand dollars, and here I am."

"Nothing wrong here," said the Sergeant.

"What happened at the session tonight?"

"Nothing much. They told a lot of funny stories. I don't mean funny *stories*, Lieutenant. I mean *funny* stories. You know, funnylike. Then the one with the beard got mad and went off to his room, and the dark nasty one got drunk and tried to start a fight until Jackson told him he'd better go to bed. I guess that sort of broke up the party."

"They're all here now?"

"All but the German and the professor. You said I could let them go if they wanted to."

"I know. We've got no legal right to detain them, and we might get into trouble with Metropolis. But I hoped they'd stick around anyway. Well, it can't be helped. And you're sure nothing happened?"

"Not a thing, Lieutenant."

Finch smiled at his own foolishness. "This'll teach me to play hunches. Well, Sergeant," his eye lit on the pulp cover, and the smile broadened, "enjoy yourself." He turned back to the door.

"Just a minute. There was something. The worst one—what's his name?"

"I take it you mean Harrison Ridgly III?" Finch's tone was almost as unpleasant as Ridgly's own.

"That's it. Ridgly. He came down and said his automatic was missing and we searched all the rooms, only we didn't find it."

Finch was at once alert. " 'Nothing happened'!" he quoted. "Why, man, do you realize—? Another gun loose in this house, and you say—"

"But it isn't in this house, Lieutenant. We looked—"

"Never mind where you looked. Come on with me. We're looking again." Finch turned to the stairs, but stopped short as a sudden sharp explosion came from the second floor.

Someone had found the automatic.

Lieutenant Jackson reverently raised the lid from a fresh stein. "You see, it's like I started to tell you before you went dancing. This is a very pleasant place, but . . . Well, the *but* is this. There's a lot of talk going the rounds that this is a Nazi hangout, sort of gathering place for secret agents and such. It used to be avowedly a German restaurant. Then when public feeling got strong it changed to Austrian. After the *Anschluss* it began calling itself 'The Original Luxemburg Restaurant.' But it's been under the same management all the time. A lot of liberals are boycotting it. I don't know a thing for sure; but Sergeant Levine won't touch their kosher salami. He says the name on the menu's a trap to lead him into eating impure food."

"Then what happened to me this morning—" Drew Furness began excitedly.

Jackson smiled at him. "Do you really believe all that, Furness?"

Furness hesitated. "In this case," he said "it's hard to know what to believe."

"I know. Someday when I write *My Fifty Years in the Los Angeles Police Department,* this'll have a chapter all to itself. The Murder Case Without a Killing."

"Listen," said Judith. "A polka! Oh, Andy, please."

A minute later Maureen wrenched her eyes from the athletic choreography of the Lieutenant. "I'd like to know just what he meant by that," she murmured.

"Do you suppose he's really solved it?" Furness asked nervously.

" 'The murder case without a killing.' It doesn't make sense."

"You don't imagine that he might mean that Worth wasn't really killed?"

"But I've told you I saw him." She saw him again in her mind and shuddered. She took a quick gulp of beer but it didn't help. "I saw him. Do you think a man's going to get up and just wander away with a bullet in his heart? I saw the blood coming out— here."

Furness looked at the indicated spot. Blood was not what he saw.

"Don't you believe me? Is that it? Do you think I've just made up this whole thing?"

Drew Furness looked in her face intently. "I do believe you, Maureen," he said.

Maureen smiled part of a smile. "You're sweet," she said gently.

Even a small glass of white wine can work wonders under the proper circumstances. There is no telling what untoward effect that and a part of a smile might have had on Drew Furness at that moment had there not suddenly sounded above the polka the sound of loud and vigorous German cursing.

"It's Mr. Federhut!" Maureen exclaimed. "He's in trouble. I think we'd better . . ."

It did look like trouble. His face alight with exalted indignation, the white-maned refugee faced the headwaiter, holding his ground firmly while waiters bore down on him from all directions.

" 'Raus!" the headwaiter was saying. "Verdammter Juden-hund, du! So was darf nicht . . .!"

"Please," Furness ventured in hesitant German. "This gentleman is my friend; I am sure that he—"

"From such people," the *Herr Ober* snapped in insolent English, "we do not want the friends. He has made an insult which is not to tolerate. He goes, and you with him." He beckoned the waiters to draw nearer.

"What goes on here?" Lieutenant Jackson shoved his way past the hovering waiters.

"And who are you?" the headwaiter demanded.

Jackson silently showed his badge.

It worked. With true German respect for authority, the *Ober* smiled and backed. "I give him into your custody, sir," he said. "But I am warning you: let him not come here again."

"What happened?" Judith demanded as they led Federhut back to their own table.

"It is most kind of you all to come in this way to my help. I thank you from the heart—all of you."

"But what happened?"

"It was most unfortunate. The *Herr Ober*—the head-waiter— he comes over to greet me. Hearing his accent in English, I reply to him in German. He smiles and says, *'Ach, Sie sind deutsch?'*— You are German?—*'Also, Heil Hitler!'* I do not wish to make a scene; I say only in reply, *'Grüss' Gott!'* But he would not have it so. He asks questions—why I the Fatherland abandoned, why I his greeting refused, what my thoughts of the *Führer* are—and as he goes on we grow both more angry. I know not what would have happened had you not come. I did not know I had friends to support me."

"Hm," said Jackson. "Sort of settles my doubts about this place, doesn't it? And also, I hope, Furness' doubts about you. But the beer is still first-rate. Let's all have another round and forget our troubles. Will you join us, Herr Federhut?"

But at that moment, through the loud-speaker which amplified the music came a plaintive speaking voice: "Telephone call for Lieutenant Jackson."

Abruptly Jackson became serious. "I'm afraid that cancels the next round. There's only one person who knows I'm here tonight. I was half afraid he might want to call me."

"I'm glad you said 'he,'" said Judith. "But who's that?"

"Sergeant Watson."

Lieutenant Finch went up the dark staircase at the double, service pistol drawn and ready. The heavier Sergeant all but matched his speed.

Even as they ran the lights came on in the upper hall. In their light Finch saw two men—Bottomley and Evans—standing before one of the bedroom doors. The two simply stood there.

They said nothing, even when they saw the officers. As Finch reached the door, little Mr. Evans suddenly turned away, still silent, and hurried to the bathroom.

The door was ajar. Looking into the room, Finch had for an instant a terrible feeling of a recurring nightmare. It was Worth's room over again—the gory RACHE scrawled on the wall, the pool of fresh blood on the floor, the black arm band dropped beside it, even (he was to discover later) the nick on the window sill.

But this time there was a body. Sprawled in the middle of the room, fountain and origin of that blood, lay Harrison Ridgly III.

Chapter 18

"AND TOMORROW we start shooting already!" F. X. Weinberg looked up in wistful woe from his littered desk. "Never was such a jinx on a picture! Never since I left the fur business have such things been! What's happening to us, to a dog it shouldn't happen!"

"How can you start shooting?" Maureen asked. "And I wish to goodness there was some other word for it; Lord knows there's enough shooting going on. Worth never finished the script, and the Irregulars haven't had any time to check it over yet."

"You are giving me this information?" Mr. Weinberg replied with dignity. "Don't I know we aren't ready? So A. K. says we must hold to the shooting schedule and keep production costs down. There may be war yet and we lose the rest of our foreign market. 'So how do we keep the domestic market,' I ask him, 'if we make pictures when we aren't ready to?' But he doesn't say anything—just 'You start shooting tomorrow.' That young man from England, John Zed, we've put on the script; he'll write along and we'll shoot it off the cuff."

The buzzer sounded. "Eleven thirty, Mr. Weinberg," Miss Blankenship squawked.

Mr. Weinberg reached for the carafe. "So with my headaches

I drink bicarbonate! Whisky I should be drinking and forgetting it all!"

The buzzer came again. "More reporters, Mr. Weinberg."

Maureen slipped off the chromium desk, feeling a little guilty that she hadn't even been reproved for sitting on it. "I'd better go see them."

Mr. Weinberg silently motioned her to stay where she was, gulped down his sodium bicarbonate, and cleared his throat. "No, Maureen. I'll send Feinstein to see them. He'll take over your duties here for a couple of days. Do I need you, my smartest girl, to say, 'We have nothing to say; sorry'? No. I do not."

"What am I supposed to do then?"

"Where you belong is in that house—221B. Never in my life will I forget those numbers. Thirteen, people say is unlucky; but does anybody warn me about 221B? No, they do not. So you go there. You keep in touch with these Irregulars and you let me know what happens when and I hope nothing ever happens. Go on now."

As Maureen left the office, F. X. Weinberg was crouched over his desk, calling plaintively into the speaker for Feinstein. Only on her way to the hill did she recall that Mr. Weinberg had gone through a whole conversation without one double take. Nothing could more thoroughly have attested his worried state.

Maureen was not unworried herself as she approached 221B. All she had known last night was that Lieutenant Jackson had received a sudden phone call, hustled Drew and Federhut back to the house with him, and unceremoniously bundled herself and Judith home in a taxi. Another murder was then the least of her fears. The morning paper had informed her that it was only an attempt at murder, with the victim assured a good chance of recovery; but this lesser fact, though anticlimactic, was not reassuring.

Mrs. Hudson opened the door. In a way, Maureen was relieved; she had feared lest the bell be answered by a large presence in uniform, whom she might have had difficulty in persuading to let her in. But otherwise Mrs. Hudson was not a sight to afford relief. She had changed vastly in two days. No longer was she the cooly efficient housekeeper, secure in the confidence of her B.S. She was now just a worried woman, with some what scraggly hair and purple patches under her eyes.

"Oh, it's you, Miss O'Breen," the housekeeper burst out. "I *am* glad. Somehow you seem to be the only person around here who has any sense, aside from that nice young Lieutenant and maybe Mr. Evans. Won't you come in?"

She showed Maureen into the living room. The day was hot; but the blinds in this room had not been raised yet. It was cool in here, and likewise rather dank and deserted. Last night's glasses and ashes had been cleared away (Mrs. Hudson's efficiency was not so dissipated as all that) ; but the room still looked hung over. It had that air of a place where a good deal happened yesterday and nothing at all since then.

"Where is everybody?" Maureen asked.

"They're mostly out," Mrs. Hudson admitted, "but I do hope you'll stay anyway. The Austrian gentleman had to go to Pasadena on business; Dr. Bottomley walked down to the Boulevard with him, and I think he said he was going on out to that rest home. Mr. Ridgly's upstairs in bed of course; they thought he'd be better off there than in a hospital. And Mr. Evans is around somewhere. He was talking to me in the kitchen just a few minutes ago."

"And Mr. Furness?"

"He went out. I'm afraid I don't know where."

"Oh." Maureen hoped her disappointment didn't show too clearly in her voice. "Tell me—how is Mr. Ridgly? I was so relieved to read that they thought he'd recover. But is it serious?"

"I'm afraid it is, Miss O'Breen. You see—" She broke off as they heard steps descending the staircase. "Here's Lieutenant Finch. He'll tell you all about it."

"I hope," said Maureen doubtfully.

"And I must get back to the kitchen. Lunch is in half an hour. You'll stay, of course?"

"Thanks. I'd love to."

"Thank you, Miss O'Breen. It helps to feel that there's another woman in this house."

"And much good I've been," Maureen added to herself.

She heard the footsteps leave the staircase for the level floor of the hall. But they did not turn into the living room. Instead they seemed headed straight for the front door. Maureen hurried into the hall. "Lieutenant!" she called. "Could I speak to you for a minute?"

The little man turned around with his hand on the doorknob. "Oh!" Maureen exclaimed. "It's you."

"Sorry to disappoint you, Miss O'Breen," Jonadab Evans replied courteously. "I deeply regret that I am not your handsome young lieutenant."

"I didn't want any handsome young lieutenant," she explained afluster. "I wanted—"

The door opened inward, thrusting the knob out of Mr. Evans' hand and almost pushing him off balance. In the doorway stood Lieutenant Finch. "Somebody calling me?" he asked. "Oh, hello, Miss O'Breen."

"I was," Maureen admitted. "I didn't know you were outside."

"Went down the back stairs to have a look around. But why should you think—"

"I heard footsteps coming down the stairs, so I—" Finch turned a baleful eye on the little writer, happy that this was one of the few men over whom he could relatively tower. "So you were upstairs," he said. "Why?"

"Why?" Mr. Evans hesitated. "Why not? I wanted to see how Ridgly was getting on. After all, even though we did quarrel last night, he is a man whom I like and respect in many ways. I wished to see—"

"If you got as much out of him as I did," Finch grunted, "you wasted a lot of stair climbing. But I don't like people sneaking around to see wounded men."

"But you could hardly call this sneaking, Lieutenant. Your male nurse was there, and Sergeant Hinkle."

"Look here, goofus. The more you try to talk yourself out of this, the more I'll think there's something that needs talking out of."

"Very well." Mr. Evans face assumed a dry sort of pout. "If you'll excuse me, I think I'll have a little chat with Mrs. Hudson."

"She's busy getting lunch," Maureen warned him.

"I might even help," he said. "Rex Stout isn't the only novelist who can cook." This proud assertion seemed to restore his self-confidence; he walked off with something as close to a swagger as a man of his height could well manage.

"I've got about ten minutes to spare, Miss O'Breen," Finch announced. "If you want to step into the living room—"

The living room was not cheery to Maureen. Here she had seen Stephen Worth make his fantastic drunken entrance and heard him hurl vile insults at her. Here she had regained consciousness that awful night—was it only thirty-six hours ago? Here, last night, she had heard those five supposedly civilized men toss wild accusations at each other. What else, she wondered, could still happen in this room, now so cool and peaceful?

Lieutenant Finch looked up sharply from his pipe filling. "I suppose Weinberg sent you?" he began.

"Naturally," Maureen replied, a trifle nettled by this opening. "But I assure you I'm not spying or anything sinister like that. After all, Metropolis brought these men out here. We have a certain responsibility to look after them."

"Sure, Peaches, sure" said Finch in a mollifying tone.

"But instead," Maureen went on, "of seeing the men I'm supposed to look out for, I find that you've let them go wondering all over the face of Southern California. Aren't two shootings enough for you?"

A slow burn was spreading over Finch's face. "Look," he said heavily. "You produce a movie about a murder. You have so many suspects—one, two, three, four, five." He ticked them off on his fingers. "Then you keep them all in one place under police guard, in a nice solid clump." He clenched the five fingers into a fist by way of demonstration. "That's fine. Then everybody can keep an eye on them—and a camera."

"And one set," Maureen contributed, "holds down the budget."

"Sure. That's beautiful. But by what law do you do that? We're just policemen—we aren't the Cheka or the Ogpu or the Gestapo. The only way we can keep a man in one place is to arrest him. Now we've got no evidence to arrest anybody for this murder. Sure, we could hold any one of them as a material witness; but what would happen? Along comes a smart lawyer and pulls him out on a writ—the papers raise a stink all over the country (these are big men)—and what have we got? Not," he added in his archaic idiom, "not even magnolia."

"I guess you're right. But what happened last night? The papers weren't very clear."

"The papers weren't clear! And wouldn't *I* like to know what happened last night? All I know is what they told me, and I don't believe that."

"Please tell me anyway."

"All right. It went like this: first Jackson left. Then you and Furness. Sergeant Watson settled down in the front hall for the night. The kitchen door and the door to the back stairs were locked. Mrs. Hudson had checked them and I'd take her word for it. Ridgly and Evans went to bed—Bottomley was already there—and Federhut goes off to the Rathskeller. Pretty soon Ridgly comes hurrying downstairs to Watson and reports that his automatic's been stolen. They make a search and can't find it. That proves nothing—two men can't go through a house thoroughly enough to make sure. Then everything quiets down again. Meanwhile I get a goofy kind of a hunch and drop in to check up. Watson tells me that nothing has happened—nothing, mind you, except that somebody has a stolen automatic. While we're talking, there's a shot. I run upstairs and find Bottomley and Evans at the door of Ridgly's room. On the floor is Ridgly, streaming blood. And the rest is just what you read in the paper."

"I thought," Maureen said slowly, "that some of that might be just a reporter's imagination. But it was all just like—like Worth's room?"

"All," Finch groaned. "On the wall was RACHE written in blood. On the window sill was a nick in the wood. Under the window was the stolen gun, with a book of Furness' tied to it. On the floor was a black arm band."

242 · ANTHONY BOUCHER

"There were some other things in Worth's room, weren't there? There was the brief case with that list of numbers in it."

"That's right. No brief case here. And no fragment of glass in the wastebasket either, if you're going to be so particular. But all the rest was the same. Ridgly was unconscious when we found him, but he wasn't any more help when the ambulance boys did bring him around. He says all he knows is that he was almost asleep when he heard his door open. He got out of bed and saw a figure step into the room. The light was still on in the hall and the room was dark; so all he could see was a black shape. Before he could even speak, the man fired. That's the last he knows, or anyways the last he's saying."

"Do you think he's shielding somebody?"

"Foolish question number thirty-seven. He must have some idea of who shot him even if he only saw a shadow. He won't even say how big the figure was—it might be Evans or Federhut or even Mrs. Hudson from all he'll say. But you can take it from me, if he's shielding anybody, it isn't out of human kindness. He knows what he's about, that baby; he's no Boy Scout."

"Did you see," Maureen ventured tentatively, "if there were any other wounds on his body?"

Finch smilingly tamped his corncob. "I suppose you think, young lady, that that's a cryptic question. You want to be mysterious with the police, like all the clever heroines. I hate to disappoint you, but that other wound was the first thing the police thought of. It's a frame, I said to myself. He's pulling an alibi out of a book—stage an attack on yourself and you seem innocent. And if we do notice how the gun got out the window, we're supposed to think the murderer is just confusing things like with Worth. But then! I said, he couldn't have written on the wall after a wound like that. He'd have to get blood some other way. So is there maybe another wound? Am I right—that's what you're after?"

"Yes. Only please, I wasn't trying to be a smarty. I just wanted—"

"I know. I never saw a case with so many people trying to solve it. Hell and Maria, we've even got a member of our own police force working as an amateur! All detectives and no suspects, that's what's the matter."

"But was there another wound?"

"There was. A cut on the upper lip—pretty bad. On the one hand, it could easily have been caused while shaving. On the other, it would have furnished enough blood to do that writing. This RACHE was smaller than the other, and pretty faint."

"Then he did do it himself!"

"Horse feathers! I thought so too, till I got the doctor's report. Nobody could have faked that shot. He only lived because the bullet glanced off a rib. The least fraction of an inch to one side and it would have been fatal. If you fake a shooting you pick the shoulder or the leg; you don't aim at just missing the heart by a hairsbreadth. No, whoever fired that shot meant business."

"I guess that's that then." Maureen sounded regretful. "It would have been so simple. And I'd soonest he was the murderer out of all of them."

"He still might be. Because somebody tried to kill him doesn't mean he's innocent of Worth's murder; it just means we've maybe got two of 'em on our hands."

"But," Maureen insisted, "men don't shave at night just before they go to bed. It isn't natural. I've watched my brother. He always shaves either first thing in the morning or before he goes out in the evening—sometimes both, but he hates that. He wouldn't think of shaving before he went to bed."

Lieutenant Finch rubbed his chin reminiscently. "Wait till he's married," he said. "Wait till you're married yourself; you'll find out why men shave at night."

"But Mr. Ridgly is a bachelor. He wouldn't have any habits like that."

Lieutenant Finch rose from his chair. "You know, Miss O'Breen, you may know a lot of stories that a nice girl shouldn't; but I guess you're pretty pure at heart after all." With which he took his departure.

Chapter 19

THE MAIN dish at lunch puzzled Maureen. On either end of a large platter were heaps of green peas and of crisp fried noodles; but the mass in the center she could not place. It looked like scrambled eggs, but not quite. She was still uncertain after she had sampled it. It tasted like Welsh rabbit, but not quite.

"What is it?" she finally asked Jonadab Evans. They were lunching alone, while Mrs. Hudson, clinging to class distinction as one small chunk of solidity in chaos, fed Sergeant Hinkle in the kitchen.

"Do you like it?" Mr. Evans was solicitous.

"Very much indeed. It's delicious."

"I'm very glad." He hemmed an instant. "You see—I made it."

"You did?"

"Yes. There was a certain satisfaction in accomplishing something. I had been losing confidence in myself. In such a state, I frequently find it advisable to reassert my ability in the kitchen; and since I particularly pride myself on my fondue, I attempted that."

"How do you make it? I must try it on my brother sometime. You see, I go on the principle that if you can please a brother with your cooking, a husband, when the time comes, will be a cinch."

Mr. Evans beamed. "Take a small skillet," he began. "Iron, preferably. Melt therein a sizable chunk of butter. Add broken lumps of cheese—whatever sort you prefer—and melt them slowly. You will forgive me if my quantities are not precise? I am not what you might call a metric chef."

"I'm afraid I am," said Maureen, "but I'll try to get the idea."

"Now," Mr. Evans' voice grew warmer as he spoke, "the cheese is melted—a golden lava. Take the skillet from the fire—an essential and often neglected step. Break into it the eggs—one or one and a half per person—and add salt and Worcester source 'to taste,' as sensible cookbooks should say. Mix eggs and cheese together with a fork and return to a very low fire. Cook as slowly as possible and never cease stirring; for it should be—and, I trust, is—impossible to say where cheese leaves off and egg begins. When the mass, of its own consistency, frees itself from the pan, the fondue is done. If you wish to add a final tribute to the eye as well as the tongue, a few dots of paprika will do. For my sake, however, do not add sprigs of parsley; for I hold with the eminent Alexis Soyer that no food should be garnished with anything which will remain on the plate uneaten."

Maureen smiled. "You make it sound even better than it tastes."

"I hope not!" Mr. Evans exclaimed in horror. "I abominate these cooks whose sole artistry lies in glowing words. The ideal cook should be a deaf-mute and preferably illiterate, so that he might create freely with no end save the palate."

Maureen took another mouthful of the fondue and let its cheeseful richness dissolve against her rejoicing taste buds. "But

I've had what they called a fondue," she said. "It was a baked dish with bread crumbs and things."

"I know." Mr. Evans shook his head. "In modern cookbooks that puddingy abomination is known by the splendid name of fondue. But Brillat-Savarin," he said with not unjustified pride, "supports my usage."

"And do you feel happy and self-satisfied again now? You certainly should after this."

"I don't know. Of course I feel better, but still—I know that I am a reasonably good writer and a somewhat better cook; but there was once a time when I thought that I was a passable amateur cryptanalyst."

"Crypt—?"

"Code solver. Interpreter of ciphers—though pray do not think that I confuse the words."

"I see. You mean you're stumped on something. Would it be that list of numbers in the brief case?"

"My dear young lady, not only would it be; it is. I have spent much of two days on those absurd figures, and still do not know even whether they form a code message or a cipher." He hesitated.

"Is there anything I could do?" Maureen asked. "Not that I know anything about crypt—"

"—analysis," he finished for her. "Yes, there is. You listened so kindly to my few comments on cookery. I wonder if you could be equally kind and hear me outline my futile endeavors to interpret those numbers. Sometimes the lay mind . . ."

"Of course," Maureen said, and regretfully took the last remaining bite of fondue.

"Very well." The little man took from his vest pocket a sheaf of papers and spread them on the table. "First of all, here is a copy of the list:

20518
25414
25723
20974
25191
25585
22394
25237

Now what do you think those numbers must indicate?"

"Lord only knows. Maybe they're a listing of bonds, or numbers of counterfeit bills."

"The numbers of bills, I fear, are much longer and contain letters as well as figures. For instance," he produced his wallet, "here is a five which reads E41619027A. About bonds I cannot be so sure; but if this were a list of the numbers of anything, those numbers would be arranged in their proper numerical sequence. No; consider the circumstances under which this was found. It was in Stephen Worth's brief case, from which whatever else it contained has been carefully removed. It is barely possible, of course, that this slip of paper may have been overlooked; but it is far more likely that we found this list because it was deliberately left for us to find. Now everything else in that room, with the possible exception of that confusing shard of glass, was a purposeful clue, however misleading, and usually of a Holmesian origin. Is it illogical, then, to assume that this paper as well is a clue, and that its solution is to be found by the application of Holmesian methods?"

Maureen frowned. "I guess that's all right so far."

"Now when, I asked myself, did Holmes decipher a message similar to this? Obviously the interpretation of such simple ciphers as the dancing men or the candle movements in *The*

Adventure of the Red Circle would be of no use to us. But I quickly recalled the magnificent opening chapter of *The Valley of Fear*, that strange calumny on the American labor movement. You will of course remember the message which Holmes had received from Porlock, the one flaw in the chain of Professor Moriarty's organization."

"I'm afraid I don't," Maureen confessed.

Mr. Evans regarded her with the mild but somewhat wounded surprise of the enthusiast who encounters the ignorance prevalent outside his blessed sphere. "One moment," he said, and sped into the living room, whence he returned in a moment with the complete volume of the Holmes stories. "Here we are," and he laid before her the page bearing the message referred to.

" '534,' " Maureen read, " 'C2 13 127 . . .' And your Mr. Holmes really read that?"

"Of course," Mr. Evens replied with as much pride as though he had accomplished the feat himself. "He observed at once that these numbers referred to the words on a given page of some book, and by several rapid steps of deduction he concluded the identity of the book and from that the meaning of the message."

"And you think you can do that with these numbers?"

"I thought so," he sighed. "But have the kindness to go along with me as I follow the Holmesian line and tell me, if you can, where I have slipped. These earlier calculations we can disregard; they were based on cipher probabilities (which gave ridiculous results, as you can see) before I realized the possibility of this book code. Now let us assume that 20518 means page 205, 18th word, or possibly word 20, page 518; for it is likely that the word would be the smaller number, the page the larger. This indicates a book, in one case of average size—at least 257 pages; in the other of epic proportions, for the page numbers would run as high as 974. It must be a book which is certain to be available to us. Unfortunately, Americans outside of the Middle West are not certain to possess an almanac, in which Holmes found his solution; and as the Master himself pointed out, the Bible cannot have been used because of the variable pagination of its different editions. I toyed with various other possibilities, until at last I decided that the one book certain to be in our possession, the one volume to which reference could be made with absolute certainty, was the Los Angeles telephone directory. Names may frequently also be common nouns; to construct an intelligible message from such a directory would be nowise impossible. But here my train of logic comes up against hard fact. Behold my lists: if we follow the form of page 205, word 18, we get:

COOPER DOMECQ DORT COSGROVE DIXON
DONNELL CUNNINGHAM DOCKINS

And if we try the form of word 20, page 518, the result is:

KNOX HELM PEACOCK WALKER COFFER MAIBEN
HAPIP DEAN"

"The second list's much better," said Maureen. "PEACOCK and MAIBEN are good enough in themselves; but I just love HAPIP."

"That," said Mr. Evans, "is all very well; but can you tell me where I went wrong? Why should this logical attack produce gibberish?"

"Well then, I will tell you. You got the wrong book."

"Thank you." His tone was not friendly. "And could you tell me the right one?"

"Of course," said Maureen unexpectedly. "There." And she indicated *The Complete Sherlock Holmes.*

"Of course!" Mr. Evans exclaimed. "Miss O'Breen, you put me to shame. Holmes—the one volume that everyone in this house would be sure to have access to. And naturally in that one-volume Doubleday edition—anything else would have entailed a volume reference. Undoubtedly you have hit it! Now let us see. If you will be so kind as to read the numbers to me—" He fumbled eagerly with book, pencil, paper.

Maureen picked up the list. "What shall we try first—the 205, 18 division?"

"As you will. Page 205—plumb in the middle of *The Red-headed League.* The eighteenth word is—SLOWLY." He noted it down on the paper beside him. "Not in itself significant but surely a possible beginning. Next?"

"Page 254, word 14."

"Two—fifty—four. Ha! *The Five Orange Pips,* which our friend has quoted once already. This is familiar ground. The fourteenth word—THE. SLOWLY THE—the what, I wonder? Go on."

"This is exciting, isn't it? No wonder your Holmes loved his work. Page 257 next—word 23."

"Still *The Orange Pips.* And the word is—" Suddenly his voice fell. "The twenty-third word on page 257, Miss O'Breen, is IT. SLOWLY THE IT—There must be some mistake."

But there was no mistake. After the most careful checking and recounting, the message as transcribed read:

SLOWLY THE IT UNPACK ORDERS OPPOSED TO
DESCRIBED

"I feel," said Jonadab Evans, "as Holmes himself must have

felt when he sought to decipher Porlock's message by means of the wrong Whittaker, and received the answer:

MAHRATTA GOVERNMENT PIG'S-BRISTLES

But we are not through yet; let us try the 20, 518 division. The twentieth word on page 518 is—LETTER. That is encouraging enough. Next?"

"That would be page 414, word 25."

"And that is—oh dear!"

"What is it?"

"IT again. Wretched word! But let us persevere."

The result this time was even less coherent than the first. It read:

LETTER IT WERE A LEAD THERE HOLMES'S HOLMES

"But it must be this book," Mr. Evans insisted plaintively. "Do you suppose it could be some tricky arrangement of numbers, such as the twenty-eighth word on page 51, or the fifty-first on page 208?"

"Why?"

"This way. You see?" He drew on the page 2(051)8 and 20(51)8. "We can at least try."

They tried. The 2(051)8 arrangement gave them:

UNTIL AFTER FRONT BLONDE HE (*) PROBABLY TO

And the 20(51)8, most discouraging of all, resulted in this choice array of monosyllables:

---

*   P. 558 is blank.

IN THAT BUT BY THAT ITS THE IT

Maureen was tired of the game by this time. It had started out to be exciting, but now it was just silly drudgery. The spirit of the chase was still hot in Mr. Evans, but he was close to tears with exasperation at its hopelessness.

"There *must* be an answer," he lamented. "But I am too exhausted and annoyed even to think any longer. Sometimes when I am in this state over a chapter in which I am forced to revise a snag in my friend's plot, I can stimulate my lagging mind with music; but I have tried the radio here and all I can find is what I think is known as swing. If only I could—"

"If you wanted to walk down to the Boulevard with me," Maureen suggested, "we could listen to records. Do you think that might help?"

Mr. Evans looked more cheerful. "Thank you, Miss O'Breen. It might at that. I do feel sure that if we could only break down this message—"

"I beg your pardon, Miss O'Breen." Mrs. Hudson had entered silently and was regarding the paper-strewn table with manifest disapproval. "Do you think I could clear away? I've been waiting for you to ring."

"I'm so sorry," Maureen apologized. "We got to working on a code, and—"

"There's a lot of codes in this house," Mrs. Hudson announced, in something the same tones in which she would have proclaimed an incursion of rats.

Mr. Evans pricked up his ears. "What do you mean? Have my colleagues been—"

"This wasn't writing codes," the housekeeper explained. "It was the Austrian gentleman on the telephone this morning. I don't know who he was talking to, but he didn't say anything but numbers. Just a lot of numbers, and waiting in between like he was listening to something, and at the end he said thank you. That's a code, I said to myself. And there's enough going on in this house, I said, without foreigners talking codes over the phone." And with this profound dictum she began to clear away the dishes.

"And one hell of a murder case this is!" Burly, rednecked Captain Norris, in charge of homicide, towered over Lieutenant Finch and thundered at him. "You haven't even got a body to show for it. How the hell do you know anybody was murdered at all?"

"There's the girl's evidence—"

"And who's the girl for Christ's sake? Publicity agent for Metropolis Pictures, that's who she is. Goddamn it, Finch, I tell you they're making a monkey out of you. The whole stinking thing's a gag, and you've fallen for it."

"Ridgly's shooting wasn't any gag."

"So what? What's that got to do with Worth? Go ahead—find out who shot Ridgly if it makes you happy. But Jesus Christ with wheels on! Stop futzing around this Worth frame-up. Call their bluff and be damned to them."

The phone rang. "For you, Finch," Captain Norris grunted in a moment.

"Listen, Herman," Finch heard. "This is Andy Jackson speaking. I'm still on vacation, so I want you right away, and a whole squad with you."

"What's up?"

"What's up? Merry hell and all. I've just found Stephen Worth's body."

Finch suppressed a gleeful chortle and started to retail this information to the doubting Captain. But Jackson's next words stopped him short.

"The nice thing about it is," Jackson went on, "the corpse is still warm."

Chapter 20

"WE'D LIKE to hear the newest recording of the Brahms Second," Maureen told the clerk in the record store. Mr. Evans, from long experience, had recommended that placid symphony as one of the best for stimulating thought processes.

"I am more than ever certain," he insisted as they waited, "that the key to it all lies in those numbers. It must be more than coincidence that another of our group uses a number code for telephonic communication. I cannot help feeling that we are on the verge of a great discovery. This little piece of paper—" He stopped short, and panic began to creep into his face. Hurriedly he started to explore his pockets. "Where *is* the paper?" he gasped.

"You had it in your hand," said Maureen. "Maybe you laid it down on the counter."

"It isn't there. And who would take it? Who could have taken it, except—Miss O'Breen, we've been followed! He realizes how close we are to a solution!"

"Who realizes?"

"If only we had that paper we should know. But we are in danger now—frightful, immeasurable danger."

"Don't be silly, Mr. Evans. This isn't Victorian London on a foggy night. This is Hollywood Boulevard, now, on a bright summer day. Nothing can happen to us."

"Can't it? Then what happened to that paper?"

"There'd be no point to stealing that. It's only a copy—Lieutenant Finch has the original. You must have dropped it."

A clerk (not the one Maureen had given the order to) approached them with a stack of records. "If you'll just step into this booth here—" he began.

Maureen looked at the top record. *Two Dukes on a Pier,* fox trot, by Larry Wagner and his Rhythmasters. "Good heavens!" she exclaimed. "These aren't what we wanted."

"I beg your pardon," the youth insisted, "but here is your list. You can check the numbers." And he handed them the now all-too-familiar code message.

Maureen began to laugh so wholeheartedly that the clerk stared openmouthed. "So that's what our wonderful code is! We rack our brains for hours trying out all our most ingenious ideas, and what are we working on? A list of dance records that Stephen Worth meant to buy."

For a moment Jonadab Evans had seemed dejected, but now his eyes were alight again. Maureen could almost swear she saw his nose twitch. "Miss O'Breen," he announced, "this is the greatest discovery since Stephen Worth was shot."

"What is? That Worth bought dance records? That's no surprise; he probably used them for aphrodisiacs."

"You honestly believe that this is merely a shopping list? Come now: do people who mean to buy records list them by number? No; they jot down the title, perhaps the performer. And remember when and where and under what circumstances this list was found. No, Miss O'Breen; these records are no haphazard group of tunes. They are a message!"

"Do you want to hear them?" the clerk asked patiently.

"Go away!" said Mr. Evans sharply.

258 · ANTHONY BOUCHER

"I beg your pardon, sir!" The clerk was not unjustifiably indignant.

"Sorry." Mr. Evans relapsed into his milder self. "Eight records at seventy-five—one fifty—three—That would be six dollars. Here you are. Now go away."

"And where will you find this message?" Maureen asked. "Do we have to play them all and maybe pick out the forty-third word in each lyric or something? Or is it in the tunes? That would be Holmesian; you could settle down with your violin and solve the whole case."

"No. It can't be that. It must be something relatively simple— something that any one of us could read once he had stumbled on the idea that these were record numbers. Now the first thing we must do—"

"Excuse me, please." It was the first clerk again. "Here's the Brahms album. Now if you'll step right in here—"

"You go away, too," said Mr. Evans, "and stay away."

"Please excuse us," Maureen added, "but this is really important. Maybe," she murmured doubtfully to herself.

"The first thing," Mr. Evans went right on, "is to arrange the records in the order of the list. What is the first one—number 20518?"

"Go Down Moses," Maureen read from the label, "and I Want to Be Like Jesus, sung by the Tuskegee Quartet. This isn't even a dance record, like all the others."

"Then it must be the words. Go Down Moses—I Want to Be Like Jesus—GO—I—Either one of those is a plausible beginning for a message. What is the next—25414?"

"My Kingdom for a Kiss and To You, Sweetheart, Aloha, played by—"

"Never mind. I think we want only titles. MY—TO—I—

TO—I MY—No. Ah, this fits! GO TO—Go on, what's the next one—25723?"

"Autopsy on Schubert and—"

"That's perfect! GO TO AUTOPSY—We'll have a message yet. Now the next."

Each step meant trial and error—weighing the merits of the two initial words and rejecting the one which made no sense. And after eight such steps, the paper before Mr. Evans bore the message:

STEIN

GO TO AUTOPSY THREE TWO SOUTH STREET SONG

"That's it!" he calloohed. "Now all we need is a map-find out where Stein Street is, or Song Street—it's hard to know which it should be—and hurry there before anyone else has the sense to see what these numbers mean."

Maureen had caught his excitement by now. She did not even stop to point out that it was chance, not sense, which had shown them the meaning of the list. "There's a bank across the street," she contributed. "They have maps."

Clutching the precious records to him, Mr. Evans started out of the store like a back in the clear with the goal posts straight ahead. But in the path hovered a safety man—the second clerk.

"Excuse me, sir," said this youth, "but do you have eighteen cents?"

Mr. Evans halted abruptly and stared at this monument of effrontery. "And what business is it of yours, young man?"

"The sales tax on six dollars," the clerk explained patiently, "is eighteen cents."

Maureen already had her purse out and handed him the

change. "Though I don't know where," she added as they left the store, "I'll put that in my budget."

"It's strange," observed Mr. Evans, dodging through Boulevard traffic. "In the East we always hear of California as such a prosperous state, and all people do here is ask you for pennies."

"Anyway," Maureen consoled him, "this is a prosperous bank. They give you maps free gratis for nothing."

Some minutes later she looked up in despair. "It's no use," she said. "Somerset Place, Somma Way, Sonora Avenue, Soper Drive—no Song Street."

"Try Stein then."

"I did. Stearns Drive, Steele Avenue, Stelle Place, Stephenson Avenue. No Stein either. I never heard of one, but that wouldn't prove anything. I never heard of any of those I just read either. Funny how you can live in a town for years and not know the names of streets."

"I know," said Mr. Evans. "All you can be sure of is that there'll be a Main Street. Main Street—Miss O'Breen! There is a Main Street in Los Angeles, isn't there?"

"I'll say there is," Maureen laughed. "It's the City Council's greatest problem. Burlesque theaters, flophouses, Beer Five Cents a Glass—you know the kind of street."

"And it runs north and south?"

"Yes."

"Then that's where we're going. Come on. How can we get to 32 South Main Street?"

"But why Main Street?"

"Don't you see? What is the full name of the *Stein Song*? *The Maine Stein Song.* Probably there isn't any record beginning with

Main; the man who wrote the message had to substitute Stein and trust to luck. Now how do we get there?"

"These red cars on the Boulevard would take us to Fifth and Hill. We could walk from there."

"And how long would that take?"

"A good three quarters of an hour in traffic."

"Too long," said Mr. Evans decisively. "Taxi!"

Maureen, as they rolled down Hollywood and turned onto Sunset, kept sneaking sidelong glances at her companion. The success of his cryptanalysis, even though brought about by pure chance, seemed to have changed him completely. He was no longer a pale and wistful rabbit. Instead he was abruptly a Man of Action and Few Words. This, she reflected, must be the author's own interpretation of the Honorable Derring Drew.

"Miss O'Breen," he turned to her sharply, "what is on the other side of the *Autopsy on Schubert?*"

She looked at the discs on her lap. *"Two Dukes on a Pier—* which sounds terribly like Lucky Louie to me." (Lieutenant Finch, she thought, would disapprove of that crack.)

Mr. Evans rapped authoritatively on the glass. "Driver," he commanded, "change your destination to 232 South Main."

He sat back in self-satisfied silence. "But why?" Maureen asked, feeling foolishly stooging.

"An autopsy," he explained with only a trace of condescension, "would be held in a known building and the address would not be needed. Therefore the numeral on the other side must have been intended."

"And if that isn't right," Maureen said, "we can go back and try number 32 anyway."

"We won't need to," said the Honorable Derring Drew.

Nor did they. The cab driver had to let them out a half block from the desired address, such was the confusion in front of that building. Maureen saw official cars and men in uniform and for a moment even thought that she glimpsed a now familiar tall and rangy figure, which seemed impossible. She looked at the men in the gathering crowd. If she asked anything of them, she thought with a shudder, they'd think she was—A Salvation Army uniform was more encouraging.

"I beg your pardon," she ventured, "but could you tell me what's happening in that building there—the hotel, I think it is, at 232?"

The man gave a friendly smile and tipped his cap. "If I were you, Miss, I'd stay away from there. There's just been a murder."

Chapter 21

IN THE small third-floor bedroom of the Hotel Elite (232 S. Main St.—Beds 25¢, Rooms 50¢ And Up) stood Detective Lieutenants Herman Finch and A. Jackson. The squad had already gone over the room minutely, with the result that it was accidentally cleaner than it had been in years; but it was still not an appetizing abode. A little afternoon sun penetrated through the cracked window giving onto the air shaft, picked out glistening motes in the dusty air, and fell inert on the uncarpeted wooden floor, burned and stained by past smokers and chewers.

The man who had registered as James Moriarty had left little impress of his own personality on the room during his brief tenancy. He had brought no baggage, added nothing to the room's shabby furnishings save a tablet of yellow paper, a pencil, *The Complete Sherlock Holmes,* and two quart bottles of whisky—one now empty and the other still half full. The rest was the same as when he had arrived—the washstand with its tarnished mirror and rude bathing utensils, the chair with the partial cane bottom, the bed with the creaking springs and the tattered spread.

To be precise, the bed was not the same. It was bloodstained now and half hidden by a ragged screen, and on it lay the body of the man who had called himself Moriarty.

"It's impossible," said Finch. "The man who was murdered twice—"

"Double Jeopardy," said Jackson grimly. "Un-American, that's what it is. But it's what comes of a gag sense like his. Playing with murder is like what Catholics believe about playing with magic—there's no telling when it will turn into the real thing."

"And Norris was right, damn him," Finch grunted. "But now that you've found him, Andy—and a smart piece of work that was—what have we got? He tried to leave a clue to his murderer—that much is clear."

"Is it? I'm doubtful about these dying clues ever since the Garnett case. That crumpled knave was a perfect pointer if ever there was one, and look at the trouble it gave us. Let me have another look at our priceless clue." Lieutenant Jackson took up a piece of paper—half of a plain yellow sheet from a tablet, with nothing on it but cavorting stick men.

"Mind if I think aloud? I want to repeat this and make sure it's straight. When I walked in here, he was dead but still warm, and this was clenched in his hand. The other half of the sheet was on the floor along with those other papers. They're all fake messages of one sort and another, mostly with a Holmesian flavor; so it looks as though he was going to make a few more mysteries for us if nobody found him. But somebody did find him—Anyway, Herman, your idea is this: he was still barely alive when his murderer left. He hadn't strength enough to reach the pad and pencil, so he took one of these papers and tore it in half. What he tore off is supposed to tell us who killed him."

"If we could figure it. Of course it might be the other half. With a bullet in your chest, you could easy keep the wrong scrap of paper."

"Right enough. Let's see the other one, too."

Jackson spread the two yellow halves on the dresser and contemplated them. Both were part of the same message, written in the now-familiar cipher of the dancing men. With the aid of *The Complete Sherlock Holmes,* the officers had already translated them and penciled the clear message beneath. The first half, which had been tossed onto the floor beside the bed, gave the result:

R E M E M B E R | T H E | P O L I C E

The other, the half that had been clutched in the dying hand of the so-called Moriarty, read:

A N D | A M Y | G R A Y

"Amy Gray," said Jackson. "According to Federhut's story, that was the stepdaughter that died as in *The Speckled Band.* And that name cropped up in one of those strange phone calls the day of the fake murder. It must all tie in somehow, but I'm damned if I can see—"

"There's another little gathering tonight at 221B. We'll see what happens then. And in the meantime I've got plenty to do on this new development. So until tonight, Andy—"

"Excuse me, Lieutenant," said a uniformed man in the doorway.

"Well, Gomez? What is it?"

"There's a girl downstairs trying to crash. She was just about giving up when she heard your name and says you know her and want to see her."

"Herman," said Jackson, "I've got a crawling hunch. The name isn't O'Breen, is it?"

266 · ANTHONY BOUCHER

"That's the name," said Gomez. "And there's a man name of Evans with her."

"Bring 'em both up," Finch ordered. "So Evans is around here, is he? Isn't that nice? Right handy for us. We'll just do a little alibi checking right now."

Maureen entered hesitantly, still balancing the precious records; but her entrance was bravura itself compared to the timorous manner in which Jonadab Evans followed her. The momentary incarnation of the Honorable Derring Drew had vanished, and there remained only a meek old man who had got into deep waters.

"Lieutenant Finch," Maureen ventured, "what *has* happened? Downstairs they wouldn't—And Andy!"

"Andy?" Finch repeated. "What is this?"

"We drank beer together last night," the young Lieutenant explained. "It plays hell with the professional relationship. What's happened, Maureen, is that I've just found Stephen Worth."

"Oh." Maureen looked relieved. "Is that all? A Salvation Army man told me there'd been another murder. But why should anybody have brought Worth's body here to this awful place? No thank you, Lieutenant Finch, I'd sooner not sit down here."

"You see," said Jackson, "the trouble is we're both right, the Salvationist and me. I did find Worth and there has been a murder."

"Oh!" Her relief had evaporated. "Oh, this is awful. Who—"

"Was it one of the—one of *us?*" Mr. Evans faltered.

"The man who was killed in this room, Miss O'Breen," Finch said, "roughly three hours ago, was Stephen Worth."

"No!" Maureen gasped. "I *will* sit down!"

"But Lieutenant," Mr. Evans expostulated, "that's impossible.

This young lady *saw* Worth shot at 221B night before last. That is," slowly he drew away from Maureen's chair, "do you mean that she—"

"No," said Jackson. "Miss O'Breen's in the clear. I believe her story is in good faith, just as I might believe a man who told me he saw the Indian rope trick. That doesn't mean I believe in the trick. I know what you think you saw that night, Maureen; but I still don't know what you did see. I just figured it like this: supposing, in some freak way that I don't understand yet, this whole thing is a colossal hoax of Worth's. That made sense. That fitted in with his character. He could stage a fake murder and then frame all these weird adventures that the group went through yesterday, just to show up the Irregulars as a bunch of bungling amateurs."

Maureen nodded. "That does make sense. That's like him. He was all for ribs. Remember what he did to Drew in the commissary?"

"I remembered that. So I said, if this is a hoax, how did he get away from 221B? He wouldn't take his own car; if that was missing, it might arouse suspicions. His hide-out probably wouldn't be within walking distance; and writers in the film colony have forgotten years ago that there are such things as streetcars and busses. He probably took a taxi. Well, he did, and the rest was easy. The driver dropped him a block from here. I checked all these hotels, and when I saw *James Moriarty* on this register, there wasn't any doubt who that was. So I found him—but somebody else had found him first, somebody who was smart enough to—and by the way! Just how did you two find this place?"

Maureen held up the records. "With these," she said.

"Criminate!" said Lieutenant Finch. "It's bad enough that a

detective on his vacation should beat the working police to this hide-out. But if a couple of amateurs can find it with phonograph records . . .!"

So Maureen had to explain, and in the fullest detail, all about the list of numbers.

"So he did leave a clue!" said Jackson. "There the address was if we could only read it. Worth may have been a rat—"

"*May* have?" said Maureen.

"—but he did have a sporting kind of gag sense. What could be fairer?"

Finch crammed his pipe with concentrated vicious pokes. "That isn't what interests me so much. You've been with Evans, Miss O'Breen, working on this cockeyed list ever since I left you this noon?"

"Yes."

"And before that," Finch recapitulated, turning to Mr. Evans, "Hinkle saw you upstairs and Mrs. Hudson talked to you in the kitchen, which takes us back to around eleven o'clock. Right?"

"Yes, Lieutenant," the little man admitted. "But why?"

"Why? You've got an airtight alibi, that's why. With Ridgly in bed under guard, that leaves only three of you; and before we have our little conference tonight, I'll—"

"Lieutenant," Maureen protested, "you don't still think it's one of the Irregulars?"

"I know what I think," said Lieutenant Finch.

BY TELEPHONE

"Hello. Withers Rest Home."

"Hello. This is Lieutenant Finch of the Police Department speaking. Is Dr. Rufus Bottomley there?"

"Sorry. Dr. Bottomley has just left."

"May I speak to Dr. Withers, then?"

"Sorry. Dr. Withers is—"

"This is urgent. Official business."

"Very well. I'll see if I can reach him."

"Hello. Withers speaking."

"Dr. Withers, this is Lieutenant Finch of the police. Can you tell me when Dr. Bottomley reached your sanitarium today?"

"Why not ask him yourself?"

"He hasn't got back here yet, and this is urgent. Can you please tell me when he got there?"

"I suppose you know what you're about, Lieutenant, and I don't see what harm it can do. He reached here around two."

"Do you know where he was before then? We've checked his movements up to eleven thirty and—"

"Oh. I thought you wanted to know what time he got *here*. I met him in Hollywood for lunch at about a quarter to twelve. He's been with me ever since till about ten minutes ago. Anything else I can do for you, Lieutenant?"

"Hello. Mr. Arbuthnot's secretary speaking."

"Hello. Is this the Association for the Placement of Refugees in the Professions?"

"Mr. Arbuthnot is the western secretary of the APRP. Did you wish to speak to him?"

"Yes, I did. This is—"

"Sorry, but Mr. Arbuthnot is out at present. Do you care to leave a message?"

"This is Lieutenant Finch of the Los Angeles Police. I—"

"How do you spell that, please?"

"I don't want to leave any message. I—"

"Very well. I shall tell Mr. Arbuthnot you called."

"Just a minute, Peaches. Don't hang up. Do you know a man called Otto Federhut?"

"Whom did you say you were?"

"Whom hell! I'm Lieutenant Finch of the Los Angeles Police Department, and I—"

"Oh, the *police!* Can I help?"

"Now you're talking. You sound almost human. Look, Peaches, if you want to, maybe you can help solve a murder."

"Ooh!"

"Now listen. Do you know a man named Otto Federhut?"

"Yes. He was in here today."

"What time?"

"Just a minute. I have it here in the schedule. He came at 12:35. Mr. Arbuthnot was just going out to lunch, so they went together. He came back and stayed until—until 2:45."

"Now one more question. We know he left Hollywood on the 11:32 bus. Does that jibe?"

"I'll look at our timetable. The 11:32 (that's from Cahuenga?) gets into Pasadena at 12:25. He must have taken a taxi from the station to get here as soon as he did—we're some distance south. There! Have I solved your murder?"

"University of California at Los Angeles."

"Department of English, please."

"Department of English."

"Hello. Is the department secretary there?"

"This is Miss Freeze speaking."

"This is Lieutenant Finch of the Los Angeles Police Department. Could you tell me if Professor Furness was in your office today?"

"Why, yes. He was here from about eleven to two thirty."

"Was he in the office all that time?"

"No, not exactly. He went to the library for a half-hour and he went out to lunch. The rest of the time he was reading here or dictating letters to me."

"Thank you, Miss Freeze."

"Oh, Lieutenant. There isn't anything the matter, is there? He seemed such a nice young man, I'm sure he couldn't be in any real trouble."

"No, nothing much. There—ah, there was an accident involving his car. We're checking to see that he wasn't mixed up in it."

"Oh. That's good, And Lieutenant—"

"Yes?"

"When you see Professor Furness, please remind him that he forgot to sign those letters he dictated."

Lieutenant Finch looked at his notes:

WORTH DIED 11:30–2:30

Irregular	Alibi	
HARRISON RIDGLY	11:30–2:30	Hinkle, nurse
JONADAB EVANS	11:30–12:30 12:30–2:30	Hinkle, Hudson, me O'Breen
RUFUS BOTTOMLEY	11:45–2:30	Withers
OTTO FEDERHUT	11:30 12:35–2:30	gets on Pasadena bus (Bottomley) APRP
DREW FURNESS	11:30–2:30 (with short gaps)	English Dept., U.C.L.A.

"And all of them," he muttered, "so damned far away from Main Street that what gaps there are no help at all. Well, we'll see what happens tonight."

BY ASMODEUS

The conference that night was scheduled for 8:30. At 7:30:

Dr. Rufus Bottomley was brushing his rich imperial and thinking with bitter tenderness of the girl in Dr. Withers' office.

Drew Furness was trying to select a tie and wondering if his clothes really seemed overconservative to Miss O'Breen.

Jonadab Evans was writing a letter to his publishers and meditating if the splendid flavor of Mrs. Hudson's soup had been due to a pinch of saffron.

Herr Otto Federhut was in the shower, a bright-green bath cap over his white mane, asking himself if his visit to APRP would actually accomplish anything.

Harrison Ridgly was in bed, wishing that the nurse would go away and let him finish the plan he had started.

Maureen O'Breen was deciding, in view of the nature of the meeting, that a high neck would be better.

F. X. Weinberg was protesting to A. K. that they'd start shooting tomorrow positively.

Mrs. Hudson was deciding that no matter what the conference was for they'd want something to eat afterwards.

Lieutenant A. Jackson was just having a bright idea, which could be most appropriately symbolized by the cartoonist's conventional light bulb.

Lieutenant Herman Finch, who was not a markedly religious man, thanked his wife for a good dinner, kissed her good-by, and asked her to pray for him.

Vernon Crews, ribber extraordinary, sat behind the black whiskers of Commissar V. N. Plotnikov at the banquet of the Friends of Soviet Democracy, pondering his speech on the defense of capitalism and wondering also why he hadn't received that check yet.

Sergeant Watson, on his way to duty, stopped to play a game of pinball. He knew the druggist wouldn't pay off to a cop; but he liked to watch the balls go round. He was thinking of nothing at all.

Even Asmodeus, that limping devil who looked through rooftops at men's most secret actions, could not have told which of these thoughts masked an undercurrent of joy—the joy of the man who knows that he has killed wisely and well.

Chapter 22

"It appears," Jonadab Evans began timorously, "that I am to take the chair tonight. Dr. Bottomley, after last night's disturbance, is still unwilling, Herr Federhut pleads discomfort in the language, Mr. Ridgly is physically unable, and Professor Furness finds the chair too reminiscent of the classroom. I fear, therefore, that you must indulge my own poor fumbling with the situation."

The living room of 221B, which had seen so much happen in the past forty-eight hours, was again filled with an intent group. The other four Irregulars (even Harrison Ridgly, who had insisted upon being moved downstairs at whatever risk), the two police Lieutenants, Maureen (as representative of Metropolis), and the faithful door-watching Sergeant Watson—all sat in patient silence, all waited eagerly on the outcome of this session. Only Mrs. Hudson had declined to attend the gathering; there was enough going on around here, she said, without her meddling in it, and besides if they wanted some refreshments later they'd better leave her alone now.

"Lieutenant Finch," Mr. Evans went on with growing confidence, "has asked us to help him. He confesses that the police are nowhere near a solution to this case, and he asks us to apply to its complexities such deductive faculties as we have acquired through our study of the Master."

"Herman," Jackson whispered to his fellow Lieutenant, "have you gone nuts?"

"Shh," Finch cautioned him. "This is the best way on earth to pit them against each other. They'll be trying so damned hard to produce brilliant solutions that they won't care what they say. Keep your ears open—no telling what we might learn from this."

"With your permission," said the chair, "I shall sum up what we know before we take up the conclusions to be drawn therefrom. It is now evident that the 'murder' which started this whole investigation was a hoax planned by Stephen Worth himself to expose us as incompetent amateurs—all the more reason, I may add, why we should now seek to display our real ability."

"But Mr. Evans—"

"I know, Miss O'Breen. You are about to protest that you did see Worth killed night before last. How he effected that illusion I still do not know, though I hope someone may provide an explanation this evening; but we have the positive medical evidence that Worth died some time between eleven thirty and two thirty today. There is no question about that.

"It is clear, then, that someone saw through this hoax, tracked Worth to his Main Street hide-out, and there turned the jest into murderous reality. It is our purpose to discover who that someone was. The police doubtless would not have entrusted that task to us were they not convinced that this murderer, brilliant though he was, could not have been one of the Irregulars. Allow me to recapitulate our alibis:

"I myself was with Miss O'Breen at the time of the killing.

Herr Federhut was either on the 11:32 bus to Pasadena, which Dr. Bottomley saw him enter, or at the APRP office in Pasadena. Dr. Bottomley was with the eminently reliable Dr. Withers, and Professor Furness is vouched for by the secretary of the English department at U.C.L.A. Mr. Ridgly, of course, has the most perfect alibi of all, the presence of a police nurse in his room."

Ridgly twisted his mouth into a sort of a grin. "There's your case, Lieutenant," he said. "Look for the man with the perfect alibi. Would somebody mind passing me that bottle?"

"The doctor says no," declared Lieutenant Finch with conclusive sterness.

Ridgly grimaced. "Do I have to make dazzling deductions cold sober?"

"If you don't mind, Mr. Ridgly," said Mr. Evans stiffly, "we shall get on with the discussion. Our murderer, you will all agree, must fulfill two conditions. He must have a sufficiently ingenious mind to solve Stephen Worth's hoax, and he must have been at Second and Main within the specified time limits."

"I might also suggest," Dr. Bottomley offered, "that he have a motive for killing, Mr. Worth. Though from what we know of that individual's character, or lack thereof, a motive should be reasonably simple to find for almost anyone. Mrmfk. Particularly if we consider Mr. Evans' masculine pronoun as a mere convention."

"It was intended as such, Dr. Bottomley. But before we go on, I should like to consider another question of identity. I am sure that each of us recalls, with fascinated horror, the singular adventure in which he was involved yesterday. There can be no doubt that the mind behind those adventures was that of Stephen Worth. Their purpose was to confuse us with Holmesian byplay while carefully casting a doubt upon the reputation of each of us, with the possible further intent of sowing among us mutual distrust and suspicion. But surely Worth himself was not an actor in these macabre little farces. Even he could not have been so incredibly self-confident as to believe that not one of us could recognize him.

"The more I consider those adventures, the more I am convinced of this: that the five character leads, if I may use a theatrical expression, of those episodes—the terrible spy Grossmann, the weary Captain Fairdale Agar, the absurd Colonel Warburton, the villainous Dr. Royal Farncroft, and my own Russian Orthodox priest—were all one person, and that that one person was the most protean impersonator in Hollywood, known to us to have aided Worth in previous hoaxes—in other words, Vernon Crews, assisted, of course, by a small troupe of actors for such minor parts as Anna Trepovna, Larry Gargan, and the German chess players. Does that seem plausible to you, Miss O'Breen?"

"I wouldn't be surprised. Crews can get away with anything, and he'd love a setup like that."

"Good. I simply wished to make that point clear, since I may desire to refer to it later. Now, when we have realized that everything that took place in this fantastic case up to eleven o'clock this morning was part of a weird plot contrived by Stephen Worth and executed by Vernon Crews and assistants, the picture becomes clearer. Unnumbered confusions may be stricken out of the record as irrelevant—though I confess that I should still like to know how Worth learned of my young collaborator, Larry Gargan. I think we may assume, however, that his malice had inspired and his detective associations enabled him to collect, for some time, any derogatory information relating to the members of our organization, which information he turned to

278 · ANTHONY BOUCHER

good account in the concocting of certain of these adventures. I should dearly like," Mr. Evans added thoughtfully, "to see his file on Alec Woollcott.

"But now, setting all these reflections to one side, it is high time that we fulfill the Lieutenant's request. Professor Furness, you look as though you were struggling with an inspiration. Will you confide its nature to us?"

Drew Furness hemmed and tugged gingerly at his shirt collar. "I was merely thinking—That is—But it was nothing of importance."

"Come on, Furness," Finch said encouragingly. "Try it on us."

"I—Really I would rather wait."

Maureen smiled. "Go on, Drew. Show Worth's ghost you're not the dope he thought you were."

"Very well. But remember that you asked me to. Mr. Chairman, Miss O'Breen, gentlemen!" He halted.

Voices throughout the room urged him on. He gave his collar a stronger tug, distorting it in a manner to affront Ridgly's *Sirrah*-accustomed eyes, and began. "I think," he said, "that we have been neglecting a suspect. To my mind, Dr. Bottomley was right when he insisted on motive. It's all very well to say that Worth was the sort of man that anybody would want to kill, but it's much more convincing if you can show a real motive in black and white, instead of simply saying, 'Oh, Worth was such a terrible fellow.' And that's why I think—mind you, I'm not trying to offer a solution or anything like that—but it seems to me—Oh, I know I should build this up dramatically and surprise you all but what I'm trying to say is—well, maybe it was F. X. Weinberg."

"Mr. Furness!" Maureen sounded shocked.

Finch seemed exceedingly interested. "That's what you think, is it, Professor? Now that's an idea, that is. Quite an idea. In fact, if you could disprove the evidence of his secretary and his superior producer and the gateman at Metropolis that he never left the studio between ten and five today, that would be a brilliant idea."

Furness seemed too downcast to reply. The chair hastily cleared its throat and went on. "Dr. Bottomley, have you anything to contribute?"

Bottomley rose, stocky, vigorous, and imperialed. "By the Lord Harry, sir," he exclaimed, "I have. And no fumbling guess like Furness', either. Your aunt, young man, may be hovering on the verge of madness, but she has more spunk in her little finger than—"

"You hush up!" said Maureen. "I'd like to know what you'd have done if instead of having a crazy old woman lock you up in a closet you'd been shut up in a den of what you thought were Nazi spies."

"I have no doubt," Dr. Bottomley replied acidly, "that I should have done just as Mr. Furness claims to have done." There was only the slightest possible stress on *claims*. "But enough of this stupid bickering. If one of Worth's aims was to sow dissension among us, I can only say that he has done that part of his work too damned well. We are, in fact, so wrapped up in what Mr. Evans has termed mutual mistrust that we tend to be all too trustful of the others outside of our little group.

"Now the outstandingly hateful characteristic of Stephen Worth, as I now know definitely, was his incurable satyriasis. No one had more motive to kill him than a woman whom he had outraged. I have been morally certain from the first, even in the days of our innocence when we were still deceived by the hoax, that Worth's death was caused, directly or indirectly, by a woman. Now, gentlemen, let us forget our mistrust for a moment. Let us hunt for a woman; and may I rot forever if I utter that banal phrase in my bad French. Let us hunt for a woman who has been with us throughout this affair, a woman who is shrewd and intelligent enough to pierce through Mr. Worth's phonograph riddle, a woman who is brave enough to track down the man who assaulted her and to avenge herself in cold blood. Is there such a woman?"

He paused. Maureen looked fixedly at her hands folded in her lap. She felt certain that every eye in the room was on her. She wanted to jump up and scream, "But I was with Mr. Evans!" The rhetorical pause seemed to last for minutes.

"Hell and death, sirs, there is! She has been with us all the time, and never once have we thought of her as anything but that staunch and loyal housekeeper, Mrs. Hudson! Her spirit," he plunged on, riding recklessly over the murmurs of astonishment, "has been more than demonstrated on the occasion of the encounter with the supposed Ricoletti in the garret. She is obviously a far more attractive woman than she allows herself to seem; why should that be if she were not seeking deliberately to minimize her beauty and the dire consequences which it brought her in the past? The poor woman was one of Worth's victims, she sought this position (under the assumed name which was the chief qualification for the job) in order to confront him again, and when she saw through the plot which he was perpetrating, she realized that her moment of vengeance had come."

"I refuse to believe," said Jonadab Evans reverently, "that such a cook could be guilty of the slightest offense."

"At least you'll admit," Ridgly contributed from his couch, "that it's in the best Doyle tradition. Vengeance dating back into the past, disguises, a Woman's Honor—"

Rufus Bottomley stroked his beard. "What do the rest of you think?"

"I think," said Lieutenant Jackson, "that this has gone just about far enough. Dr. Bottomley, did you once have in your employ a girl named Ann Larsen?"

Dr. Bottomley turned in surprise. "I—that is—"

"Please, Doctor. I've checked this with the New York police. Don't bluff. Did you?"

"Yes."

"And was Ann Larsen found in your office one day, unconscious as the result of a peculiarly vicious attack?"

"Yes."

"And did Ann Larsen never fully recover her sanity, so that you had to send her to the rest home of your friend, Dr. Withers?"

"Yes, but—"

"And was Stephen Worth a patient of yours at that time?"

"He had consulted me about—"

"So that he might have come into your office, accidentally or otherwise, while you were out? And did you not realize, from Mr. Ridgly's story of the office assistant who suffered a relapse on hearing Worth's name, that he must have been Ann Larsen's assailant?"

The imperial was all that was left of the former Dr. Rufus Bottomley. Behind it was a drawn old face above a saggy body. "I fail to see, Lieutenant—" he said hopelessly.

Jackson turned to Lieutenant Finch. "There you are, Herman. There's your case."

The senior Lieutenant looked undecided. "Good work digging up all that stuff, Andy. But remember the man's alibi."

"And who gives him that alibi? Dr. Withers, who has seen

Ann Larsen relapse from an almost cured patient to a helpless wreck at the sound of Worth's name. Do you think, after that, he would betray Worth's murderer?"

"I can say nothing, gentlemen." Bottomley was seated now. His voice was thin and old. "It is true that from the moment I knew him for Ann's attacker, I wanted to kill Worth. That girl was a daughter to me, and the man who destroyed her life deserved even greater punishment than any that I could inflict upon him. My only defense is that I believed Worth to be already dead. If I had seen through his hoax, you may rest assured that I should have made it come true. I did not. You may believe that or not as you choose. Since Worth and Crews and Ridgly among them drove Ann back to madness, I do not care."

Ridgly laughed. "So now I'm a villain too, Bottomley? Very well; but I think you're a bit hard on Worth. If wanting to ravish that blonde is a stamp of villainy, I'm a member of the club. Won't somebody give me a drink?"

"No," said Lieutenant Finch.

"Well, Herman?" Jackson asked. "I'm sorry as hell for the poor devil, but—"

"But you want to clear your good name as a detective," said Ridgly courteously.

"Look here, you foulmouthed rat! Because you're laid up on a couch with a—"

"Andy, Andy." Finch's tone was the one he used to employ on drunks in the old days on the beat—soothing but stern. "Hold your horses. Let's hear what the others have to say. Go on, Evans."

"I must confess," the chair resumed, "that I have been a bit shaken by these accusations, and not a little surprised. Herr

Federhut, do you have some further startling denouncement to make?"

The Austrian shook his white head. "As you know, I was a jurist in my own land. To my mind only in the stories should the amateur solve the crime. In reality I am contented with the police. To them belongs the task; I am only a poor *émigré* who sits and listens."

"That is kind of you, Herr Federhut." Mr. Evans' words bore a strong emphasis which seemed meaningless at the moment. In the pause following them came a sudden glurp from the door.

"Did you speak, Sergeant?"

For a moment everyone turned. They had quite forgotten their Watson. Under this cluster of glances, the Sergeant looked embarrassed. "I didn't say a thing," he muttered. "Just swallowed a piece of Lifesaver. Sorry I sort of busted into things."

"That's quite all right, my dear Watson."

The Sergeant frowned. "Say. As long as I interrupted. What's that he said he was?"

"Who said?"

"He said he was only a poor something-or-other."

"Herr Federhut said that he was an *émigré*—a person who had left his native land. It is a French word."

"But I thought he was a German." Sergeant Watson seemed to find this a suspicious circumstance.

Federhut smiled. "In the Third Reich, the poor writers are supposed to use *bloss echt deutsche Wörter*—only truly German words. But we *émigrés, Gott sei Dank,* we can speak as we please. It is, you perceive, elementary, my dear Watson."

The Sergeant's frown deepened. "I guess you guys got to have your fun," he said darkly.

"Mr. Ridgly?" the chair asked.

"So John O'Dab wants to save his big Derring Drew set piece for the grand finale? Let all the rest of us speak our little pieces and then—boom! comes the blaze of glory. Fun and games for all! All right, I'll stooge, if I can have a drink."

"No," said Finch patiently.

Ridgly shrugged. "Now one thing hurts me about all this. You're so exclusively worried about Stephen Worth. None of your solutions yet gives a damn about who shot me. I don't want to seem conceited—a Ridgly never puts on airs, not even a Ridgly III—but I do think my case ought to be considered, even if I didn't die. Attempted murder's a crime too, isn't it, Lieutenant? And now can I have a drink?"

"Yes," answered Finch, "to your first question. The answer to the second is still no."

"Very well," said Harrison Ridgly III. "Then I won't tell you who shot me."

Chapter 23

"What the hell!" Lieutenant Finch's was the loudest of the various similar exclamations which sounded through the room. "Then you do know, and you've been holding out on us? Come clean, Ridgly."

"For one small drink. Not too small."

"You'll tell us without anything or you'll be liable as an accessory," said Finch with fine disregard for the stricter points of law.

"Let him have his drink, Herman," Jackson urged. "It won't kill him."

Finch grunted. "All right. Pour him a shot, Miss O'Breen, if you please. Now, Ridgly, who did you recognize?"

Ridgly downed his shot straight and looked wistfully at the bottle. "No one, Lieutenant," he smiled.

"But you said—"

"I said I'd tell you who shot me. I will, too; but by reconstruction, not by recognition. Listen, my children: last night, when I was shot, there were only five other people in this house: Mrs. Hudson, Evans, Bottomley, Sergeant Watson, and Lieutenant Finch. We can strike you out, Lieutenant, and with you our dear, if somewhat elemental, Watson; and despite

286 · ANTHONY BOUCHER

Dr. Bottomley's astounding conclusions, I refuse to take Mrs. Hudson seriously as a person of this drama. Though I might have had some motive for attacking Evans over his absurd accusation of sororicide (for at the time I thought it his own invention; I realize now that it was part of Worth's little game), there was no earthly reason why he should try to shoot me. That leaves us with—come now, gentlemen, on your toes! Whom does that leave? Exactly—Dr. Rufus Bottomley."

"Very neat," said Finch skeptically. "Excepting that he had no earthly reason either."

"No? You have seen how fanatical he is on the subject of the tragedy of Ann Larsen. In my Warburtonian adventure I had come near the truth of that tragedy, and worse, I had made mock of it and vaunted my own—to use the doctor's term—satyriac thoughts concerning that lovely wench. I was guilty of sacrilege against his darling."

For a moment Dr. Bottomley's old spirit flared again. "Hell and death!" he cried. "Will you stop tormenting me?"

"I have learned my lesson," said Ridgly. "I never torment snakes that may strike back." He laid his hand on his wound.

"Then you're with Jackson on this," said Finch judiciously. "It's all Bottomley?"

"Oh no. Not at all. I've met Dr. Withers. I'm sure he would never endanger his professional standing by supplying a murderer, however noble, with an alibi. Our eminent literary medico is merely a would-be murderer, and a bungler at that."

"Then who—?"

"It's quite simple really. Whose movements have been completely unchecked? Who has displayed the training and ability to track Worth down? Who held a deep-rooted grudge against him because he had been made ridiculous and because his whole professional career had been imperiled by Worth's hoax? Who was indicated by half of the dancing men?"

"OK," said Sergeant Watson out of the blue. "Who?"

"To put it most simply, my dear Watson—*who found Worth?*"

Jackson rose suddenly and loomed over the couch, a towering monument of ire. Then slowly the wrath faded from his face, and a good-natured grin took its place. "All right," he said slowly. "*Touché.* That's a pretty job, Ridgly, especially that about the dancing men. The other half did say, 'Remember the police,' didn't it? Well, I'm not saying there mightn't have been trouble if I'd found Worth alive. But it would have been fists—not a gun."

"Have you more to add, Mr. Ridgly?" the chair inquired.

"Isn't that enough? Look how the Cossacks stick together; not a peep out of our respected Lieutenant Finch. Jackson's a copper, so he's got to be innocent."

"What do you expect me to do?" Finch demanded. "If I made an arrest every time one of you boys has a bright idea, I'd have to hire a bus to take the mob to the station. I'm biding my time. Go on, Mr. Evans."

"Hm." The chair paused. "I should like now to present my own notion of what may have happened this morning at the Hotel Elite. And like some of those who have spoken before me, I feel that your great fault has been in overlooking a logical candidate.

"Gentlemen, I have said, and you agreed with me, that our suspect should be clever enough to see through Stephen Worth's plan. But how much simpler it is if we consider a man who *knew* that plan—a man who was in Worth's confidence, who could approach him, even in his hide-out, without suspicion, who could keep in touch with him by code communication and know where he was at any moment. The motive, I admit, must be a matter of conjecture; but any business dealings with Worth, as I am certain F. X. Weinberg would assure us, are in themselves quite as valid presumptions of motivation as are Dr. Bottomley's conjectures of assault. With such overwhelming evidence of opportunity, even though motives remain obscure, I offer for your consideration the name of Vernon Crews."

"Vernon Crews?" Finch did not look pleased. "But he hasn't even been under consideration."

"Exactly, Lieutenant. Therein lay his safety. And what is your opinion of this—I believe you term him a 'ribber'—as our leading candidate, Miss O'Breen?"

"I—I don't rightly know. You sprang it so out-of-the-blue-like. I think and always have thought that Vernon Crews is a very low form of life, but a murderer—"

"And you, Herr Doktor Otto Federhut, what do you think of the notion?"

"I am at a loss, Herr Evans. What is it that I should know of this impersonator, this—ah, this boner?"

"I think that you should know a great deal, Herr Federhut. Because, you see, you *are* Vernon Crews!"

If the room had been startled before, it was now reduced to chaos. Over the babbling babel rose the heavy voice of the white-maned Austrian, swearing intently in a dialect which no one understood.

"Quiet!" said Lieutenant Finch forcefully. "Now Evans— what do you mean? Even if the man's an imposter, he can't be a murderer. He was in Pasadena at the APRP."

"There are other members of the Crews Acting Company, as we know from our adventures. He could easily send one of them to the APRP, apparently on an ordinary hoaxing excursion, while he attended to—ah, to the matter in hand."

"Andy, get Arbuthnot on the phone. Find out if he'd ever met Federhut before."

"OK, Herman."

"This," Mr. Evans went on explaining, "was the start and focus of all Worth's trick—to plant a confederate in our very midst. He knew of Federhut's European reputation and his monograph on the *Holmes-Mythos*. It was not unnatural that a man of his attainments should be in exile, voluntary or otherwise. Actually, the authentic Federhut is probably now in a concentration camp. Crews was sent to New York to present himself to us. Worth knew all along that we would naturally suggest that 'Federhut' be added to Mr. Weinberg's list of guests.

"I might add two more points, small in themselves but nonetheless contributory. He was heard this morning talking over the phone in a number code. What could this have been but some communication with Worth, who, as we know, used such a code? And his refusal to advance a hypothesis is indicative in reverse: he was afraid that if he advanced too cogent a case to incriminate someone else, the police might suspect a purpose in it. Here, however, he underplayed his hand dangerously; a refusal to make intellectual conjectures about a mystery is completely out of character for a Baker Street Irregular."

"And the clue?" asked Harrison Ridgly. "The squiggle men and Amy Gray?"

"Simplicity itself. Grasping that fake Holmes message meant simply, 'My murderer is the man who played my fake Holmes tricks.' "

The old *émigré* had stopped swearing. Now he was laughing

so heartily that his white mane was like a mop being shaken out. "*Herr Leutnant,*" he gasped, "do you wish to pull at my hair that you may assure yourself of its reality?"

"Just a minute," Maureen interposed. "Dr. Bottomley, when was the party when you initiated Federhut?"

Bottomley roused himself from his melancholy contemplations. "Let me see. It was the night before the Fourth—the third of July, I think. Yes, I am certain."

"That was the night that Crews spoke before the Daughters of the British Lion. He was supposed to be the man who makes all Chamberlain's umbrellas, and he told them the *strangest* things."

Jackson came back in. "Arbuthnot says he's known Federhut since the '20's in Vienna."

"That I could have told you," Federhut laughed. "But everyone must you ask save only me. More I could have told you also about those numbers. I am delighted that I am suspect of the ability to talk in code—truly a rare achievement. But I must confess that all I was doing was to ask the omnibus company the times of their vehicles, repeating the hours as they to me read them. I am sad that it is so simple."

Finch looked at Mr. Evans. It might almost have been called a glare. "I thought," he said with measured scorn, "that I might get something out of this little see-ance, but I guess I'm wrong. Each of you's trying so all-fired hard to find out the most impossible answer that we're getting nowhere fast."

"But Lieutenant," Mr. Evans protested, "it was your own suggestion that we—"

"I know. Andy said I was crazy and I guess I was. It's about time to tell you that I came here tonight with a warrant in my pocket. Don't all jump. I'm not going to use it. You've done that much for me; you've shown me what happens when you go off half cocked. I want to get my facts straight before I do anything definite. But if it isn't out of parliamentary procedure, Mr. Chairman, I'd like to ask a couple of questions."

"I assure you, Lieutenant, you need not be so bitterly ironic. The floor is yours."

"Fine. Now, Professor Furness, who's the secretary of the Department of English at U.C.L.A.?"

"I believe," said Drew Furness, "that her name is Gwendolyn Abercrombie. I am afraid that no one ever speaks of her save as Abbie."

"And did she take your dictation today?"

"Naturally. No—just a moment. Abbie is away for the summer. There was a strange girl, I don't know her name."

"What did she look like?"

"I think that she was smallish."

"What was she wearing?"

"Heavens, Lieutenant, I don't notice women's clothes. I never have."

"Was she blonde or brunette?"

"She—Frankly, I don't know."

"Of course you don't know. Because, Professor Furness, you never saw her."

"I never saw her?" The academician's echo floated feebly through the silent room.

"Of all those five perfect alibis, Furness, yours was the one with the hole in it. *You never signed the letters you dictated.* And why? Because you weren't there, and you didn't dare risk a false signature going into the files and maybe being spotted later. You knew that a substitute secretary would be in the office for the summer. You aren't teaching summer school; she would only know that there was a Drew Furness on the regular staff, and if a man came in, gave that name, and started dictating letters, she'd never know the difference. I don't know who your accomplice was, but the scheme wasn't quite good enough. Tomorrow we'll confront you with this girl, and we'll have the whole story."

Finch brushed away the questions which arose. "I've got the floor now, and I'm going to go on with my exposition—just the way you boys play, only this is for keeps. This wasn't planned as a murder; this alibi was just in case any of the rest of you checked up on where Furness was. He'd solved the phonograph code and he wanted to be the first and only one to find Worth. He wouldn't have taken the chance on an accomplice if he'd had murder in mind; but now that accomplice is in so deep that Furness figures he'll keep quiet. The one mistake the professor made was in going armed. He was afraid of Worth—Worth had attacked him twice, and Professor Furness isn't so hot with his fists. So he took along a gun, just in case.

"When he confronted Worth, either Worth did take a sock at him again or maybe started infuriating him with cracks about Miss O'Breen. The gun was there, so he used it. He must have been scared as hell to start with, but then he realized that his little trick with the secretary gave him, as he thought, the perfect alibi, and he decided to bluff it through. As to his fumbling with his solution just now, the same reason holds as Evans gave for Federhut—he didn't want it to seem too good."

"But how about our priceless clue, Lieutenant?" Harrison Ridgly objected. "How do dancing men mean Professor Furness?"

"A clue, Mr. Ridgly, is any unexplained fact, which usually

hasn't got a damned thing to do with anything. I've got plenty without the clue—and without knowing how Worth pulled his hoax, either. A broken alibi's worth a hundred clues. But if you really want a nice storybook Sherlock Holmes ending, how's about this:

"Worth couldn't reach a pencil. He couldn't write his murderer's name. So to indicate it to us, he grabbed (and tore in the grabbing) a piece of paper. And what was on that sheet of paper? It was something he *drew*."

"Darling," Maureen was pleading, "say something. Tell the man—"

"What can I say? He'll find out his mistake tomorrow. In the meantime—"

"In the meantime," said Lieutenant Finch, "you're coming along with me. Material witness, you understand; the other comes later when we've checked things. Watson, the handcuffs."

There came an irreverent snort from Ridgly's couch. "And my dear Watson, pray do not forget the needle."

"Just a moment!" said Drew Furness with a certain sudden strength. "I need my hands for a minute." He turned to Maureen and laid those hands on her shoulders. "Tomorrow, my dear," he said gently, "when all this is settled, I want to say something to you."

"Pretend you said it now," Maureen murmured, "and pretend I said yes."

They pretended.

"Break it up," said Finch, not without a suggestion of sympathy under his gruffness. "It's time we got going."

In the silence the click of the handcuffs drowned out the crunch of a fresh Watsonian peppermint. Finch turned to the door with his prisoner. Then came another sound, sharp and decisive.

Knock! Knock!

"Who's there!" Finch barked.

The door opened and Mrs. Hudson entered with a mountainous tray of sandwiches. "Who wants tea," she asked, "and who wants coffee?"

Chapter 24

"I'll leave you to your party," Lieutenant Finch announced. "We've got to get going. Come on, Sergeant."

But Sergeant Watson hesitated. "Lieutenant," he said tentatively.

"Come on, Watson. I want to get some sleep tonight."

"But wouldn't you maybe sleep easier, Lieutenant, if you were sure you had the right man?"

Finch started incredulously at his subordinate. "Good Lord, Watson. Have you caught it too? Are you going to start delivering a deductive hypothesis?"

The Sergeant blinked. "No sir, Lieutenant. I don't want to do that. Nothing like it. I just want to say who done it."

"Horse feathers!" Finch snorted. "If I hadn't known you for seventeen years, I'd start thinking you were Vernon Crews and this was some bright new rib. Come on."

"All right," said Watson reluctantly. "But when Mrs. Hudson up and knocked on the door and you said, 'Who's there?' then all of a sudden like I knew the answer."

"Come on," Finch urged, with a little of his drunk-wheedling tone. "We'll talk about it later."

"But Lieutenant," Ridgely protested. "That's not fair to us. Certainly we want to hear what theory the Sergeant advances.

Think of it: The Case Solved by Watson. A title of titles, my dear Finch; you couldn't deprive us of the pleasure."

Watson gave Ridgly a black scowl. "I ain't kidding," he said.

"Go on, Herman," Jackson urged. "No harm done."

"No? We'd make a laughingstock of the police department, that's all the harm we'd do."

This seemed to decide the Sergeant. He turned facing the room and blocked the doorway with his bulky body. Drew Furness, chained to Watson's left wrist, found himself abruptly jerked about by the maneuver, so that he too directly faced the group's curious stares.

"Sorry, Professor," said the Sergeant. "You'll get unlocked pretty soon."

"Watson," Finch snapped, "this is insubordination. I'll break you for this."

"OK, sir," Watson replied submissively. "But I just want to tell you what I thought. You see when Mrs. Hudson knocked on that door—"

"Don't be a fool, Watson. Come on. How can knocking on a door tell you who killed Worth?"

"When she knocked on that door," the Sergeant went right on, "she just knocked twice, like this: *knock! knock!* And you said, 'Who's there?' just like in the game."

"Game!" Finch snorted.

"So I was still worrying about that clue. I know what you think about clues, Lieutenant, but a guy does have to explain them, don't he, or else there's no telling what the defense'll do, and it seemed to me a good lawyer, like Max Farrington say, mightn't like your explanation so much. So I was thinking about Amy Gray, and Mrs. Hudson went *knock! knock!* and you said, who's there, and I said Amy, and then like I was playing the game, I said Amy who? and right like a flash I knew who killed him. It was just like watching the ball shoot into the ten-thousand hole and all of a sudden the lights go on."

"For heaven's sake, Sergeant," Jonadab Evans exclaimed, "do come clean, as the Lieutenant might say. Are you trying to beat us at our own suspense tricks?" The Sergeant looked surprised. "You still don't get it? Look, you know that game. Sure you do. You say, knock! knock! and this other guy says, who's there? and you say Goldy, and he says Goldy who? and you say Goldy's where you find it. It's a gag, see?"

"The whole damned thing's a gag if you ask me," said Finch. "Just what the hell, Sergeant, are you blethering about?"

"Amy who?" said Watson. "Amy Gray. See? It's just like in the game. It's a gag. Amy Gray doesn't mean a name. It's a word. Like a pun, sort of. Amy Gray means what you said. That French word."

"French word!" Finch was near exploding.

But the others saw. "Amy Gray!" Furness gasped. "Why, of course—*émigré!* It couldn't mean anything else."

"But why on earth?" demanded Jonadab Evans, seemingly a little puzzled at hearing his own accusation repeated. "If he really is Herr Doktor Otto Federhut—"

"He's a Nazzy," said Sergeant Watson simply.

"Sergeant," Harrison Ridgly laughed, "this is too beautiful to spoil, but you're simply crazy. Herr Federhut was thrown out of Austria and his whole professional career shot to hell merely because he refused to be what you call a Nazzy."

"Sure. I know. They do that. A friend of mine, he was working on a detail investigating the Bund. That's a trick of theirs. They throw a guy out and then he comes over to this country, and on account of he's an amy-gray he gets to know all the people who're working over here against the Nazzies. So he sends reports back home and they get to work on their relatives and that stops them. Sure, that's what he was up to. Remember how anxious he was all the time for Weinberg to introduce him to the Germans in the anti-Nazzy movement here?"

"But my dear Watson," Ridgly smilingly protested, "what about the scene at the Rathskeller? Surely he and the headwaiter should have fallen on each other's necks and burst into the *Horst Wessel Lied*."

"An act," the Sergeant said patiently. "He'd spotted the Lieutenant and the others. It was a swell chance to wipe out any doubts they might have after Furness' adventure with the spies."

"And you explain his refusal to give a solution incriminating someone else in the same way that Evans did?"

"No. I don't think so. I just think maybe he has a conscience."

Finch was beginning to look interested. "What have you got to say to all this, Mr. Federhut?"

"What I have to say?" Federhut rose in all his whitemaned juristic dignity and walked to the door, where he stood calmly confronting the burly Sergeant. "This have I to say, my dear Watson. I was at the Office of the Association for the Placement of Refugees in the Professions. Your own police have with Herr Arbuthnot spoken. He knew me in Wien; there is of impersonation no question. I was there."

"Sure," said Sergeant Watson. "You were there. Later on."

"And before that," Federhut continued, "I was on the omnibus to Pasadena and then in a taxi to the Association."

"Look," the Sergeant objected. "Dr. Bottomley saw you get on the bus, sure. But that don't mean you went to Pasadena. You got off a couple of blocks later and took a taxi to Second and Main. You left Hollywood at 11:32. That'd get you downtown about 11:50. What happened there wouldn't take more than ten minutes. That still leaves you thirty-five minutes to get to Pasadena, with another taxi."

Federhut laughed. "It is *komisch* that twice in one evening I the judge must the defendant be, but it is fortunate that my prosecutors are so stupid. Why should I wish to kill Herr Worth?"

"You didn't. Not at first. It's like the Lieutenant said about the professor. You just wanted to steal a march on the others. That's what you were doing at the phone—reading numbers to a music store and asking them what those records were. So you give Bottomley the slip and sneak down to the Hotel Elite to see what goes on. But when you find Worth, he's drunk and he gets to boasting and you see he really know's what you're up to and he can prove it. So you kill him. You see, sir," he turned to Finch, "that's what we kept forgetting. We've found out that what Worth planted about Bottomley and Evans and Furness was all true, so hadn't it ought to seem that the rest was true, too?"

"As a Holmesian," said Federhut, "I am delighted by this Watson solution. As a jurist, I am unimpressed. It is conjecture, and else nothing. If you were in court, my dear Watson, how would you attempt of this the proof?"

"That's a cinch. I'd round up both those taxi drivers and put them on the stand. They'd fix you right on the scene of the crime."

"That is true," Federhut reflected judiciously. "Their testimony would be of great weight, is it not so? And therefore, my dear Watson, I am going to have to ask you to move out of that doorway while I leave the house, or I shall be regretfully forced to fire into you as one might through a lock."

He turned just enough to let them see the gun in his hand. "I had no fear, gentlemen, of your collective cleverness. So hard did you strain that I knew the simple truth was safe from discovery. But our cherished Sergeant has altered my plans. He has unfortunately destroyed the work for which I came here; let that be to him some consolation if he is wise enough to move from that door and live."

No one spoke, not even Harrison Ridgly. The twist had come so suddenly, so quietly, that speech was meaningless.

"Let it also be to him a consolation that he has guessed shrewdly. It is even as he said. I found that Worth was of certain documents in possession. These I removed, and with them some few others. I am generous, you see. There was an affidavit—I do not know how obtained—proving that Mr. Evans was not the true John O'Dab; and there were other statements which might to Herr Ridgly have been of interest. I like you gentlemen, and was glad to serve you. But of what I was most glad was that I had served the Third Reich and our Leader." He said this simply, without fanaticism.

"You speak in this country too much of the wickedness of the Nazis. You make of them ogres and monsters. We are human, *meine Herren,* and what you will not understand—we wish you well. It is your fight, too, that we are fighting. Your fight against the Jews and the international moneylenders who suck you dry. We do not want war and hatred, though the Chamberlains and the Roosevelts and the other warmongers—the petty tyrants like Smigly-Rydz and Beck—may yet drive us to it. But if war comes, remember that it is for you too that we are fighting; and that when we are through we shall help you to create a new America, a free America purged at long last of its oppressors and defilers."

"I'll be damned," Ridgly murmured. "He believes it."

"Of course." Federhut was surprised. "Because I have killed such a low thing as Stephen Worth, do you think me a villain? I killed him because he would have ruined my mission here. That mission is now, alas, fully ruined. You all know of it, and I could not kill you all. You are my friends. Besides, it would be very foolish. I must escape now."

"Don't be a fool," Finch grunted. "You can't get far."

"You do not know our power, *Herr Leutnant*. I can get very far indeed. Otto Federhut shall forever vanish. But I shall continue his work somewhere. It does not matter where. For myself, I should willingly pay for my crime. In my young days as a judge, I should have despised a man who sought his death to escape. But I know now that there are higher obligations than a man to his life owes, or even to his death. I must go on. And therefore must I again ask you, Sergeant, to move from that door or to be shot."

"I'm staying here," said Sergeant Watson stolidly.

"Put up that gun, Federhut," Finch warned, "or I'll drill you."

"By the time you had your gun drawn, *Herr Leutnant*, your Sergeant would be dead. Do you too care so little for human life?"

For an instant Federhut had turned his head to answer Finch. In that instant everything happened. Furness and Ridgly moved at once, as though some extrasensory perception had coordinated their actions. Furness gave a sudden twist to his right arm which flung the handcuffed Sergeant flat to the floor. At the same time the professor's free left arm grasped the Austrian.

It was an heroic gesture; but though it saved the Sergeant, it would have been fatal for his prisoner had not Ridgly also acted. A desperate lunge from the couch hurled him at Federhut's right hand, which held the automatic. Both his hands seized that wrist and held it motionless.

But they could not hold the trigger finger. Even as Furness dragged the jurist to the floor and Finch, service revolver drawn, stood over him, that finger tightened its grip, the automatic spewed forth its full load, and fresh blood spread over the bandages of Harrison Ridgly III.

Federhut seemed to look with horror on his own murdering hand. "I had not meant that," he gasped. "It has nothing accomplished. *Herr Leutnant!*" he cried. "Why do you not shoot?"

"I think," Finch reflected aloud, "that I'd sooner see you stand trial. It'll help purge America."

Chapter 25

The living room of 221B was again almost deserted. Finch and Watson had done their duty; Otto Federhut was by now on his way to the county jail. An ambulance had come and gone; *Sirrah* would have to find a new editor. Only Jackson, Furness, and Maureen lingered in that event-crammed room.

"Time you were off to bed, Maureen," said the Lieutenant. "Finch is a good guy; he'll try to keep this quiet as long as he can. But the reporters will be around here soon."

"Please," said Maureen. "I'm still sort of dizzy and all jangly inside. And tomorrow I have to face F. X. and the press and I really don't know yet what's happened. Won't you sit down a minute and let me ask questions?"

"I don't know if I can answer them all myself," Jackson grinned. "But I'm game for a try."

"I still can't believe that nice old man was a spy and a murderer. He didn't leave us much doubt, though, did he? But what I really don't understand is Mr. Ridgly. Federhut can't have shot him—he was at the Rathskeller when it happened. All three of us saw him there. Does that mean that it was Dr. Bottomley, the way Ridgly said? And why did Ridgly jump at Federhut that way? He must have known it was certain death. And I know we ought to speak well of—of the dead, but he didn't seem to me like a man who would sacrifice his life for Sergeant Watson's."

"Whoa," Jackson protested. "That's enough for a start."

"Sorry, Andy. I'm still all tangled. But why—?"

"I think it makes sense. Remember what the Sergeant said. We'd learned that three of Worth's planted scandals were true. Isn't it probable that the others were, too? All right; therefore Federhut *was* a spy, and Ridgly *had* killed his sister. It isn't a pretty thought, but it makes everything else come out logically. Evans' old Russian woman was a fraud, but her story was close enough to the truth to make Ridgly worry. He had killed his sister out of jealousy, and found that life wasn't worth much without her. All his bitterness and drunkenness stemmed from that. Now it looked as though the truth would come out. So he tried to commit suicide; only it pleased his sardonic gag sense to make that suicide look like Worth's murder. Fortunately for him, that *Thor Bridge* plant made it possible. He cut his lip, painted RACHE on the wall, and shot himself with the automatic attached to a weight hanging out the window. He probably held the gun with the black mourning band so as to fool the parafin test. Then, by the damnedest chance, he lived and had to go through with it by pretending it had been attempted murder. When he went for Federhut, he wasn't sacrificing his life for justice; he was grabbing the opportunity to finish off the suicide that had gone wrong."

Maureen's face was serious and her voice low. "The poor man," she said.

"It was tragic," said Furness. "Worth's hoax hasn't had very pleasant results for anyone. Think of that poor Larsen girl and her relapse from the shock."

"Any more questions?" Jackson asked.

"Yes. One. How on earth did Worth pull off that hoax in the first place? I saw him—"

"Oh," said the Lieutenant. "That. Look—you wait here like good children. I can expound better after a trip upstairs."

Drew Furness broke the silence almost a minute after the departure of Jackson. "While the Lieutenant is gone, are there any questions that I might attempt to answer?"

"Yes, Drew. One."

"And what is that?"

"Tonight—oh, years and years ago—when they were putting the handcuffs on you, you said—"

Furness turned his eyes away from her. "It wasn't fair, my dear. It was taking advantage of an emotional situation. You could never—"

"Drew! Look at me! Now. Did you mean it—what you didn't quite say?"

"You know I did."

Maureen smiled. "Then for my sake act like you meant it!"

"I think," said Drew Furness a happy eternity later, "that someone is calling us."

"Damn," said Maureen, and listened. "It's upstairs. Must be Andy—maybe he's found something."

"I suppose that we'd better—"

"I guess so. But please, darling, remember to wipe off that lipstick. I'm afraid," she said reflectively, "you're going to be hell to housebreak."

Light came from the door of the empty room which they still thought of as Worth's. A few feet back from the door stood Lieutenant Jackson, weaving drunkenly.

"Andy!" Maureen gasped. "What are you up to?"

Suddenly the Lieutenant seemed to stagger and clutched at the air in front of him. As he did so there was the sound of a shot. He crumpled, clutching his hands to his heart. Wet redness seeped out between his fingers.

Maureen turned pale and grasped Drew Furness' arm. "Oh, God, he's—" Then abruptly she laughed. "Swell, Andy! Magnificent."

Another door opened, and Dr. Bottomley rushed out, calabash in hand. "Don't tell me," he exclaimed, "that *that* was a backfire!"

"I thought," Jackson explained rising, "that it might be more impressive if I demonstrated than if I just told you. Was that what you saw, Maureen, the night Worth was supposed to be murdered?"

"Exactly," said Maureen.

"You mean," Dr. Bottomley broke in, "that you've solved the hoax?"

"Apparently I have. Come on in and I'll show you. Where's Evans, by the way?"

"I believe that he is in the kitchen with our fair housekeeper. Mrmfk. But we can inform him later." Dr. Bottomley's melancholy was slowly being dissipated by this new achievement of ingenuity.

"A chair, Doctor," said Jackson. "You two can sit on the bed."

Maureen did so at once. Furness hesitated until she took his hand and drew him down beside her. "You'll get used to it," she whispered. "Now, Pride of the Force, expound."

"The essential clue was that glass shard. Remember what it said on it?"

"Yes," said Bottomley. "The letters OV, with a segment of an arc above them."

"And where," Jackson demanded, "will you find a piece of glass with the letters OV on it? Where but on an electric-light globe! The O isn't a letter; it's the figure O, part of the inscription 120V or whatever the voltage is. Add that to the way Worth clutched at the air just before he 'was shot,' and it's easy. Look." He proceeded to demonstrate, talking, in his triumph, much faster and more excitedly than Maureen would have thought possible for him. "You take a fine thread and hang in across the room like this. (See the two chipped places on the wall—that's where the tacks go in.) Then you twist some more thread around a light bulb and fasten a ring to it. Run the ring along the thread across the room and adjust it so that the bulb hangs down at one end, just over the metal wastebasket. Then you clutch at the air, break the thread, bulb falls into basket, goes *boom!* You clutch your heart, break a sac in your breast pocket (I just used ink; Worth probably used the real thing—you can buy it in labs— same like your ear, Doctor), and there you are."

Furness frowned. "I'm not quite certain that I—"

"Look. Here are the notes I made on the way out here tonight. This is a bird's-eye view:

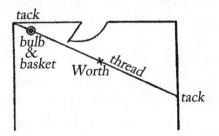

And this is the view if you are facing the door looking straight
at the setup:

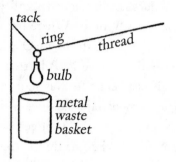

Of course you couldn't see any of that. The door hid the bulb, and
you wouldn't notice that very light thread. Afterwards Worth
cleaned it all up, only he left the chipped places on the wall and
the fragment of glass in the basket."

"Lieutenant," said Drew Furness, "that is brilliant."

"And therefore," Dr. Bottomley added, "a fit occasion for
celebration despite all that has gone before it this night. If you
care to adjourn to my room, where there is a bottle—"

Once back in his own room, Dr. Bottomley carefully placed
the calabash back in its cradle, took one of his villainous black
torpedoes, and lit it happily. Dr. Withers would have rejoiced
at this action; there could be no better indication of successful
mental convalescence. With gleeful if mephitic puffs, the Doctor
brustled about the room as the Perfect Host, setting out ash trays
and glasses.

"Our Buy Laws," he announced when the drinks were
poured, "prescribe that the first toast shall be drunk to *The
Woman*—Irene Adler, to you, Lieutenant, who caused the
Scandal in Bohemia. But under the present circumstances, I give

you a toast not included, strangely enough, in our usual ritual. Gentlemen—and Miss O'Breen—to Watson!"

"Drew," Maureen protested. "You just barely sipped it."

"That was not," he assured her, "out of any lack of reverence for the name of Watson, now doubly hallowed as it is. It was only that I can conceive of but one toast worthy of my first full drink of straight whisky."

"Then make it, man," Bottomley urged.

"Very well. To the future Mrs. Furness!"

He downed the whisky bravely, glurped only a little, and pulled out his handkerchief to wipe his lips. A scrap of paper floated to the floor. Smiling, Maureen picked it up.

Both Bottomley and Jackson were offering profuse congratulations. "Wait a minute," said Maureen. "Here's a loose thread."

"A thread?"

"In our plot, I mean. This is the message from the aluminum crutch, isn't it?"

"Oh yes. I jotted that down while I still remembered it. So much else has happened since that I've never thought of deciphering it. Do you suppose we might make a stab at it now?"

They looked at the paper and read:

HTR OWMOR FEVOL HTI WTEE RT
SREKA BOTST UN

"Worth's last words," Dr. Bottomley mused. "That outrageous voice speaking to us anew from whatever confines it now dwells within. Mrmfk. Lieutenant, what on earth are you laughing at?"

Jackson was not so much laughing as howling. "Oh Lord," he managed to gasp between spasms, "this is marvelous."

"Marvelous?" said Furness. "You mean you've read it already—the cipher is that simple?"

"Cipher? That's the trouble all through this case; we've tried too hard." Laughter choked him again. "Look. Just read it backwards."

Slowly they spelled out the message from end to beginning. Maureen giggled. Drew Furness frowned. Dr. Rufus Bottomley looked annoyed, then smiled, at last grew solemn.

"I think," said the Doctor gravely, "that Stephen Worth has his perfect epitaph."

THE END

DISCUSSION QUESTIONS

- Were you able to predict any part of the solution to the case?

- Did your knowledge of Sherlock Holmes stories (or lack thereof) help (or hinder) your understanding of the story in any way? Elaborate.

- This book is bursting with esoteric and obscure references; did you encounter anything that surprised you?

- Did any aspects of the plot date the story? If so, which ones?

- Would the story be different if it were set in the present day? If so, how?

- What role did the setting play in the narrative?

- If you were one of the main characters, would you have acted differently at any point in the story?

- Did you identify with any of the characters? If so, who?

- Did this novel remind you of anything else you've read? If so, what?

- If you've read others of Anthony Boucher's novels, how does this compare with what you know of his work?

AMERICAN MYSTERY CLASSICS

from

*Available now
in hardcover and paperback:*

AMERICAN
MYSTERY
CLASSICS

from

PENZLER PUBLISHERS